SLEEPING BIG
IN
SMALLVILLE
A Telluride Story

Jerry Vass

Edited by Rachel Vass

VASS Publishing, Saint Augustine, FL 32080
www.sleepingbig.com

Printed in the United States of America.

For information, contact:
VASS Publishing
1093 A1A Beach Blvd., #448, Saint Augustine, FL 32080
www.sleepingbig.com

Cover design by: Christine Giraud, GenuineImagery.com

Cover photograph by Jerry VASS
"Telluride in 1970"

ISBN: 978-0-9629610-5-2/Book

ISBN: 978-0-9629610-6-9/eBook

10 9 8 7 6 5 4 3 2

SLEEPING BIG
IN
SMALLVILLE

Some of this actually happened …

"Every man has his own threshold of impossibility ... ."

—Napoleon Bonaparte

TABLE OF CONTENTS

PREFACE

In the 1970s, Telluride, Colorado, was an extreme place populated by extreme people made crazier by each other. It was the last bastion of the Old West where living was fun and death was nigh. I was another person—an obsessive, a cheater, a lover, a love addict, an imposter and a phony guru who some people believed was real.

I was a man obsessed by two things: the reality of loving a high mountain town and the fantasy of loving a perfect woman. This one incredible place, the bona fide and provable center of the universe, is where one entrancing woman-child delivered love beyond reason, pain and anger, disappointment, guilt, loss of control and the slow, undetectable descent into a private purgatory.

What is truth? In love, there is no fact and in war, there is no fiction. In Telluride, there was neither.

—Jerry Vass, 2015

PROLOGUE

Ed Cross is compelling but not handsome, a man's man, a John Wayne character and a crack shot. A hero from central casting, he is tall, well over 6 feet, lean frame with an important walk. He projects a fearless aura, which, when I get to know him, is well-earned from a life of cowboying, poison gas, crime, death and other adventures perhaps too interesting to admit. In 1968, almost by accident, Ed Cross had come to own an option contract to buy 3,200 acres of prime development real estate in San Miguel County, Colorado. He paid the ranch owner pocket money for the option.

A couple months later, away in his winter quarters, a trailer house parked in southern Utah, Ed takes a phone call from a man in Aspen who wishes to speak to him about his option contract on the McLeod Ranch.

As often happens with ideas, a mystical message flies through the air and the same idea occurs to two strangers at precisely the same moment.

Unknown to Ed, the race was on between the man on the phone and his developer rival. Both contestants had created small developments around Aspen; both had the wherewithal to buy the land package to develop a ski area. Control of the land controls the concept. No land, no concept. Thus, Ed Cross has to be found in his trailer house under a cottonwood tree in a red rock draw with an intimate canyon view in the middle of nowhere somewhere near a wide spot named Panguitch, Utah, wherever the hell that is.

Within minutes of each other, the two competitors charter airplanes in Aspen, race off to southeastern Utah, rent cars and begin a needle-in-a-haystack search, raising dust plumes along unmarked dirt roads in their hunt for the single-wide hidden out of sight of the road.

Morey Stein finds it first, arriving in a burst of thrown sand, sliding to a stop in front of the sheet metal door that opens and fills with an imposing Westerner in a snappy-button shirt and Levis.

"Are you Mr. Cross?"

"Yep."

The visitor scans up and down the length of the paint-peeled mobile home sitting on cinder blocks, obviously the home of a poor man.

"May I talk some business with you?"

"Yep, C'mon in," Ed smiles.

Stein steps up into the smallish living space.

Ed waves him to the couch that sits across the front of the trailer. "Have a seat. Like some water?"

"I'd love some. God, you live in a dusty part of the country."

Ed draws a cup of water from a cooler sitting on the kitchen counter.

Stein drinks it in one gulp. He looks around the trailer, taking in the spare nature of the space. Papers are neatly stacked on the table. A leather holster wrapped in a wide leather belt makes a bump on the table.

"You are a hard man to find. You live in a spectacular place out here," Stein says.

"Yep. I grew up around here, so it's home to me." Ed sits at the table.

4

"I am given to understand that you own a contract on a piece of land near Telluride I am interested in buying, the McLeod Ranch."

"Yep."

"I would like to buy that option contract from you. I am prepared to offer you $10,000 in cash for it!" He holds his breath, watches Ed's eyes.

Ed laughs heartily, "I'll take $50,000 for it."

Stein feigns shock. "Oh, Mr. Cross, that is way more than it is worth!" he exclaims dramatically.

Ed shrugs. "Well, I just got a call from another man who's on his way to make an offer, so we'll see what it's worth, won't we?"

"Well, can we discuss this?"

"I'm gonna have a cup of coffee. Want one?"

Big, white roadside cafe mugs of oily coffee are served black. There is no offer of cream or sugar.

Stein takes a big slug of the disgustingly vile liquid and controls the violent rejection that yearns to show in his face. "Great coffee. How do you make it like this?"

"Sheepherder's coffee. Kept me alive for years on the high mesas. Secret recipe. Throw a handful of grounds in a pot of water and boil it until it's black." Ed smiles.

There is a long silence.

Stein thinks surely this man is bluffing. There isn't anyone else on the way. This unschooled cracker can't fool me, he thinks. I did not go to Harvard B-school to negotiate with a fool, but here I am.

"Please forgive my asking: Who's the other man that's on his way?"

"No, I don't mind. He said his name was Dick Kirk from Aspen."

Stein blanches and in a serious tone says, "I know him. He doesn't have any money. He's been broke for years. And he's a crook."

Ed stares at him through lidded eyes, waiting unmoved, unwavering and unresponsive.

Stein falls silent and leans back on the couch. I'll just wait him out, he thinks. He'll come around. This redneck has never seen $10,000 in cash at one time in his whole worthless life; he's just hardheaded. I know that the winner in a negotiation is the side with the walkaway power. Will he let me walk away? I don't think so.

Slowly, Stein stands. "Well, Mr. Cross, it was nice meeting you. When you want to make a deal, give me a call. Here's my card. You can call me day or night. My money is always ready, and I can do a deal on the spot."

"Yep." Ed takes the card, slides it into his shirt pocket and sticks out his hand. They shake.

Stein opens the door and steps to the ground.

Ed says, "Thanks for stopping by. Have a good trip back. You might stop at the hamburger place on your way into town. Minnie makes the best burgers in this part of the world. The motel is good, too. Clean."

With his hand on the handle of the car door, Stein looks back at the lanky Westerner who fills the trailer door above him, an older man with a weathered face that shows no emotion except a small, friendly smile that yields nothing.

Stein's resolve folds. Taking a briefcase from the passenger seat, he says, "OK, you win. I'll tell you what I am going to do. Against my better judgment, I will double my offer. $20,000!" he exclaims, smiles broadly and nods his head.

A dust devil whirls up out by the big road. A wisp of dust spins around the trailer enveloping the two men. A window rattles and the cottonwood leaves rustle.

Ed's expression doesn't change. He looks at Stein with steady eyes, making no move.

For minutes, neither man speaks. They stand listening to the brittle leaves talking, the only sound.

Stein breaks the silence. "OK. OK. I'll give you double that. How about $40,000?" he says without enthusiasm.

Ed's face is stone, unreadable; his smile freezes and his eyes go hard and dark.

After another minute, Stein tips his palms to the sky. "OK. $50,000 it is. Let's go inside and finish this."

On the way through the door, Stein says, "May I see the original contract you and McLeod signed?"

They sit at the battered kitchen table.

"Yep." Ed fishes around on the table and finds the folded envelope under a stack of bills. He pushes aside the holster and belt, a round leather package with the smooth pistol grip exposed.

Stein looks at the pistol grip. "What do you use the gun for, Ed?"

He laughs. "Oh, occasionally beautiful 20-year-old women come out to see me but when they don't leave, I have to make them go home. It's just insurance to keep me faithful to my wife."

Stein laughs courteously and carefully spreads out the wrinkled envelope with both hands and reads the five lines and pencil-scrawled signatures. Ed doesn't move. His eyes never shift from the disappointed face.

With a sigh, Stein says, "I took the liberty of preparing a simple contract assignment before I left Aspen." He fills in the date and amount with a Mont Blanc pen, signs two copies and pushes the legal-looking documents across the table.

Ed reads it over slowly. "It looks all right to me except for this one line."

"Oh?"

"This 'held-harmless' clause. Remove it. I won't sign this when you have a side door out of this agreement and a way to tie up my property. You don't have to put this part in. If your check doesn't clear, I will come and collect in person. Do you understand?"

Ed holds the man's eyes steady in his, dropping his chin slightly to look over his half-glasses.

"Strike through that clause and initial it in the margin."

In a single stroke, Stein inks through the offending words and initials the omission.

Stein looks into Ed's hard eyes, then back at the paper, then back into Ed's face that still holds a slight smile. This guy is nobody's fool, smarter than he looks. Damn these country boys. Where do they learn these things?

"How do I make the check out?"

"Just make it out to cash," Ed answers. "I'll run it to the bank in the morning."

Stein writes the check for $50,000 and slides it across the table. "Mr. Cross, thank you very much for your hospitality. I'll see you in Telluride I suppose?"

"Yep. In the summer. That's the best time."

Stein drives away in a dust cloud knowing he has been beaten at every move by this old man. He is angry about losing to a goy yet happy knowing that with this document, he can turn his fifty thou into millions. Damn, that old man looks quite capable of collecting, too, if he is so inclined. How could you not respect a fucking local cowboy who lives in a $500 trailer on a $500 lot and has turned $50 into $50,000 cash in two months and keeps a pistol on his kitchen table?

Within an hour, Dick Kirk arrives at the isolated outpost. "Are you Ed Cross? I've come down here to talk to you about your option contract on the McLeod Ranch."

"Yep. But you're too late. I just sold it to another man. He just left."

Kirk's face falls.

"Who was it?"

"A Mr. Stein."

Kirk's face reddens with anger. He looks into the sky and through clenched teeth screams, "Yaaaaaaaaah!"

"Would you like to come in and take a load off? Have a cup of coffee?"

The visitor takes off his new cowboy hat, slams it to his thigh, then hurls it to the sand and stomps on it with his hand-tooled cowboy boots, leaving it deformed like roadkill. He screams again and turns away shaking.

Turning back, he says tightly, "No." He waves his hands in frustration. "Well, fuck Stein! And fuck you, too!" As he drives away, his wheels spin violently, shooting gravel up against the aluminum wall of the trailer.

As the car disappears into the dust cloud, Ed raises his hand high above his head, laughs and raises his middle finger, saluting the man who is the big loser in the race for millions and ski area history.

1

THE DEAL

The streets are dusty and empty, populated only by the occasional wandering dog. A parked car looks out of place. A triangular Conoco sign stands like a silent sentinel over the boarded-up and empty buildings. A lone gas pump stands at rusty attention.

I visit Telluride in 1968 and buy three corner lots with a house on the main street for $700 down and three years to pay the $800 balance.

I have a feeling about this place; it will be an enormous success when discovered by the moneyed classes. I will buy these commercial lots now and by the time my 6-year-old son is ready to go to college, the town will have blossomed and selling the lots will pay for his education. "I just paid for the kid's education for $1,500!" I would tell my wife.

It would have cost several hundred dollars more had the house not been the luckless victim of a blaze started by the volunteer firemen on their monthly drunken fire practice in which they set empty houses on fire and then squirt water from leaky hoses and put it out. It's a charred hulk, open to the alpine weather with no roof or windows or hope. Behind it hangs one of the most-dramatic mountain backdrops in all of Colorado. The vision projects itself through the blackened studs, dangling joists and melted shingles dripping black. Behind the hulk, a precipitous canyon with sharp peaks lightly floured with snow highlights the golden fall aspens vibrating against a sea blue sky; where cloud ships sail languorously by.

By blocking out the ruins with my extended hand, the remaining image is a calendar photograph of idealized nature, pristine peaks, breathtakingly lovely. The flames have done their work. The first floor is more or less intact, but the summer rains have loosened the flowered wallpaper, and some has peeled and hangs limply onto the linoleum floor. The kitchen sink is there, but the appliances are gone leaving gaps like missing teeth. Everything stinks of smoke.

One day I can build this back, I think. I can come over from my big city life, spend the summer, find myself a carpenter and we can put this place back together. My family can use it to escape the hot city and enjoy the cool days here. Yeah, it's a junker, a miner's house, even intact it was just a shack. But it has a history. I am going to save it, just for the incomparable view if nothing else.

Telluride is nearly a ghost town; however, the mine at the end of the canyon puts out a good-size payroll to the miners, the breadwinners in this settlement of 450. Most structures are empty, but there is a movie house, a tiny liquor store, a barbershop, the seamy Sheridan Hotel, the Elks Club and two cafes, all looking like tired old hookers forlornly beckoning the unsuspecting and naive.

Take away the magnificent backdrop and it is no town in particular, just one of those isolated gatherings that dot the West: dirty, dusty, falling-in buildings, vacant houses with blind eyes that reflect past glories. The streets are empty and cracked; the cubic false-fronted commercial buildings faded, broken and boarded up. At the end of the valley, the mine spills its guts into a tailings pond—ground rock that creates acres of gray sand hovering over the east end of the main street like a 10-story, flat-roofed warehouse. When the wind blows, the dust swirls and spirals into the canyon, air fuzzing out the trees and mountains that overhang the box canyon in which the village sleeps among the gravel streets and fractured pavement of the main drag.

It is the surrounding mountain peaks that squeeze the town into its pocket, their biblical presence of bigness, of importance, of "being there" that imprint the town, then and forever more on its visitors. The settlement, 400 acres of decayed dreams, nestles in the protective and cupped hands of God, which, for its people, make it the unique power point in the universe. Without the looming mountains punching up into a breathlessly blue sky, without the vertical canyon walls, without the river and the waterfalls that ribbon noisily down the red cliffs, without the groves of aspen and pine, without the high peaks that shoulder the valley, this town—the empty buildings, the streets, the people—could be any tumbled down prairie town in Kansas.

But here among the high mountain peaks, there is a vibration about the place, an expectation, the mountains waiting patiently for something to happen.

The seller of the lots is also the town lender, an unusual, petite woman named Rosalie. She and her crop-duster husband moved to the valley from Texas some years before and started dealing in land and houses, speculating on the economic wildfire that would surely engulf southwestern Colorado. But it has taken longer than she expected, and now she is tired of it all and ready to do other as yet unidentified things in her life. While signing the contract for the lots, she mentions that her loan and insurance business is for sale.

My Denver life is comfortable. I have a wife, three kids, girlfriends, a Victorian house full of antiques on Observatory Park, a good advertising business, real estate holdings. But none of it makes me happy.

I feel a prisoner in the American Dream, unable to wake myself so I might experience the happiness that has to be here somewhere. At 33, I am a tired old businessman with a heart murmur. I don't like myself. I have become an egotistical asshole, using and discarding talent and women—the American Dream turned bad.

The black population is angry over racial matters. The whites are angry about the Vietnam War. Cities are burning: Watts is on fire. Detroit is smoky. Riots and gunshots echo around Denver's black neighborhoods, and the chaos frightens me—I fear for my family's safety.

Just owning a little piece of a mountain town, the escape from the pressures of my city business, is worth 10 times the cost. America has changed. It is more crowded, faster, more immoral, more plastic, more violent, more used.

My kids could grow up here, away from all that craziness. They could be the last of the mountain-bred children. Most of the high country towns are being quickly overrun by refugees from the burning cities, and they bring with them the gentrification and city ways that are transforming the old west towns into trilevel-house-with-paved-driveway suburbs where the adults dress correctly and learn to meditate, and the kids all have straight teeth and take dance lessons.

But that hasn't happened here ... yet.

In explaining the promised profits of her loan and insurance business, Rosalie says some guy from Aspen has bought land and is in the planning stages of a great ski area to be built on a ranch south of town. If that is true, there's no way this place can avoid becoming one of the most famous recreation centers in the country. It is too pretty a woman not to get hit on by big money. If I buy Rosalie's business, I will be here to watch, to participate and maybe become a developer myself. Here shines the bright prospect of wealth.

It is then that the idea gels—move to the mountains, bring my kids and wife and the whole modern debacle of life to this place of romance, history and mystery. And adventure.

I accept her offer on the spot.

It is a handshake deal with Rosalie. The business will transfer to me some 18 months hence. I need time to sell my business, sell the home on the park, gather my money, move from Denver and tape-record as much classical FM music as I can. There is only one AM radio signal from Grand Junction that plays pure country music interrupted by furniture ads, garage sales, lost pets and strident Christian preachers.

The thought that my family will move here to spend every day in the high country to live and work is a thrill like discovering young love.

I know something about lending. I had been a lender in the Navy, illegally, of course, lending $5 for $6 back on payday, which turns out to be 20 percent compounded every two weeks. I was never able to calculate the interest rate then, but I knew it was very profitable. Sure as hell I can learn insurance. There are people dumber than me in the insurance business. And up to this point I have never failed at anything.

I stand in the middle of Colorado Avenue, the main street, in front of my burned-out ruin, and do a slow pan of the entire scene. This high country is the best Colorado has to offer: 800 feet of layer cake strata, mostly red, with peaks above, sharp, defined; real mountains that show a mile of raw rock from top to bottom, not the shallow, feminine, flowing mountains of the Eastern Slope, but real upthrusts, gutsy and uncompromising, masculine mountains.

The town feels almost holy. Everything looks close through the transparent air; it smells fresh with a hint of wood smoke.

The sun low over the ridgeline brightly blesses me and cheers at my conversion from city boy to mountain man. I feel complete. My chest swells and somewhere down deep I feel stirrings of love for this place.

I can visualize this isolated place bursting like a new bud and flowering dramatically, opening up to once-in-a-lifetime opportunities. I just can't say no to all of this glory. So I don't.

It is the spectacular scenery that captivates all who crest Keystone Hill, 3 miles to the west. While it is called a hill, it is a terminal moraine, a place where an ancient glacier cut the rut that became a canyon, a monumental grinding wheel powered by the infinite thrust of freeze and thaw that ground out the walls and floor. It became tired of doing that work and finally, after thousands of years of labor, sat down to rest and melt in the sun. Like an old man, it laid down its load of rock on the canyon floor that formed a natural barrier 600 feet high and a quarter-mile across, enclosing the valley. Once the load was released, the snowmelt flowing down filled the canyon for 3 miles upstream. It had to have been a lovely sight, that mirroring lake and the ragged mountain backdrop with the gossamer waterfalls. But the lake is gone now, silted in by the spring torrents carrying debris from the high peaks, leveled by 500 feet of sharp little gray stones and many large ones until it is a flat floor even with the top of the dam. Across the floor on top of 50 stories of ancient entrapped water now meanders the San Miguel River, or it did meander, until the narrow gauge railroad builders redirected the river into chalk-line straight railroad right of way.

Keystone Hill is the first glimpse a visitor has of Telluride. Once seen, that view is forever etched into memory. The San Juan peaks fill the windshield from door to door. Low down, underneath a mile of raw rock, and avalanche runs and waterfalls and pearlescent mountain streams is a tiny town, a toy town, a town made for adult play, a town exactly the right size for an ordinary person to own.

The rush … what a hell of a rush to top out Keystone and watch the valley expand.

Telluride is a place to be possessed. It is a place that can and will possess. I want to be possessed. So I yield myself up to the whispered seductions of the overwhelming mountains, the village, a new adventure, a new love.

I close my Denver business, sell our house there and buy one of the handful of brick houses on the sunny side of Telluride for the record price of $10,000, build an office in the basement and hang a sign that announces that Tomboy Finance and Insurance is open for business.

Home has finally found me.

2
DOYLE'S HAIRCUT

After six weeks in town, I badly need a haircut. Shaggy hair droops over my ears, falls into my eyes and makes me look like a hippie. I hate it.

Down on the main street, next to the 10-foot-wide liquor store, is a 10-foot-wide barbershop operated by the same owner. Driven by hair fatigue, I drop by Doyle's Barber Shop, in which I have never seen a live customer. Not only is it the only barbershop in town, it is the cheapest.

As I enter the empty shop, the barber shuffles the 10 feet from his liquor store with a friendly greeting.

"Good mornin'. Lookin' for a haircut?" he asks in a slow way, pulling each word out of the air like a helium-filled balloon.

"Yep, I am."

"You jus' moved to Joe Hardy's house, dincha?" He flips the cape over me and fastens it with a clothespin.

"Yep, I did."

"Whaddya think of Telluride?"

"I love this place."

"Well, you'll git over that." With that conversation killer, he begins to cut.

His dull clippers pull hairs as it mows. Hair falls in big lumps, covering the floor and the cape. He is fast, his clippers never slow, always moving, and they seem to go unusually high on my head.

In the city, there are many haircutters to choose from: men, women, gays, straights, switch hitters and unidentifieds that will give one a passable businessman's haircut—short, but not too short, modest sideburns, tapered in the back, shaved neck—an honest, upstanding look.

In the city, I always questioned: "Is this barber going too high on the sides? Is he buzzing a bit overlong? Do his scissors seem quick and sure or hesitant? Is he pausing to calculate his next move or does he know those moves from experience?"

Like picking a doctor, you want neither a young one nor an old one, but one who is old enough to learn his specialty and still young enough to be up-to-date.

Doyle is in his 60s and has lived in this dead-end canyon all his life. After a surprisingly short time, the clippers stop, the hair combed, sweet water sprayed onto my neck. The cape flies off my body with a flourish. Wads of hair float to the floor, adding to the piles around the chair.

Look at all that hair, I think. I needed a haircut. Checking in the mirror, I am startled. I look like a marine with a military white wall. I have no hair.

"How is it?" Doyle asks expectantly.

The image in the mirror is not me. It is a military recruit who has stood in line with 50 other guys and watched hair of various colors stack up around the feet of the single military barber who, every 60 seconds, yells, "Next!" As each man crawls into the chair, the barber asks, "How do you like it cut?" and before the victim can form an answer, the greasy glory of his dating life falls away in chunks and half his head shines like a light bulb. The barber laughs at his joke. None of us line-standers thinks it is funny. His clippers never break their racing pace. Discouraged, we recruits watch the hair fall and know we will live baldly naked for weeks to come.

"So, how is it?" Doyle repeats.

My answer is slow to develop. "It's OK," I reply without conviction. One does not want to insult the only barber and liquor store owner within 65 miles.

"Good!" he says. "It's the style most miners like."

I step into the empty street, glad that it is empty. I have no hair left except a little tuft on top with the approximate dimensions and depth of a coffee saucer. Sun shines on skin that hasn't been kissed by Old Sol in 15 years; white skin climbs up the side of my head and then stops abruptly like a snowline. My sideburns are missing. The only thing left to do is drive to the Navy recruiting office and swear in for four more years. I am ready to attend boot camp again.

I turn to look at my pitiful reflection in the narrow shop window, which reads

BARBER SHOP

in peeling paint. A hand-lettered sign in child's scrawl is taped in the lower corner:

haircuts 50¢

3
RECIPE FOR DISASTER

I'm up early this morning. I love the town this time of day. A layer of wood smoke hangs over the still street; the gray buildings sit silent in the morning shadows. Colorado Avenue, a street of broken pavement, is as snaggle-toothed as a Kentucky coal miner. Weeds grow in empty lots.

There are only two cafés in town. One café, the S&S, is decorated in a high-linoleum theme with bright yellow walls and a subtle counterpoint of ragged barn wood framing the windows. It serves thin, naked hamburgers and chicken-fried steaks fresh from the freezer, delicately drizzled with gourmet canned gravy.

The other café, The Roma, lives in a corner building that leans up canyon toward the mine. It has a Formica counter with eight round Naugahyde stools rimmed in shiny metal, three plywood booths, a gritty wood floor and a serving window in the back wall that opens onto the kitchen where I can see black, stringy hair rustling around. The cafe is empty of customers so it appears that I will breakfast alone.

A plain but smiling waitress in a flowered apron wanders out.

"How are your bacon and eggs?" I ask cheerily.

Closely considering the question, she looks at me for a long time. "They're the best in town," she says without enthusiasm.

"Then I'll have bacon and eggs, sunny side up."

Thelma, the café cook, is a true Old West woman: built like a tank, short, stocky, tough as armor plate and not very pretty with a heart as strong as a diesel engine. She speaks loudly and confidently and occasionally obscenely. She is fearless and fits Telluride like a glove—rough, untutored, unsubtle. When she laughs, there is no place to hide from her vocal volume. Her voice permeates the building, the windows rattle, and everyone within hearing laughs with her even if they don't hear the joke.

Her father was a professional gambler, and she had grown up rough-and-tumble during the '30s in the small mining camps of the Rockies and dangerous settlements around the Indian reservations where her father made a living in the saloons and card parlors. She married a miner and had babies. I am very fond of her.

A young couple walks in cuddling a ball wrapped in a blue blanket.

"Hey, Thelma!" the mother screeches. "Come see what we got here!"

The black hair pops up, and dark eyes strain to peer over the kitchen sill. They go wide.

Thelma skids out of the kitchen door and around the corner like a fat, grease-spattered white Porsche and screams, "Oh! Oh! Oh!" She scoops up the newborn wad, gives its tiny cheek a big smack and, an inch from the baby's face yells, "Yore th' cutest li'l sumbitch I ever seen!" The baby crunches back and begins to cry. The mother grins.

My order arrives, bacon like weathered house siding and eggs floating in grease, yellow eyes that stare back from their brown fringes looking like they had overtrained at the Elks Club bar last night.

I hear from breakfast in the form of serious stomach cramps. I jolt from a noon nap, jump from the bed and with an inspired and quick dance step trot to the bathroom.

It is a very close call.

We hire Thelma to clean our house, but we never let her cook.

4

ED CROSS, WESTERNER

I am thrilled to be his friend. Ed Cross is the last remnant of the Old West, that time when there were fewer laws and more spirit, where survival of the fittest sometimes meant outside the law, not inside.

Two miles high, surrounded by Silver Pick Basin at the foot of Mount Wilson, in the gray slide rock at the rim of a vertical defile that herds the raucous rushing creek, he tells me about panning for gold there.

"My son and I found a nugget as big as your fist. I filed mining claims on this basin years ago and the whole side of Wilson there. I pioneered that Z road going up the cliff there with a Dee-four Cat." He points with his chin at the scar in the slide rock clinging to the shoulder of the mountain.

He gazes out over the green and brown mesas of western Colorado toward a final touch of blue in the far distance 100 miles away, the La Sal Mountains in Utah. The air is clean and crisp, snappy cool even on this summer day.

"But we ran outta money."

"What happened to the fist-sized nugget?"

"Somebody stole it," he says without regret. He falls silent and slowly lets his eyes drift around the slide rock and sharp angles of this tough place.

"How did you get to Colorado, anyway? Where did you grow up?" I ask.

He seems pleased to be asked. Perhaps he is so daunting that people are afraid to ask. Certainly, I am cautious in my curiosity.

"Well, I was born on a ranch in southeastern Utah sometime around 1900. My daddy was a federal marshal who chased cattle rustlers during the day and rustled a few head for himself at night."

"He worked both sides of the law?"

"Yeah. The law was pretty shaky out in the cedar breaks. Us Mormons finally rustled so many cattle from the rich Limeys that owned all the good grazing land that they finally went broke and went back to England leaving us Mormons to steal from each other," he chuckles.

"That means you grew up as a cowboy?"

"Oh, hell yes. It was a dryland ranch. I was punching cows and wrangling from the time I could sit a saddle. I love it out there where the wind blows and it rains sideways."

He nods, agreeing with himself.

"When I was 12, my daddy sent me off to boarding school in St. George. I couldn't stand it. I felt like a prisoner there. On the second night, I went outta th' window and took off."

He scratches his jaw with a crooked forefinger.

"I walked that night and the next day I was walking along a wagon track and a man on a buckboard comes along and asks me where I was going. I said I don't know. Then he asks if I had any food. I said no. Then he asks me if I have any water. I say not anymore. He asks me how I thought I was going to live. I said I don't know that neither.

"So he picked me up and took me to his ranch. That night I slept behind the cook stove and worked for him for the next three years as a horse wrangler and fence rider."

"So did your folks come looking for you?"

"Yeah. They found me but left me alone. I was happy working there, and I liked the man. He was a good man." His faded blue eyes went into the distance. "He died."

"Then what happened?"

Sitting on a big flat rock, he shifts to a place more comfortable. He looks like a movie star that has been slammed in the face with a shovel. His once aquiline nose shows that it had been broken several times and is now a bit crooked, and the skin around his dark eyes is taut and terminally leathered from a lifetime lived in the sun.

"I left the ranch when he died. Then I was 15 going on 16 and I heard that Black Jack Pershing was going to Mexico to hunt Pancho Villa. That silly-assed greaser had come across into New Mexico, attacked the army fort in Columbus and killed some people. Can you imagine? Came across the border and attacked the United States," he says, seemingly still surprised again after all this time.

"Black Jack was going down there with some soldiers to kick Pancho's ass and was looking for horse wranglers. So I hired on to one of his wrangler outfits and ended up down in Mexico with his herd."

He digs deep in his jacket pocket and brings out a muslin bag of Bull Durham and a flat of rolling papers. Curling a rolling paper in his fingers, he carefully dumps a tan line of tobacco into the crease, pulls the tobacco bag closed with his teeth, runs the paper expertly along his tongue and rolls it into a slim cylinder.

I have never seen him smoke before.

As he strikes a kitchen match on a rock and fires the cigarette, he catches my eye. "Peg don't want me to smoke, so I have to sneak around." He chuckles at his duplicity.

"I hadn't been down there long when one night I was playing poker with some Mexicans and one of 'em pulled a knife on me. So I pulled a pistol from my belt and shot him from under the table. I never knew if I killed him. I took off running.

"I go find my lieutenant and tell him what happened. He says to me, 'You go pick out the two best horses in the remuda and run for it.' I roped two tough horses and rode north hell-for-leather toward the Rio Grande riding one and pulling one and switching off every hour." He nods slowly, remembering. "I rode hard that night and the next morning and I could still see the greasers. They were gaining and when I got to the river, they were pretty close, but I thought they wouldn't cross the river.

"But when they came up to it, they didn't even slow down. So I dropped down behind this big log and when they came splashing across I laid my rifle across it and started shooting 'em with my 30-30."

He doesn't say shooting *at* them; he says *shooting* them. I feel my brain go funny. Is this story true or is he just having fun with this awestruck flatlander?

"So how many did you shoot?"

His face goes immobile, unreadable. "Six."

"Did you kill 'em?"

He shrugs, "I don't know. It was pretty close range, 30 or 40 yards. Some of 'em fell off their horses and were floating down the river. Two of them turned around and rode off fast and so did I."

He stands, curls his arm around, scratches his back with his thumb and scans around the gray rock cirque and up at the peak in front of us. I look upward, and I see him as the ultimate westerner, a tall man in a worn leather vest and a Stetson outlined against a background of snowy peaks in the high Rockies. He looks like a '50s movie poster. The only thing missing from the iconic image is a low-slung pistol on his hip tied off to his thigh with a thong.

"I knew I was in big trouble," he continues. "This is an international incident and everybody would be looking for me.

Then I figured out where is the last place on earth they could find me was in the Army. So I joined up, got gassed in France and spent two years in the army hospital."

"So nobody ever found you for the border thing?"

He shakes his head, "Nah."

He looked out to the horizon, remembering. "After that, I worked on the Hoover Dam mucking those water tunnels. I got a bit of the rock in my lungs, so I quit that and went up to Washington and tie-hacked. Then I trapped around Jackson Hole for a while. The winters were bad but the trapping was good. Several of us were trapping out of season when a game warden got shot. So I moved on."

"Did you shoot him?"

He takes on the poker face. After a long pause, he says, "No. But I know who did."

An awkward silence falls on us. The creek races and tumbles, the sound reflects off the rock walls and makes background music to a quiet long moment. Had I gotten too close?

I break the silence. "So how did you end up here in Colorado?"

"Well, during the Depression, a partner and I set up a sawmill cutting railroad ties down here in what is now Sawpit. We went broke." He peers hard down the canyon as if he has spotted something. "I've been in and out of this country for a long time," he says, almost to himself.

"So how did you end up with a contract on the McLeod Ranch?"

"Oh, I've known Buster McLeod for years. We used to get drunk together back when I was drinking. I was a Jack Mormon then. I went by his ranch to talk about some water rights one day and he told me he had a big dustup with his wife. They been married 30 years and she was going to leave him and he might have to sell the ranch to settle the divorce.

Just right there I told him I would buy it and he said all right and we shook hands on it and wrote out a deal on the back of an envelope on the hood of his pickup. The only thing we could find to write with was a short-assed little pencil. I gave him $50 cash as earnest money because that was all I had on me."

The McLeod Ranch, above the town, over a ridgeline, is higher pastureland interrupted by aspen and evergreen groves and open parks populated by grazing sheep and cattle. McLeod's father and mother had homesteaded the ranch back in the 1800s. Cattle prices are down and now it produces only a thin living for Buster McLeod, a real rancher who dresses like one, thinks like one and takes great pride in living like one.

Buster had lived the idyllic western life until he was caught in the act with the county clerk in the bed of his pickup truck parked way out on lonely Good Enough Mesa. Nothing but the woman's head could be seen bobbing in a carnal rhythm. This nasty news traveled fast and the public hilarity that raced around the county annoyed his wife so much she filed for divorce.

Ed continues, "I think McLeod was ready to move on anyway. He got throwed a couple of years ago and his horse stomped on his kidney and broke some ribs. And he's got some age on him now, too. Said he had rheumatiz in his back from rodeoing when he was a youngster. It hurts when he rides. Wanted to go to the low country because it was getting harder and harder to make a living up here."

"Then I came along and he saw a way out of his troubles. He took my $50 as a down stroke to buy his whole ranch for $177 an acre." He smiles slyly.

The ranch is a spectacular 3,200 acres in the last largely ignored part of southwestern Colorado right where the sandy edge of the Colorado Plateau drifts up against the San Juan range of the southern Rockies. The terrain is perfectly suited for a large ski development and all the associated real estate scams that blossom from it. The topography flows down from the high craggy peaks into rolling foothills, then into gentler and easier pitches, all of which look into the face of the 14,000-foot Wilson Peak, the most-photographed mountain in Colorado. At this moment, we sit 3,000 feet below that summit.

Is this guy for real? Has he actually done all of this stuff or is he aggrandizing himself for my benefit? He can tell that I soak up his stories. I encourage him at every opportunity. Am I being played for a fool?

As the shadows stretch out, we amble to the pickup in silence and drive back out of the slide rock and the scrub trees and across Wilson Mesa to Telluride.

For a year, Ed and I hang out together in the hills, mesas and canyons, and he regales me with stories of his past and I am an appreciative audience. Now 72, he is still straight, strong and vibrant. He moves quickly, athletically. His eyes are clear, and it is obvious that he will live many years if he stays out of trouble. Apparently, trouble for him is now more remote than it has ever been.

As older folks often do, Ed repeats stories told months before. The details never vary. Either they are true or he has a wonderful memory.

I opt for the memory theory. But somehow, the doubter in me never rests. Ed is tender with his wife. He gives coins to children and speaks respectfully to them. He is habitually polite.

He is a hard man to figure.

5

GOING BROKE

On this cloudy morning a week before Christmas, 1970, I watch the town come alive and shift into gear for the business day. Gray clouds hang in the high peaks behind the town, a dowdy and stained curtain of hard weather wet with moisture from the south now being made pregnant with arctic air from Wyoming, fitfully birthing yet another storm.

I have much on my mind. Fear is a goodly part of my preoccupation, for I am now broke. My first year in the town has been a monetary disaster. It is depressing. I am broke with a wife and three kids, a failing insurance business that I hate in my bones, and we're stuck here in paradise.

And the only road out is downhill. To leave, one has to flow like water from the high peaks, race back out through the chiseled valleys, swirl down through the desert slick rock, through the prickly pear and rabbitbrush and finally to the toasted beach of the Gulf of California. Like spring snowmelt, my life is going downhill fast. Only my beach is the dry, hot, bubbling black pavement of Denver. God, I don't want to go back. I can't go back and admit failure, give it all up—the dream, the effort, the loss of community and the individual identification I have developed—to return to the nameless, faceless millions slaving away, having heart attacks to pay their life insurance. I don't want to end this love affair I have with Telluride.

Making the money to move here had been hard. It was the aggregate of 15 years of work, risk, 90-hour weeks and late nights. And now I have blown it all, my whole friggin' wad, in less than a year. Obviously, the way to make a small fortune in Telluride is to start with a large one.

With an effort, I push the thought away.

I stumble and catch myself on the crumbled sidewalk that is no longer a sidewalk but blocks of broken concrete lying at angles along the edge of the dirt street. The town itself is crumbling, fragile, aged, colorless, warped, settling winter by winter into the alluvium of Coronet Creek and her side-canyon waterfalls, white strings of erosion rolling gray gravel, pebbles, pills and thumb-size rocks yanked by force out of the conglomerate that hangs above the town and tumbles down in the summer downpours and flash floods.

The town used to sit atop this alluvial trash but over the past 80 years of rushing snowmelt, it has become an integral part of the trash, more embedded, more indebted to the valley, sinking lower into the gravel flows. Some of the houses have sunk to window level, the gravel and weeds reaching nearly to the sills, growing high enough to show through the wavy glass windows and paint-flaked mullions, making each reflection a little tourist painting.

Many of these wrecks are purchased for $500 or $1,000 and used for summer escapes by people from the deserts to the south. In summer, Phoenix is a solar cooker; the Texas Panhandle, desiccated; and these "shining mountains," as the Ute Indians call them, are the air-conditioned playground for schoolteachers and retired college professors with a few bucks and a sense of not very adventuresome adventure.

The village is kin to the primitive piles of sharply broken rocks, the miniature town, craggy, cubic clapboard buildings, piles of lumber twisted by rain and snow and blazing mountain sun, all gray, broken and sinking into the valley floor together, returning to the earth and while not dying, certainly looking extremely ill.

As a newly arrived flatlander, I'm an outcast from the town's high society—the longtime locals, the miners, the Rotarians, the Elks, the Masons, the Odd Fellows—all the fraternal clubs that are the warp and woof of the town, ignore me.

Arising before sunrise each morning is not particularly difficult since the sun does not creep stealthily over a flat horizon but scrambles by its fingernails up over the peaks above the town. Sunrise never occurs before 8 o'clock or so. In the winter, it can be 10 o'clock before the town feels the warmth of direct sunlight. I often watch the sun's rays scrape across the canyon walls on the low side of town, rubbing heat into the aspens and ponderosa. Except for the shadows, nothing moves at this time of day.

My spirits rise with the sun. At night I worry. In the daytime I work at the losing business I have bought from a very smart local. The newly opened bank is decimating my loan business; it gets the good loans. The deadbeats have spotted me as an easy mark, a patsy for small loans that immediately go uncollectible. The insurance agency is a detail business I hate and ignore and lose money on every day. So I feel stupid all around—the finance company and insurance agency—losers in a mining town in the middle of the mountains in southwestern Colorado, a million miles from any way to make money. And I love the place in spite of it all.

Our dream of a home in the mountains is dying a painful death. We will not have the luxury of living in the high Rockies. Life will have to visit us in the lower altitude in an ordinary place.

The thought of returning to the crowded city just to make a living makes my stomach churn. It is an impossible thought yet it is here, a living possibility.

I raise my eyes to the jagged ridgeline above the town where the rock invades the blue sky. I wonder how long I will get to admire this spectacular scene.

But I'm going to worry about that tonight. Today I have to make a buck.

6

CRIBS

Watching the ancient madam creep across the main street is an exercise in patience. Dressed in layers of ankle-length print skirts as old as the whorehouse line itself, her bulk moves with the quiet, almost imperceptible motion of a high valley glacier: first one foot, a slow drag, then the other, feet encased in frayed black canvas slippers. A bandana corrals her gray hair, her tan face rutted and crevassed. She is the picture of straight-backed dignity. She looks neither right nor left at the stopped cars in the street. Drivers wait patiently for her to achieve the crossing.

Stopping at the high curb, she contemplates the big step for a minute or two, moves her hand from the crook of the cane to the middle and plants the stick firmly on top of the curb. When Rita finally makes her move, she hunches over the step and in a mighty effort, ascends in one smooth motion that carries her to the summit where she stands straight and proud.

One morning I tag along with my across-the-street neighbor who takes food to her grandmother on Pacific Street. We knock on the door of the grandmother's house, a narrow two-room clapboard structure without paint, the wooden boards eroded by wind and snow until they show the silver hills and valleys of the grain. Two windows and a door are the only openings in the shack. It is what remains of a whorehouse crib in the red light district on the low side of Telluride.

Rita opens the door wide. Her fearless, heavily weathered face with a big smile and bad teeth greets us. The room is dim; the curtains, thin and limp from age, are closed but losing the fight against the light. With a dying fire in the stove, the room fills with the edgy patina of old people.

Across one end of the room, a blanket hangs on a sagging wire. A hidden hand slowly slides it open to reveal a sickbed. In the dim light, a man half rises on his elbow; an apparition, wild white hair, white arms like sticks, claw-like hands, deformed fingers frozen into hooks. It is obvious the withered man is living out his last days.

"Who is it?" he wheezes. She answers softly, "It's your granddaughter, Sissy." His head drops back, his mouth gasping and his coal black eyes watching us and listening.

In an old and accented voice, Rita says easily, "She brought us cake, Barney." He closes his eyes and doesn't answer.

The middle 1920s was the heyday of hard rock mining and working girls. Pacific Street was the town's shopping center of desire and debauchery. Popcorn Alley, the longest running red light district in the state, sported 20 or more cribs, two-room wooden buildings perhaps 20 feet wide. The hundred or more prostitutes serviced the 5,000 miners that emerged every Saturday night and swamped the town with a level of horniness that created a booming market in, and for, quim. Nature would not be denied, indeed, could not be delayed. So, on a busy evening, the cribs' screen doors squealed open and slammed shut throughout the night, the to-ing and fro-ing making a sound like corn popping.

Rita's business was declared illegal in 1915 as the state donned the cloak of uprightness and most fun activities were outlawed by the righteous God-fearing men who now had to sneak under the cover of deep darkness to the illegal brothels to get things done that their wives wouldn't do. Although technically the whorehouse line was illegal, a few brothels on Popcorn Alley stayed quietly in business until 1939. The whores were tolerated as long as they stayed on the shady side of the main street. Then, as now, ignoring the law was de rigueur, acceptable to Telluriders.

Watching from the sidewalk, a newcomer marvels at the old woman crossing the street, her straight figure, the commanding bearing of this obviously poor woman heavy in ancient clothes.

"Who is she?" he asks me.

"That, my man, is the last madam standing."

7

FAT JESUS DESCENDS

I'm at the end of my Telluride adventure. I am broke. Only some sort of miracle can save me, which is unlikely. Luck never shows up when you need it the most.

Then a fat man in a gravy-stained tie and a filthy fedora walks into my basement office and plumps down. His chest heaves at the altitude. He hisses at the thin air, "Are you Vass?"

"Yep."

The fat man smiles, "Good. My name is A.B. Smith. I live in Grand Junction. I've been doing some research. You have the only real estate license in San Miguel County. But it's only a salesman's license, not a broker's license. I own a broker's license that allows me to do business in my own name. So, I'm gonna do just that; I'm gonna set up a real estate office here in Telluride."

He stares out of the basement window that shows a grand view of some growing grass at the root level, several scraggly dead flowers and a patch of blue sky that, if lined up exactly right, is the size of a toilet paper roll.

I lean back in my chair. "Really?" Somebody else in the universe thinks the town might go. I'm not alone. "And where are you going to locate this new business?"

The fat man looks around with great satisfaction at the brightly lighted, freshly painted subterranean office. Slipping two fingers between the buttons of his suit vest he pronounces, "Right here. Right here in this office and you are going to run it for me!"

"I am?"

"Ya damn rights. This town is going to explode!"

"Ya think so?"

"Ya damn rights."

He takes a deep breath. The wheeze fills the room.

"This ski deal is going to change everything." He looks at me without blinking. "Here's my proposition: You work the business in town and I'll work it out of town. I keep everything I make; you keep 90 percent of everything you make." His eyebrows go up over his red face and hang there.

I look carefully at this apparition, the loose flesh under the chin, the gravy-stained tie, the black fedora with sweat rings, the old, black, vested suit with a watch chain sagging across a bloated landscape, the scarred French-toed shoes with a finish like a smoker's skin, eyebrows still at cruising altitude.

So, this is what salvation looks like. I always thought it would come in some exotic form: heaven-sent, a glorious vision with bright lights, jagged lightning, with everyone begging for forgiveness and redemption. I anticipated an effeminate guy descending from puffy cumulus clouds in a blonde wig, even a ponytail, sky-blue eyes and modest, pressed robes. There would be euphoria everywhere.

But no. It's a fat guy that just stepped off a garbage truck. And he's hustling me for free office space in a dusty, dirty, little old mining town that is nearly empty of everything, including business.

The real estate business. I have a salesman's license but it's on ice. I dallied in property as an investor, made a buck or two, couldn't buy a decent car with the profits made so far. But to actually broker it, that's an unexpected flash. And brought to me by a guy dressed as a dog dish. In this place, the people who do buy and sell land and houses are all freelancers without a state license. Brokering real estate without a license is against the law, but what the hell—a lot of things in Telluride are against the law. That is its charm.

Maybe this can work. This overweight real estate artifact has found me at the bottom of my failure curve. I have nothing to lose.

Reticently, but with a feigned smile I say, "OK. Deal." I stand and clutch the pudgy hand of redemption, perhaps holding it a bit overlong.

A week later, Fat Jesus is back, dressed exactly as before. He comes in sweating from the exertion. Obviously, at 8,800 feet, the altitude is taxing him. Breathing hard, he sags into the office couch.

He taps his chest, "Bad ticker, ya know." He gasps deeply several times.

"I requested transfer of your license from the real estate commission to here. Brought your business cards. Had them printed overnight. Need them fast 'cause we got a lotta business to do. There's gonna be a lot of money made here."

He keeps his hat on and wheezes for air, his face red from gasping. His paunch droops over his belt, which curls from the stress, and his vest buttons mercilessly strain their holes scalloping the garment. If the buttons were alive they would scream in great pain.

"You know about the old narrow gauge right of way?" he asks.

"Yes, I do."

"Tell me what you know about it."

"It originally ran from here over Lizard Head Pass to Rico and Dolores to Durango and down canyon to Placerville and over Dallas Divide to Ridgway. Must be something over 160 miles long. Abandoned in the early '50s. When the railroad went bankrupt, the county took most of the right of way back because nobody wanted it. Worthless. The rest of it reverted to the original landowners."

"OK. So it's 160 miles long. How wide is it?"

"I think it's 100 feet in most places. Skinnier in some spots."

He stares out the basement window moving his head slightly to get lined up on the toilet paper roll sky. "Can we get ahold of it?"

"You mean the right of way? To do what with, for Chrissake? The tracks have all been pulled up. Some of the grades have fallen down into the canyons; rockslides have filled in some places. The wood trestles are mostly there, I think, but they aren't safe."

I watch the fat man closely. What is his idea? Where's he going with this? Rebuild the narrow gauge? People have discussed it for years, a historic reconstruction of Otto Mears' railroad that opened southwestern Colorado to all those things that white men revere: gold and cattle and money. The right of way was dug and chiseled and dynamited out of Mother Earth, flying over white rivers on trestles, hanging from cliffs and otherwise defying gravity, a pencil line of progress drawn crookedly through the living heart of the mountains. It is a spectacular image.

Railroads make the aged, sepia, stilted scenery photographs seem unbelievable; chuffing little engines crossing shaky wooden spans hanging dangerously on vertical mountain cliffs above wild rivers. Many of those frighteningly awesome Old West images from the history books were photographed along this very railroad.

My heart skips a beat. My God, he's doing it again. Now instead of saving me, he's going to save the whole county by rebuilding the narrow gauge. What a boon to the locals. Railroad buffs will come from all over the world to see this Old West stuff; not a cardboard and plywood copy—the real thing.

There is still rolling stock around. A couple of the hand-built engines are in museums. Why hell, there is a Galloping Goose right by the courthouse and another one in Dolores, 68 miles down canyon, the hermaphrodite locomotive with its passenger coach pulled by a weird-looking school bus-like machine with a Pierce Arrow engine.

This could work. This would work.

"What are you gonna do with that right of way?"

Fat Jesus looks pleased. "You do this: Go research the title on that land." He levers himself upright with a groan and grabs the doorknob. As he is leaving, he turns and hands me a white box from his coat pocket. "Oh, here are your business cards. I'll see you next week." And he is gone.

I open the box to take out a card to see if, by any remote chance, he spelled my name right. He did.

He named our new business in bold letters: *TELLURIDE REALTY*.

8

A SHERIDAN BULLET

In the heat of the argument, the man pulls a pistol from his pocket and shoots his wife in the middle of her forehead, squarely between the eyes.

Alvin is what we locals call a spastic. With arms and legs flailing uncontrollably, he runs herky-jerky from the Sheridan Hotel into the street screaming bloody murder. His shouts are unintelligible through the spittle that sprays everyone in range, his tongue twisting into a fleshy tunnel emitting pitiful squalls.

When the marshal intercepts him and finally deciphers his story, it seems Alvin and his sister and brother-in-law had been pulling an all-nighter in the hotel room, drinking and smoking. Their family conversation escalated into an argument: whether or not to buy a Chevy pickup or a Ford. This disagreement climaxed in a point-blank headshot. According to a tearful and shaking Alvin, at this moment his sister is splayed across the bed very dead.

The marshal, Everett, is a small man straight out of the movies. He wears a leather vest, cowboy boots, a six-gun, mace, handcuffs, a billy club, lead-loaded gloves and a surly attitude. He is also a master welder and counts two mail-order degrees in law from La Salle University Extension in his curriculum vitae.

Before hiring him, the town was without a marshal, so each member of the town board had, in turn, taken over the policing duties. Eventually, they were compelled to hire somebody from the thin ranks of candidates and the field was reduced to Everett.

The new marshal is suspicious toward newcomers and downright hateful toward Jews and hippies who he thinks are subversive to the American way of life. When we first moved in, he drove his cop car past our house on North Aspen every 20 minutes, staring hard into our windows or at the kids if they were outside.

After a few days of this, I stepped into the street and waved Everett down.

"Hey Everett, how ya doin'?"

"I'm on top," he says icily. "Whaddaya need?"

"I really don't need anything. I just wanted to thank you for keeping your eye on my house. When I lived in southeast Denver, I paid $200 a month for a security service that you do for free. You're a helluva good deal for us new folks. So, again, thank you for your consistent attention. It makes me and my family feel much better about living here."

Everett's dour face fell even further and without answering, he drove away down the dusty street. After that, he turned his attentions to threatening hippies and harassing the Jews and left us alone.

Every four years there is a sheriff's election, and it is always hotly followed if not hotly contested. The present county sheriff is a tall man who goes about town unarmed and is given to wearing blue polyester blazers and staying in the office out of the weather. The last election had been between Everett and him. It came as a bitter defeat for the heavily armed marshal.

The locals feel the marshal is for picking up loose dogs, recovering cars that run over cliffs and directing traffic. But murder?

Everett's time in the sun happens on this Sunday morning.

In the middle of the main street, in a thick and nearly unintelligible Oklahoma drawl, he awkwardly questions the shaking Alvin who can hardly talk. A dozen curious citizens gather around them trying to understand what happened. After much drawling, spitting and spraying, it finally comes out that the hot-blooded killer has run away after shooting his wife and has hidden in the basement of the Floradora Bar.

Trotting down the middle of the empty street in the Sunday morning sunshine, Everett is soon in front of the bar, yelling at the murderer.

"Cum out here, Maynard. I know yer in there! Ya'll cum out with yer hands up where I kin see 'em!"

A plaintive voice comes back, "I ain't coming out, Everett."

"Ya cum out now so's I don't have to cum in after ya! If'n I have to cum in thar, it's gonna be real trouble!" Everett shouts. "Don't make me do it!"

He crouches down behind a parked car a nice safe distance from the building, his hand on his six-shooter, his 10-gallon hat pushed back, the sweat running down his face in the cool morning air.

The killer's voice quavers with terror. "I ain't comin' out, Everett!" he screams. "If I come out, you're gonna shoot me!"

"If I come in thar, I'll have ta shoot ya! I won't have no choice!" His voice quavers.

"That's whut I mean … you jus' wanna have a good reason to shoot me. I ain't givin' m'self up to you. No way in hell!"

A long silence ensues broken only by the murmur of spectators. Everett squints but doesn't move from his low and ready-for-action position, like a lawman in the movies.

"Y'all move back!" he commands a bit too loudly to the spectators. He waves his hand behind his back without taking his eyes off the dilapidated building.

"This here man is a armed fugitive an' a killer. If he starts shootin,' some of you folks might get shot, so move back outta the way."

Nobody moves a muscle, fascinated by this Old West tableau: the town marshal, now playing the Western lawman part, is terrified that his crime scene has gone horribly off script.

The weak voice from inside the building shouts, "I'll come out, but I'll only give up to the county sheriff. He ain't trigger-happy like you, Everett."

The marshal's shoulders sag. He turns and barks an order at the spectators: "Somebody go get the sheriff from the courthouse. I gotta watch this guy so he don't come out shootin'! Tell the sheriff we got a killer on th' loose anna armed standoff siteation here!"

Everett, standing as tall as he can for a short person, struts around as if he doesn't care about being replaced, but it is easy to see his relief at being substituted by a real cop.

The sheriff arrives, a tall, lean man in a double-knit blazer with a big badge and the unmistakable air of legal authority.

"Hey Maynard, it's Sheriff McMillan. Throw the gun out," he says in a calm, almost soothing voice. In a few moments, the fugitive tosses his gun outside and it bounces with a thump off a weathered board.

"Now, Maynard, you come out with your hands up. I'm not going to hurt you."

The fugitive clambers from the basement out to the sidewalk, turns and waits for the snap of the handcuffs.

Everett squares his shoulders to the crowd, his face hard and his hand on his pistol grip. "He won't give himself up to me 'cause he knows he won't live to see sundown if he makes a bad move."

The spectators nod and smile at each other. There are some chuckles from the back of the group.

The procession back to the hotel to inspect the crime scene is led by an authoritative Everett, walking as tall as his five and a half feet will allow, followed by 30 or more chattering townspeople ... and Alvin.

Waiting at the front door are the volunteer firemen who first responded to the shooting and found the woman on the bed lying deathly still, face up, eyes closed. They point Everett up the creaky stairway. Halfway up the stairs, he turns to the crowd in the lobby below. He stands on one step with a boot heroically raised to the step above. With his hat low on his forehead and his hand on his pistol grip just like John Wayne would do it, he announces loudly to those below, "Don't y'all cum up here. This here is now officially a crime scene that I hafta investigate."

At the open door of the hotel room, Everett peeks around the doorframe into his crime scene. His body stiffens. Two firemen look over his shoulder. The firemen cover their mouths to muffle their laughter. As they wend their way back down the stairs and into the street, they begin to hoot. They describe the scene; the crowd's guffaws bounce back from the hotel's glass front and fill the street.

Alvin peeks around the door. His dead sister sits on the edge of the bed smoking a cigarette. Her other hand holds a bottle of beer. A quarter-inch of gray .22 lead bullet sticks out of her forehead surrounded by a black ring of burned powder. It seems that the short tiny bullet didn't have enough power to penetrate her skull.

She weaves drunkenly. Through a billowing cloud of smoke, she hazily looks at the eyeballs peering through the doorway.

She takes a long pull from the bottle and finally focuses on the marshal.

With a sneer she looks at the small man with the shiny star affixed to his leather vest, the bawling Alvin, then around the stifling, stinking room.

"What're ... you ... fools ... lookin' ... at?"

She turns and stares absently at the dirty window and is quiet. In a moment, her glassy gaze shifts back to the slowly building crowd.

In slurred and carefully separated words, she asks, "Has … anybody … got … an … aspirin?"

9

FAT JESUS RETURNS

Telluride sits atop an alluvial fan formed by the raucous Cornet Creek. Every spring this side canyon floods and adds more rocks to the hump it has built over eons. The courthouse, an imposing brick edifice, dominates the highest point of the town's main street. It is square and two-storied and sports a prominent tower with a vent grate installed where the clock should be. Next to the courthouse sits the silver-painted Galloping Goose, a truck-like affair that carried passengers and mail on the narrow gauge railroad that serviced To-Hell-U-Ride during the mining days. It is an unusual conveyance and train buffs from all over the world come to see it. It has a working bell that tourists predictably and irritatingly ring all summer.

But the railroad lost the war against rising costs and a shrinking market. The Galloping Goose is the remains of a rail empire that had survived against all natural hazards of rock slide, avalanche and flood. But it didn't survive the fickleness of man and his misuse of money, resources and reason.

As promised, Fat Jesus returns when he said he would. He bursts into the underground office in a hurry and a flurry. Sweating as usual, he asks, "What did you find out about the right of way?"

"Well, when the railroad went broke, the railroad company abandoned it back to either the adjacent private landowners or the county."

"Good. We ought to be able to buy it cheap."

"To do what with?"

Flashing a satisfied smile, he leans back on the couch and says with conviction, "I want to build the world's longest trailer park!"

He looks at me expectantly.

I'm not sure I've heard him correctly. "You what?"

"I want to use that right of way to create the world's longest and most scenic trailer park." He chuckles at his idea; his jowls shake.

"There is plenty of room to park a 40-foot single-wide trailer and leave plenty of room for an access road. We can put several hundred trailers in this county alone! I'll bet we can put 50 or 60 with great views right out here on the valley floor." He heaves back on the couch; it groans. Looking satisfied, he suddenly stands. "That's my plan." He cocks his thumb and shoots me in the chest with a forefinger. Then he leaves pulling the door shut behind him.

I don't hear from him for a couple of weeks. I begin to run Telluride Realty advertisements in the Telluride Times. People come to my door with money and I quickly show them the two or three properties that are up for sale at any one time. They make offers. I write purchase contracts. Suddenly, it looks like I can make enough money to pay my bills, feed my family and stay in the glorious mountains. But I only get paid when sales close and titles are passed to the new owners.

Nearing the first closing date, I attempt to prepare a closing statement, that document that accounts for all the money in the transaction, which person owes what to whom and for what. Having flunked the same algebra course three times in high school, I am ill-prepared for this higher math, the plusses and minuses from buyer to seller and back. So I call on my friend, the title insurance man, one of the new pioneers like me who has gambled everything on the town. He squares me away on the math. Now, all I need is the broker's signature on the documents and the checks.

I call Fat Jesus in Grand Junction to see when he will come to sign off on the deal. It seems that he is in Veterans Hospital and will not be coming to the canyon anytime soon. He has had a heart attack. So I drive to Grand Junction, 250 miles round trip, and visit Fat Jesus in his hospital bed to get the documents signed.

"I'll be out of here next week," he says. "We can chase that railroad deal." Then he flops back on the pillow.

10

THE CATERPILLER

Teachers often take the kindergartners on field trips to such exciting and educational venues as the main street hardware store or the historic museum. Keeping them in a group and under control is stressful for the teachers, so they came upon a solution. A rope. A big, thick-as-your-wrist rope that the kids grip on their way from school to downtown adventures.

I look down the street and see a caterpillar bobbing along; the middle parts uncoordinated and held together by the rope. Little kids hold on with one hand, smile and wave to the townspeople. Everybody waves back for, while the kids technically belonged to their parents, practically speaking, they belong to the town and are therefore a community responsibility.

As they grow up and become more independent, their instructions are, "You can play anywhere you like in Telluride, just don't leave the canyon." There is always danger in the side canyons—getting lost, drowning in a rushing stream or simply disappearing, never to be seen again. So their playground is 3 miles long and a quarter mile wide, usually under the aware eye of a busy adult working nearby. Whose kid is whose, along with their dog, is street knowledge of the local. Everyone has the tacit right, even duty, to step in when things go wrong.

A big German shepherd, excited by her smell, knocks a fourth-grader on her way to school to her hands and knees. Standing astraddle, he begins to hump her lustily. A neighbor sees what is happening, kicks the big dog away, brushes off the girl's clothes and sends her on to school.

My 6-year-old son disappears for hours, which is normal. He will be somewhere in the valley. The owner of a small bar telephones and says my son is in his establishment. When I walk into the bar, a line of drinkers, their backs to the door, occupy every stool. A tiny figure sits on a stool among them, a man among men, nursing a 7-UP.

Snorky, a man of average shortness, sports for ego purposes, a bushel of black hair. It stands out from his head half a foot or more in every direction, carefully coifed into a perfectly round black ball. His stained leather cowboy hat sits floating on the very top like a UFO. As a status-seeking hippie, he speaks in riddles and talks of higher freedoms. Girls love him. All over the place.

Snorky and his girlfriend, obviously on drugs, decide to entertain the town. In the middle of the main street, just before noon, the woman strips off her jeans and stretches out, legs spread across the white centerline. Snorky drops his pants and happily goes to work; hat still perched precariously on his huge black hairball, his white buttocks glowing in the sun, her legs wrapped tightly around him. She moans.

At the critical moment of this adult display, the kindergarten caterpillar wriggles around the corner. The teacher yells, "Don't look over there!"

As one, all the kids turn and gaze in wonderment; their giggles bounce off the buildings.

Telluride is not amused.

11

FAT JESUS PASSES THE BATON

Now I'm in a crack. Fat Jesus is my only hope for survival in the mountains. If I do what he wants—locate in single file those downscale, single-wide, aluminum insults in one of the loveliest valleys in Colorado—how can I live with that? Certainly the folks in the town will ostracize me. Can it be done? There is no zoning, no building codes, no sewer and water requirements, and no master plan to stop it. In the true sense of the independent settler of the West, a landowner can do whatever he or she wants with his or her land without interference from government. Of course it can be done!

I had hoped the idea would fade away into the fog of other crazy Fat Jesus ideas, but obviously it hasn't. I am stuck. My first introduction to land development holds me in the crossfire of Conscience vs. Survival. The conflict tears at my mind. Can I sacrifice my honor and ego for the money that keeps me here in the valley? Perhaps. Do I have strong enough values to resist the money that allows me to stay?

I fret about it for days.

Then Fat Jesus' wife calls me. "He died," she says, her voice cracking. "He had nine heart attacks in a row and died yesterday at Vets Hospital. I'm going through his stuff. I think you have to return your license to the real estate commission."

I look at the wall a long, long time. What do I do now? I'm just getting started on my new profession and now it has gone away, out of business. I can't sell real estate without a broker. It's the law.

I call the real estate commission and tell them that I have deals in escrow and my broker just hit the silk. What do I do now?

A commissioner from Denver turns up in my office in a vested suit and expensive tie, takes a look around and notices that while the office is humble, even cheap, it is still a place of business with public access from the street and a sign.

"Here's what we can do," he starts. "We want this town to have a legitimate, licensed real estate broker. Right now, people are dealing illegally. We'll make you a deal. If you pass the broker's exam, we'll waive all the legal prerequisites, the two years' experience as a salesman, the law courses and all of that professional education and issue you a broker's license."

Well, screw it. I'll do real estate by myself, become a broker. It can't be that hard. There are many dumber people than me that have broker's licenses.

On east Colfax in Denver, I rent a sleazy motel room for three weeks. Knowing that I will leave the room to go out and play the instant I get dressed, I study naked. When I go crazy from studying, I drop down and do pushups to exhaustion. Each day at 4 o'clock and not before, I allow myself to get dressed and leave the room.

The grapevine says that the passing grade is 80 and only 14 percent of broker candidates pass the three-day exam on the first try. I get lucky; my score is 81.

The first thing I do is record a trade name affidavit with the county clerk on the name Telluride Realty. Thus is born the business that will keep me in Telluride for 20 years, make me a millionaire, make me broke twice and cause me endless heartache.

Thank you, Fat Jesus.

12

ED CROSS, THE SCARY

With the ski area in the beginning stages of development, Stein has spent a few dollars on surveys and land plans, and it now appears the ski mountain might become more than an empty promise. It excites the few people in town who understand what the planning means. The established citizens, the miners and their families, rarely give it a thought.

The mine pays well. Everyone who wants a job has one. There are no involuntary indigents hanging out on the only paved street. Colorado Avenue, the main street, is also Highway 145 and travels through town to dead end 2 miles later at the Pandora Mill in the closed end of the box canyon.

A ski area? The locals had heard it all before. A developer had once come to town, raised investment money from the locals by selling stock in Telluride Ski Area, Inc., and then skipped town, never to be found. The locals had been burned once and they vowed never to get burned on that kind of a scam again. Looking into their whiskeys at the Elks Club bar, they say with shaking heads, "Let's see who gets screwed this time. It ain't gonna be me."

Ed Cross buys 400 acres out on Hastings Mesa 20 miles north of town and is subdividing it into five- and 10-acre parcels. Flatlanders love to own scenic mountain property that they can photograph and show their big city friends. Out on the mesa, the land is mostly flat with aspen and evergreen trees and open areas broken by small cliffs along the draws that funnel water into tree-clogged Leopard Creek. One can see big mountains nearby, big dramatic mountains, in several directions.

Buying property in the San Juans creates a paradox: If you own land among the peaks, you can rarely, if ever, see them. The canyons are too deep, the peaks too steep and out of sight behind trees or rock walls or cliffs. If you buy land on the flatter mesas surrounding the peaks, you aren't in the mountains but, if they are several miles away, you can see them in their unobstructed magnificent glory—high, nasty-rugged, dusted white for much of the year. They appear as a scenic poster in the basement rec rooms of the owners.

On the nearby mesas, people have some access to civilization—the drugstore, the bars, the drug dealers and the naked women in hot tubs. They buy land where the ground is mostly flat with a view of the picturesque ranges.

Ed applies to the county commissioners to rezone his land to subdivide it. Since his presentation skills are admittedly weak, Ed calls on me to help him get the county commissioner's approvals; we work together to get his selling show on the road.

On a rainy fall afternoon, he phones. "Ya want to go up to the mesa with me? I've got to do something."

As usual I drop everything. I never miss an opportunity to ride along with my hero, no matter how full of bullshit he is. As it becomes more and more gentrified, the Old West is fading fast in Telluride. The Basque sheepherders no longer come to town, the herds of shaggy "mountain maggots" no longer move down from the high pastures to the low country, driven along the main street by herders on horses. The Idarado mine, the second largest base-metals mine in the state, is winding down operations and the miners are moving to work in other dark holes deep in the mineralized grounds of New Mexico and Nevada. Fancier cars and, occasionally, fancier women arrive. Young men with hard bellies from Eastern cities look for a place to play western bad man. Twenty-somethings, wannabe get-rich-quick entrepreneurs and adult children with beautifully maintained teeth and trust funds arrive. Their only ambition: to ski the steep and deep and play fantasy town in the Old West and do drugs and chase women. The real cowboys and ranchers and sheepherders give way to mountain climbers, hikers and middle-class escapees from Los Angeles, Phoenix, Chicago and points east, folks with lots of money and the burning ambition to tailor a new hometown out of rough cloth. The real West suffers a slow death from daily overdoses of money. I have to admit that I am an active participant in the coup d'etat of the New West over the Old. I listen to the death rattle and watch the final muscle twitches with conflicted emotions.

I call it involuntary superiority, the feeling that flatlanders have on arriving from the city. They bring with them the subtle but sure knowledge that city life has made them smarter and more aware than their new small-town neighbors. Obviously these ignorant mountain people need help to build their nirvana, and the city folks' altruism bursts forth from the same people who, in the city, would do almost anything to beat you away from a stoplight. They feel superior. They can't help it. The locals tolerate it. In six months, the superior feeling will go away as the newcomers realize that the people they have been gratuitously advising wrote the authoritative text on the very problem under discussion. It is a creeping embarrassment for the newcomers to realize they had been coddled like children until they grew in knowledge.

We drive up to the subdivision to discuss how the land could be subdivided to sell well and preserve the best views of the surrounding mountains and mesas.

Ed stops for me in his pickup. As I slide into the seat, my hand lands on the butt of a revolver jutting from a worn leather holster. We ride along in silence. Ed wheels expertly through the curves above the muddy San Miguel River that swirls noisily in the canyon below, hurrying on its way to the Colorado.

I study the pistol out of the corner of my eye.

"What kind of pistol is this, Ed?"

"It's a .45 Colt Peacemaker. I've owned it for 40 years," he says.

We ride along in silence until we make the turn up out of the river canyon at Sawpit.

Finally, I can't stand it any longer. "What's the canon for?"

He turns to me with a steely eye, "I'm going to meet with Marion Jackson and if he gives me shit, I'm going to kill him," he says flatly.

Certainly he's kidding me, I think. This is just more of the bluster and the personal myth. He just says that to make sure I know he is a dangerous man. "Oh. Why are you doing that?"

"He is pioneering a road in with a Dee-eight and I told him exactly where I wanted the goddamn road and when I drove by there yesterday, he was gone. The dozer was there, but he has taken the road off in a different direction right across lots I was going to sell. That son of a bitch just cost me a lot of money."

"You are going to shoot him for that? It doesn't seem like a reasonable way to handle a mistake."

"It isn't a mistake. He did it on purpose just to piss me off. He's a hardheaded son of a bitch. He was tried for attempted murder and acquitted 15 years ago. Bushwhacked a rancher from behind while the man sat in his pickup truck. Shot at him through the back window. Everybody knew he did it. He's crazy, and he isn't going to argue with me. If he does, I'm going kill 'im before he kills me. He's unpredictable."

I feel my thighs pump with adrenaline. I am a family man, three kids, a business and completely bereft of courage. A city boy. And here I am on my way to a shootout. My hands shake; I grip my knees to steady them and my foot taps involuntarily.

Perhaps Ed's stories are true. Just perhaps.

The bulldozer is working, pushing buckbrush and rocks over the side of the blade path. The engine growls with the work, belching black smoke intermittently.

We bounce down over the big rocks of the roughed out road and stop behind the huge, yellow machine. The operator looks back, puts the behemoth in neutral and jumps to the ground.

Ed opens the truck door, stands behind it, buckles the well-used pistol belt and walks to face the man. I do not move, mesmerized by what might happen next. There is a short, animated conversation between the two men, some arm waving and head shaking. Ed points along the hillside. Jackson points down the hill into the buckbrush. Ed leans over into Jackson's face, makes a final point, turns and, without a further word, returns to the truck and backs up the rocky road to the top of the mesa.

Relief flows over me like a warm shower. "What happened?"

"He's doing it my way," Ed says flatly.

Out on top, he stops the truck and steps out. "Come with me."

I follow on unsteady legs.

Ed pulls the pistol from its unadorned leather holster. No fancy cowboy decoration here. He holds it out to me tenderly like a newborn kitten.

"Can you shoot a pistol?" he asks quietly.

"I was in the Navy and had to qualify with a .45 automatic," I say tentatively.

He offers the Colt butt first. The smooth wood grip feels foreign in my hand, surprisingly heavy and serious. "See that aspen tree? See the eye about 6 feet up from the ground? Shoot that eye," he commands.

Aspen tree branches leave eye-shaped scars on the trunk when they fall off, leaving the bark with its characteristic trademarks of eyelids outlining black pupils. The tree was at least 50 feet away. Maybe more. To my eye, it's a long way away.

I raise the pistol, steady my aim and squeeze the trigger. The pistol barks and jumps. A clean miss of the tree trunk.

"Try again," he says softly.

Five more shots and, with one round, I manage to hit the tree inches from the eye.

"Let me show you," he says, almost whispering. Pulling a hand full of bullets from his pants pocket, he reloads six rounds into the shiny cylinder. With a flick of his wrist, he snaps the cylinder back into place. He holds the pistol reverently and then, at arm's length, fires six times as fast as he can pull the trigger. The explosions nearly run together into a single, crashing nerve-shattering sound.

We walk to the tree. His bullet holes are in a grouping that can be covered with a dollar bill.

13
MY LITTLE CHICKADEE

In deep winter, days are short and with only one television channel and one radio station from Grand Junction, boredom slides in to sit beside you and rests its unlovely head on your shoulder.

Two nights a week the Nugget Theater runs a movie, usually old or unknown films because they can be rented from the distributor for peanuts.

Maggiemay, a middle-aged woman with ill-designed and ill-fitting false teeth who, because of her sweet good nature, smiles at you all the time, manages the movie house. Those teeth that stand like boards in a painted fence are her trademark.

The Nugget Theater, the only picture show within 65 miles, is never crowded except when Maggiemay manages to strike a deal on a big movie intercepted in transit from Montrose to Gunnison. Then, the 60 seats fill and a sign goes up at the box office that there are no seats left.

A full house of down-insulated people raises the room temperature to uncomfortable heights. As soon as the theater empties, Maggiemay turns off the heat and the inside air rapidly drops to the temperature of the main street. If it is an old movie and the crowd is four or five entertainment-starved locals, you keep your parka on for the whole feature, quiet and unmoving, with hands in pockets, feet freezing to numbness, eyes locked onto the screen, the moving images seen gauzily through icy breaths.

The dozen people from New York who belong to the Cine Club (I call it the Sign Club just to pimp their pretensions) have a special Wednesday show every few weeks where they ooh and aah over some low-angle black and white scene of a drip of water from a faucet, symbolizing (I guess) an orgasm of lovers doing the dirty in a Paris hotel room.

"I jus' stoked the furnace. It'll warm up," says Maggiemay cheerfully, her teeth shining brightly in the glow of a single fluorescent tube inside the candy case.

Inside this frozen tomb, the walls are painted a gangrenous green with ocean scenes, cutouts of tropical fish and waving seaweed in pastel colors typical of the town's whole design motif: out of place, inappropriate, cheap, old-fashioned and weird.

For tonight's movie, Maggiemay has rented "My Little Chickadee," a 1940s classic starring Mae West and W.C. Fields.

On this frigid evening, nothing moves on the street or inside the Nugget. My breath seems to freeze in the air. I sit in the middle of the back row of the narrow hall, hoping that the slanted floor will allow all heat to flow uphill. Eino Pekkarine crabs into a seat two rows closer to the screen. We sit there, looking fat in our down parkas and wool caps, silent, shivering.

Eino, who never married, is now middle-aged, pudgy and socially awkward. He studied classical piano at an Eastern music school; his mother considered him too delicate to grow up in a mining camp insulated from the finer things in life. In a silent and empty Sheridan Opera House, I once heard him play haunting and delicate phrases that I felt came from a page of his own lonely book.

In the show, when we laugh, we are two lone voices: mine, the newcomer's—raucous with high notes; his, a local's—refined, quiet, restrained, civilized.

As we leave, Maggiemay flashes those giant Chicklet ivories at us.

"See you next time!" she says. "On Saturday morning we're gonna have cartoons. Dress warm!"

That week, in lousy winter weather thick with blowing snow, my movie partner, the Eastern-educated classical pianist, Eino, steps from between parked cars. Unable to stop, a jeep knocks him to the slick pavement. The old Plymouth ambulance takes Eino to the hospital. He never comes home.

14

ED CROSS, CRIMINAL

We drive through the gate into Ed's property on Hastings Mesa. There are grazing sheep everywhere and they reluctantly part to let us drive through. They call each other "Bob." Long, catchy and mournful sounds, "Baaaaaab-Baaaaaab." The half-grown lambs scamper around desperately trying to find Bob.

The sheepherder's tent is gray and pointed with a jutting stovepipe that exhales curling wisps of smoke above the canvas roof. The flap is open to the spectacular Mount Sneffels massif, which rises arrogantly against the low sky. As we drive up to the tent, a horse, tied to a tree, his coat shiny from the drizzling rain, shies and snorts. A dog with one blue eye and one brown eye barks at us. A slightly built man emerges from the tent, a light-skinned Basque with a growth of beard and black, greasy hair. His pants and shirt are brown with dirt. He motions us inside with a wave and slight bow.

The tent is furnished as summer sheep camps are—a cot, a bedroll, a food box, a rifle for predators and a small black stove that smells of aspen smoke.

In Spanish, he welcomes us inside, *"Buenos dias, patrón."*

"Buenos dias, Manuel. *Mi amigo,* Jerry."

The man acknowledges me with a wave of a knotty hand. He sits on the food box and Ed and I sit on the cot. In the diffused light of the tent, Ed and the sheepherder speak in fast Spanish. I can't follow any of the conversation.

Ed passes the man a bag of tobacco and rolling papers that elicit a big grin. The man stands, opens the food box, takes out a bottle of whiskey and passes it to me, making a motion to take a drink. Going down, the whiskey is flaming napalm. The Basque laughs at my grimace and I pass the bottle to Ed.

While they talk, I sit and look at the imposing gray peaks next door and listen to the rain patter softly onto the canvas roof and the Bobs endlessly calling each other. The dog eases over and I pat him on the head and he relaxes. Somewhere in the distance, a big diesel engine alternately idles and growls in full throat, rising and falling in a purposeful rhythm.

On the way home, I ask Ed what they had talked about.

"Oh, just the local gossip. A rich man from the East thought he would go into the sheep business. Bought a ranch and 1,500 head of sheep. Hired a white man as foreman who sold the sheep and ran away with all the money. I asked Manuel if his sheep were those same sheep. I told him he would get shot if they were. He said he could defend himself. These Basque sheepherders think they are tough, but they are sweet people and very responsible. The only things they shoot are coyotes."

We bounce along the dirt road across the rolling mesa.

Almost absently, I ask, "How many men have you killed?"

We rattle along the road. Minutes of silence pass as if he is totaling them up.

Finally, he says, "Not counting Mexicans?" He chuckles.

More silence.

"I nearly shot a sheriff out in Nevada one time."

"How did that happen?"

"During the Depression, me and my sidekick were out of work, broke and hungry. Jobs in western Nevada in the Depression were scarce. We decided we would go where we knew there was money, so we held up a whorehouse in Lovelock.

"We waved pistols in the madam's face, took her cashbox and rode away fast into the desert. Christ, she was mad. We rode as fast as our old plugs would go, but by sunrise the going was slow and our canteens were as dry as dust.

"Checking our backtrack, a mile or so behind, we were being followed by a Ford. We knew it was the law. About that time, my horse stumbled and fell over, so we decided to split up and meet later in Fallon. My partner took his horse and the stolen money and rode, promising he would come back to get me.

"I'm watching my horse die when the black Model T comes within range and I could see it was the sheriff. I got down behind the horse carcass and shot the Model T's radiator that blew steam into the air and hot water all over the sheriff. He had been driving with the windshield laid down on the hood. He jumped out of the car, swearing and tearing at his shirt and shooting in my general direction. I scrambled down into a shallow draw and got away.

"I was now on foot, miles from town, without water and my partner hadn't showed up to help me out of this mess.

"I walked for miles and the heat dried me to a crisp. My tongue swole up and stuck out of my mouth, and I just got madder and madder.

"I found a ranch house with water and walked into Fallon in the dark and from the across the street, I saw the double-crossing son of a bitch near the local whorehouse. In a bar, I changed a $10 bill into quarters, took off my sock and put the quarters in it. I hid around the corner of the building and when he walked by, I pulled him into the dark alley between two buildings and swung the sock hard and hit him in the forehead. He went down like a sack of potatoes. Knocked him cold. I went through his pockets and found what money was left over after his whoring around and I left him there. I think he lived."

Ed doesn't seem like a liar. Doesn't act like one. Peg, his wife of 40 years, is a wonderful, petite, outrageously tough and plainspoken woman. Would she put up with these tales if they were lies? She is very capable of leveraging her 90 pounds to stand on Ed's testicles in high heels when he doesn't act right.

15

ED CROSS' VW

Back in my office, I sit alone for a long time thinking about the events on the mesa. Or were they nonevents? Things that could have happened and didn't: a killing that didn't occur; bullets gone wild missing an aspen trunk; an old man, an artifact from another time, an anachronism who had done everything men of that time did. It feels like he is the real thing. My doubt argues with the images I have seen with my own eyes. He is an impossibly good shot. At his age? He handles that .45 Colt like it is his best friend, his pet, his child, his lover. I have been around guns all my life and have never seen a man as handy and comfortable with a big pistol as Ed Cross. Can he actually kill somebody? In all the time I have spent with him, he is still a puzzle, and I have loved his stories but never taken them too seriously.

The realization drips onto my thoughts like melting ice. Can he actually be that man that I have assembled in my brain?

In that moment on the mesa, as I inspected the tight bullet pattern in the aspen tree, I knew that his stories were true.

He is the Old West walking among us, a curious mixture of tenderness and brutality, of life and death, of yesterday's consciousness and modern awareness.

A few days later on the sidewalk outside my real estate office, a local walks by and says, "Didja hear?"

"Hear what?"

"Ed Cross was in a car wreck over by Olathe this morning."

"Oh, boy. Was he hurt?"

"Yeah. They took him up to Grand Junction. He died."

No. That can't be. I just can't believe it. Not Ed. Not my friend.

I step into my office and a hot place comes up in my chest and I need to cry, hold it back for a couple of heartbeats and then the pain comes fully, the deflating sense that this connection in my life is forever broken. The tears flood onto my wool shirt and I can't stop the sobs.

A head-on in his wife's VW. Of all the inglorious ways for the Old West to die: in a friggin' Nazi skateboard.

16
MEET CUTE

With the opening of the ski area, the old shacks and shells in town are sold and resold. The prices double, then triple, then shoot 10 and even 20 times above the old mining town prices of the late '60s. The miners and the old-timers sell out at profits beyond their wildest expectations. In many cases, it is the only old age pension they will ever receive.

From their so-called Victorians—small, simply designed and barbarously constructed little boxes—the old-timers move to larger, nondescript, flatland towns like Montrose or Cortez, where they live in trilevel homes with insulation, two-car garages, lawns without rocks and a little garden out back.

They live within reach of properly clothed doctors and two-story hospitals. They lunch with their friends of 40 years and virtually live in the discount supermarkets they love so much. The flatlands are a new home closer to the action, where winter is three months shorter and temperatures easier on creaky joints.

The first of the new pioneers are copies of the Old West pioneers. If they are lucky, they will get to subdue and rape the West like the old-timers did.

Like in the movies, there is a central figure: the ski area developer—smooth-tongued, mild-mannered, imbued with a sense of destiny and the correctness of his mission. A German Jew, graying, and in his mind, this urbane Messiah didn't come to save the community; he came to develop a ski area he would then sell and take his profit to reinvest elsewhere. As a Christ-for-hire, his personal religion is nice so long as a tidy profit can be realized in the process.

Stein's dreams, declarations and actions have caused the changes the town is now profiting from. It is not him personally; it is the symbolism, the excitement of a new happening. New things don't often occur and when they do, adventurers, malcontents, misfits and opportunists, and well-meaning and big-spirited people seeking a different way or a new life arrive soon after. Morey Stein of Chicago has built a brand new skiers' playground.

There is a small contingent of outriders and front-runners that, for spiritual reasons or escape from parents or police, preceded Stein to the valley on the rumor of his development ambitions. I and a half dozen others had arrived before Stein broke ground on his ambitious project. I know them all and even like some of them.

After the news media had announced the ski area, there had been a noticeable response of "Who cares?" from the skiing public. Beyond western Colorado, no one could remember the name of the town but worse, no one cared to. They had never heard of the place. The announcement was a sports nonevent.

The opportunists come softly, not rocking the boat, buying small businesses and houses as resources allow. A hardware store here, a long and cheap lease there, with just enough money borrowed from family to get along and open prematurely on a street without customers. Postdream prereality, the early '70s are tough years for the opportunists.

It is a wonderful time for the optimists. The town is still in its "historic" state: in poor condition but with the promise that the new ski area will become "bigger than Vail, bigger than Aspen," as Stein enthusiastically pumps his concept. Magic words like Aspen and Vail fire the imaginations of everyone except the old-timers. They have heard it all before on prior ski scams. There had always been big talk and promises of riches from underfunded developer-dreamers, but no delivery, as each idea and finance plan failed and the big talkers permanently departed back to Los Angeles or Phoenix or Chicago.

For me, life is a steady diet of the everyday duties of family and business. It is a bare living. My real estate deals click slowly along, family life is predictable and, when I think about it at all, rather boring. But hope buoys life; the town and its prospects are exciting and life is under control.

Then it blows up, an exploding bomb that sends emotional parts flying in every direction, beyond the possibility of reassembly. If Humpty Dumpty had jumped off the wall to commit suicide, he could not have done a better job of shattering his life to shards.

Hollywood's Louis B. Mayer insisted that in the movies, the boy and girl should "meet cute." Much more like real life, Crazy Shirley and I don't meet cute. She came to Telluride to marry her college boyfriend. As a favor, I photographed their wedding. Her new husband works for me so she is around a lot. She has art talent and so I hire her to run a little printing business I have set up. My yen for her doesn't start slowly or quietly but arrives with the brassy, boyish enthusiasm of a scout troop in a Fourth of July parade. It is flags and color and music and lust and laughter and jokes and overall good feelings. Just to watch her walk by makes me impossibly horny. One day as I talk with her husband, Crazy Shirley comes into the office, hands him some papers, turns and leaves. I follow her with my eyes and lose my place in the universe. I blurt out, "God, I'd love to screw that woman."

Her husband is incensed. "You're talking about the woman I love!" he says heatedly.

"Yeah, I know, but … ." I look away, but the vision of her from behind won't leave me.

I lust from afar. She is only a masturbatory fantasy, and the chances that there can ever be anything more than a distant compulsion toward this incredible young woman is as remote as flying over Ajax Peak by flapping my arms. I am longtime married with three fine children and a business in a small town where everyone's reputation is a known quantity and everyone's life is totally transparent. And I won't allow myself to do something so outrageously stupid.

I am 37; she is 23 and married to my good friend and best salesman. The town is too small a place to get entangled with another man's wife. It would be a personal and business disaster. Everyone would choose up sides, and I would go broke.

One of the compelling reasons I moved to a small town was to put women beyond my immediate reach. Women came and went every day in my Denver advertising photography studio, in all stages of high-style dress and undress. For years I had resisted their temptations. I considered myself above such professional betrayals. I liked to look at myself in the shaving mirror and see a man without guilt.

In Denver, with some lucky breaks, I had become very successful and I liked that. And women liked that. I liked that they liked it. So I wadded up my morality like worn underwear and tossed it away. I was the American dream made real. I had the largest production studio in five states; my name opened advertising agency doors, and I had more business than I could deliver. I drove a white Porsche with matching white luggage. And there were women available for sex in the afternoon. Wasn't that the reason men worked so hard—to have access to beautiful women? In a carefully separated life, my nights were spent with my wife and kids in a

Victorian home on Observatory Park in southeast Denver. Life was good. I was unbeatable. I could tolerate the guilt.

I had lived by three rules that I promised myself never to violate:

1. No married women.
2. No models.
3. Keep downtown life and family life separate.

I had kept those promises. I really did.

17

THE OLD SCHOOL

The music hits me like a wall of insects, clawing, crawling over and repulsing me at the doorway. The rock band plays hard as the joints pass and the drugs flow. The amplifiers are turned up to the maximum degree of pain. The electronics groan and scream, thumping and jumping around the historic school building, sounding like wild animals run amok inside a black cave.

Outside it is snowing lightly. Tiny flakes, each no bigger than a pinhead, swirl inside as the front doors squeal open and creep closed.

The laughter and screams of the partygoers sound above the hammer of the music. The big, old Victorian lady of a schoolhouse, a monolithic pile of bricks, had been abandoned for a modern, low-rise, solar-heated one, and the dark-eyed building was sold to a woman from Aspen with a nose for bargains. With its high ceilings, many classrooms, oak floors and wainscoting, graciously overwide stairs and hallways, this schoolhouse allows a party to roll on two floors and any number of psychological levels at the same time. It is large enough for a real bash, but the low lighting keeps it intimate. The haze of grass is everywhere.

It looks like a helluva party. If there is one thing the town does right, it is a costume party. Costume parties happen several times a year: Halloween, of course; the Coonskin Carnival; a '50s party when we can't think of anything original; and the Buzzards' Ball, a celebration of the beaux arts in Telluride. This is the granddaddy of all the parties—the biggest, the drunkest, the druggiest, the sexiest and, in the test of good taste, it fails the worst.

Most of the winter is behind us now. The ski patrolmen, waitresses, ski bums and ordinary citizens are tired of winter, and they need a break. This party is it. It has been months in the planning. Costumes were conceived weeks ago, and there has been the inevitable last minute scramble for the remaining stray pieces of ridiculous costumes and borrowed clothing for those too shortsighted to plan ahead.

I drop some bills on the ticket table. A man dressed head to foot in aluminum foil and a duck mask hands me a ticket. "Gonna do it tonight, huh?"

"Yeah, thought I'd come out and play with the children. Wintertime is gettin' to be a pain in the ass for us older folk."

Aluminum Duck crinkles as he laughs. "You play with the kids all the time, you fraud." Thinking of parties as a chore made him laugh out loud. "It's no picnic here in the West. Life can be hell." He giggles again. "Now, there's punch and booze upstairs. Just follow the drunks. The food will come out at 10."

"What's the food gonna be?"

"Our local cash crop—dog shit," he answers slyly.

"Oh. I thought it was something I wouldn't like."

I slowly climb the stairs, threading my way up through the smoke haze and the costumed people, touching this one, and that, softly helloing to each and nodding, smiling. I feel completely at home here. I have seen these people under strain, in love and heartbreak, drunk and sober, in euphoria and depression, and I feel warm in their midst this night, even if they are screaming crazies. Looking upward through the costumed cowboys and Indians, little girls, hippies and artists, cheerleaders and a whole menagerie of strange and fearsome animals, I hear shouts from the open stairway. The crowd that blocks the wide steps moves to the edges and opens a path down the middle. A man dressed as Big Bird on skis comes schussing down the wooden treads with a great clatter and a whoop. The skis shave off little curls of wood as the edges cut into the steps and then the skier runs out on the flat oak floor, checks hard and digs in the edges. The crowd hoots and claps, overwhelming the music beat. Big Bird then bows in three directions. On the fourth bow, he drops his pants and moons the onlookers. The crowd cheers again but even louder.

On the first floor, the band is raucous. A big man in a white suit and white Panama hat approaches. He wears white face makeup and a white flower in his lapel and a badge that reads "Good Toot Fairy."

"Hey, come with me. I have something to show you," he says quietly.

We step out of the crowd into a darkened schoolroom. The man fishes a tiny brown bottle from his suit coat. It has a small silver spoon on a chain attached to the lid.

"This is some good shit, just in," he says flatly.

Dipping into the small vial, he heaps the spoon and carefully knocks it inside the glass so none will spill. With a practiced motion, he thrusts the tiny dipper under my nose. With a sharp and dedicated inhalation the spoon empties instantly, a miniature magic act of disappearance. I feel the cocaine burn way up into my forehead. In seconds, the ritual is repeated in the other nostril. Again, the sharp burn and the medicinal taste in the back of my throat.

"Thanks, Hunk. Where you gettin' that toot?"

Hunk smiles and, moving quickly away, says, "This medicine is right out of Cartagena yesterday. Hey, I dig your badass costume, man," pointing to my black suit, black cape and black top hat.

I climb the stairs. Once my eyes are even with the second floor I peer through the posts of the banister. There is a pretty dark-haired girl dressed in an East Indian costume with a jewel pasted on her nose and a red dot on her forehead. She squats over a man made up like a maharaja stretched out full length on the floor. She gently rotates her hips on the man's pelvis and talks casually to the people milling around, smiling and answering questions that I can't hear. In the yellow light her placid face is that of a madonna, her nose jewel flashes.

It all seems so innocent, just children playing grownup right here in the middle of the sand pile. They could be acting, I think, not actually doing it. Everybody is acting at this party. Hell, everybody in this town is a full-time actor, playing a part, assuming a role they could not play back home in Chicago or Connecticut or small backwater towns of the East.

Everything interesting is hidden beneath the red skirt pulled demurely around the girl to the floor, covering the vital area of the action from the many prying eyes.

Well, it's a great act. Then the girl moves faster, with more determination. She stops talking to the bystanders, her eyes float shut, her chin drops to her chest, and then she utters a small, sharp cry. The bystanders stop talking to watch the magic moment. The girl's eyes flutter open and she smiles, lips wet, eyes shining brightly. The onlookers burst into spontaneous cheers. Couples in silly clothes smile and squeeze each other tighter.

I walk to find a drink. Tables covered with a hundred bottles of various sizes and colors and containing various mind-bending potions are set up in one of the schoolrooms. After several trips to the bar, I feel altogether at home. The coke has given me a lift and the volunteer bartenders pour strong drinks dedicated to getting everyone as drunk as possible as quickly as possible. I love these people. I love this town. I love this life.

I go to the restroom and return quickly. Amid endless banter and an unbroken series of one-liners, I look across the room to see the only other villain costume at the party: Mack DeJong. "DingDong," the locals call him, is dressed as a mirror image of me in a black suit, black cape, black top hat. We wave. DeJong wends his way through the writhing dancers toward me.

"Hey, what's happenin'? Looks like we got the best suits!" His dark face is menacing.

"Yeah. They're good, man. You got good taste, DingDong. How're you doin' these days?"

DingDong looks across the revelers, troubles tracing lines around his eyes. "Not too good. My old lady is giving me a lot of heat. Wants me to get a regular job and quit smoking dope. She says my kids don't have any respect for me. Do ya think that's true? Do ya think that kids lose respect for their daddy?"

"Damn if I know. I suppose they could." I stare into my drink. The drinks come in paper cups. "Aw, what the hell, you know how women are. They want to make you over into their vision of the perfect man. If I were you, I wouldn't worry about it."

He drinks the cup in one gulp and sighs, "Well, I don't know what to do. I like my kids. I even like my old lady once in a while. I have a degree in engineering, but I can't get an engineering job. I don't have a license. Even if I did, there isn't any work. All they build around here are shit houses. It doesn't take much to engineer a shit house."

"Yeah, it's a great place to live but the living can be tough."

"Sometimes I wonder if it's worth it," he says, half to himself.

"If what's worth it?" I gaze out across the swirling world of color, sound and smells.

DingDong looks into his empty cup. "Living here. Living anywhere."

This dour, ugly man is truly typecast as a villain—the black beard, the yellow teeth, the tall, menacing bearing. In reality, he is a totally harmless, dope-smoking, 35-year-old hippie, a shadow of what once had been a good-looking man.

This conversation is depressing me. I've got my own problems, I think. We need some laughs. An idea flashes on the far wall of my brain—all we have to do for some chuckles is to get DingDong into the proper situation to put on his act.

"DingDong, have you been to the toilet?"

"Yeah, the men's ain't workin' so everyone's usin' the girls'. It's dark as hell in there. No lights." He gazes at me quizzically. "Some of the guys been pissin' off the fire escape. Dangerous though. The wind is blowing the wrong way."

"Did you notice that there is a skinny little shower stall in there with a plastic shower curtain?"

"Yeah. So what?"

"The other restrooms aren't working so everybody uses that one toilet. It's dark in there, just a little candle on the back of the potty. Let's go hide in the shower stall, you and me—God, I just love this idea—and when one of these women comes in and sits down, we'll jump out of the shower and just scare the piss out of her."

DingDong begins a slow smile as the possibilities reveal themselves. "That's a hell of an idea," he says with a grin. "Let's do it."

We two villains dressed in black from head to toe casually walk down the lighted hall and wait for the door to open and for a drunken woman in a miniskirt to heel-click away and fade into the party crowd. We enter the humid toilet. It is a small room with a shower stall opposite the door, a sink and the stool.

We slip sideways into the shower stall and pull the thin plastic curtain closed. The smallness of the stall compels us to stand close, touching. So here we are, two men dressed in black, one tall and slim, one short and round, standing belly to belly. One a supposedly respectable real estate agent, the other a dissolute hippie. And both straight.

From the shower, I can see who is entering the room by placing my eye next to the curtain and looking through the tiny separation between the curtain and the shower wall.

Traffic is heavy and our wait is brief. As our eyes adjust, more and more detail can be seen. Here we are, inches apart, face to face, squeezed together. It is already getting warm. The door opens and a woman walks in. I shake my head, a definite wave off on the Big Surprise. I recognize the figure as an old local, a tough mountain woman who runs the ridges above timberline and probably can beat up both of us if provoked. It is a reasonable assumption that an unexpected toilet event might provoke some people. She sits on the toilet out of sight. We listen to the sounds of water splash into the toilet, the flush, the rustle of clothing and the door open and close.

"Jesus, DingDong, Big Mary could have beat the hell out of us if she knew we were in here."

"Yeah, I saw her hit a guy in the Roma Bar who grabbed her titty. Knocked him down. Damn near took his head off."

"OK, when I give you a nod, we do our thing and get the hell out of here." I begin to imagine the gossip flying around my little town, "Didja hear … ?"

The door opens and it is a man. I shake my head. We stand hardly breathing while the visitor does his chore. There is an extended sound like cloth ripping and a fanfare of flatulence. "Oh Telluride, what a hell of a place!" the man says aloud. He turns and leaves but before the door closes another visitor is inside. The atmosphere is ripening quickly. I begin to smell other things, too. The visitor does his splash quickly and leaves.

"Jesus, DingDong, when did you take a bath last?" I whisper.

"My water pipes froze in December, man," DingDong answers evenly.

"This is March, DingDong, can't you find someplace with a shower? How about the bathhouse?"

"The owner won't let me in there. The girls wouldn't get in the Jacuzzi when I was in there so they won't let me back in."

I sigh despondently as does DingDong, who exhales his foul breath right into my face. I try to turn away but there is no escape. The air quality is definitely going bad. My mouth is dry.

"I need a drink, DingDong. I give up. I'm going outside."

As I move to step out of the shower, the door opens and a man enters. Instead of turning toward the toilet like the others, he stands in front of the shower curtain barely a foot away from us. The door opens again. It is a waitress I recognize, a girl not yet 21. She stumbles through the door and falls into the shower stall; the curtain bulges inward. As if we had rehearsed it a hundred times, DingDong and I place our hands flat against the curtain and gently ease the girl and the protective curtain back into a vertical position. She never feels a thing. There are giggles and clothes rustling and a zipper chases down its tiny track. A teeny point of light coming through the keyhole projects their two shadows onto the curtain. Looking over our shoulders, we villains can see the girl's shadow slip down to its knees.

I shake my head slowly. I feel my eyes flare and try to control my breathing so I make no sound. I am thankful for the bass thump-thump-thump of the band.

The door rattles and there is an urgent knock. I roll my eyes at DingDong. I feel a laugh tremble up in his belly. Then I feel a laugh start in my own, building like a volcano. I look at the dark ceiling trying to think about unfunny things—auto crashes, cancer and deformed babies—anything bad. I imagine the consequences of being caught doing this. DingDong doesn't care. This asshole DingDong can blow our cover because he doesn't care about getting caught. He might expose himself at the worst possible moment just for the laughs.

I look up at DingDong's face half a foot away. He's biting his lip hard. We gaze wide-eyed at each other, each fighting our own desperate and lonely battle, our efforts being felt through our touching bellies.

There is a short silence as the shadow of the woman's head moves back and forth.

A big sigh and an easy groan and the man's head snaps back. "Oh, God!" he says tightly. There is a quiet moment. "Thanks, honey," he says earnestly. "You are the best!"

"Just for you, cowboy," she says softly. Clothes rustle. The two shadows merge in a kiss and then the door opens, floods the curtain with light and they disappear, talking over their shoulders to the woman waiting.

My attitude is failing fast. The prospect of getting caught in a shower stall with this hairy, crazed hippie is wearing on me. The joke I have so carefully prepared might trap me in embarrassment that could take years to explain away. Just try to explain this over beers at the Sheridan Bar, I think grimly.

The coke is wearing off and DingDong is revolting, smelling of liquor and body odor. The air is ripe with farts and the smell of sex. My head hurts. I want out where I can breathe.

The lady is the gorgeous, buxom wife of the local photographer. She enters briskly, sits down and heaves a sigh of relief. I nod the signal: The Big Surprise.

Throwing the curtain back, we two black figures step out of the gloom and hover over the totally vulnerable, urinating blonde.

DingDong raises his arms and waggles his fingers like the boogie man. "YA-YA-YA-YA-YA!" he screams at her.

Wide-eyed and terrified, the woman screams back, a screech like a rusty gate slowly opening: extended, heartfelt, deeply moving, escalating into the shriek of a dying house cat caught in an electrical circuit.

I escape into the hall, laughing at the top of my voice, at the relief of being out of the shower, away from the foul DingDong, getting away without being discovered.

Three days later I walk down Colorado Avenue, my head nearly healed from the party. A local stops me.

"Didja hear about DingDong?" he asks.

My ears go up. In Telluride, when the sentence starts with "Didja hear ..." it's important news.

"Hear what?" I chuckle, remembering the beautiful blonde with the big breasts sitting petrified on the potty, her eyes wide and her mouth shaped in a perfect O screaming an electrocuted cat yowl and DingDong hovering over her madly waggling his fingers and screaming his ya-yas at the top of his lungs. "What's that worthless bastard up to now?"

"He borrowed 50 bucks from his wife and went and bought a pistol."

"What the hell did he do that for?" I laugh at the absurdity of this peacenik buying a gun.

"... and his oldest kid found him this morning in their basement. He blew his brains out all over the cinder block wall."

Five years before this party, there were hardly enough people in town to throw a party. Or a reason to. And certainly nothing worth dying for. Or was there?

18

THE DECLARATION

It is a dance at the Roma Bar but there are few actually dancing. Mostly it is just the local skiers standing around shooting the breeze, shifting their weight from foot to foot, hands involuntarily twisting in front of them as they explain their skiing heroics. The tables are pushed back against the walls leaving the beat-up wooden floor open for the dancers.

The disco music is teeth-cracking loud and few people in the town are mentally equipped to move to this cool, new beat.

Since I am a poor dancer, if one can call it that, I stand on the sidelines and look over the shoulders of the males and detect little enthusiasm for this diversion. Men talk together, heads looking inward in little uninterested groups, ignoring the moving bodies completely.

The music shifts to a new backbeat and I notice a few heads turn toward the action. Then more eyes move to the dancers. Then the whole crowd of watchers stops and stares.

There is Crazy Shirley dancing like a pro, her butt in a pair of tight jeans moving in rhythm, back and forth. It makes a little circle in the air, athletic, graceful, mesmerizing. Neither I nor any man in the room can take his eyes off the action of this wild, graceful, sexual child letting her inhibitions loose.

I can't shift my eyes away. Her movements are entrancing, fascinating and nightclub sexy. I can't stand this. I would do anything to have this woman, keep her locked up in a bedroom to make love to her whenever the notion strikes me—or every 20 minutes, whichever comes first. Just dream on, man, I think to myself. That's another man's wife, and you can't ever have her, can never touch her, can't even visualize her while masturbating.

I think I'll just go quietly crazy. In all my travels, I have never seen such a sexual animal. I know I'll never be able to go to sleep again without her sweet little butt intruding on my otherwise dry-as-dust life. I love the vision and hate it at the same moment. Maybe I'll just slash my wrists or drink some hemlock.

As she walks off the floor, a friend looks at me and rolls his eyes in horny appreciation. I slowly shake my head and curl my lip against my teeth in response. There is nothing to say except "Jeeezus!" under my breath.

My life disaster starts one night when my friend John and I are running silk-screen posters. We had put together one of those ideas that come to bright-but-bored minds in late winter when it's still cold and snowy and you haven't seen bare dirt in six months. Your mind does tricks and you sit for hours pounding out mostly bad ideas with your more intelligent buddies. Usually the question is, "What does Telluride need that it doesn't have now?"

Souvenirs, of course. There is little you can buy in Telluride with the town's name on it. So we print ski posters, a black and white photograph of the town that says "Ski Telluride" in the sky. Simple, effective, and they sell, readily giving us money to run away and play. Occasionally we run low and print a new supply that involves a team effort of silk-screen printing and hanging wet prints and drinking beer and getting ripped on the volatile brain-rotting ink fumes. There is always too much laughing and hoorawing and horseplay. While John and I always get the job done, by the time we use all the paper stock and the drying line is full of wet prints hanging from clothespins, we are doing acrobatics in the ozone.

On this night, as a lark, Shirley comes along to help print. It is a big mistake. We all go into space on fumes. We laugh, we giggle, we print and hang, and finally, fully ripped, we run out of paper stock. The whole evening I listen to her tinkling laugh and surreptitiously stare at her little rear end tightly wrapped in denim shorts. At 5'2", light brown hair cropped close, faultless skin and blue eyes, she is captivating. During our work in tight quarters, occasionally our hands touch or our bodies graze each other. Each time it happens, I get a buzz, some mystical energy transfer, a chemical rush. Is she feeling it too? Are her nerves on edge or is it just mine? When she flashes me that Broadway smile, does it have any deeper meaning for me? For her?

By the time we finish printing, I am insane for this woman who is so far out of reach.

Driving her home in my Toyota jeep, I stop in the deep, dark bottomland along the river behind the new Telluride Lodge. The engine idles.

Filled to the brim with ink-fumed courage, I turn to her. "Shirley, I think you are the most magnificent woman I've ever met and I would give anything to make love to you!"

I lean over and kiss her lips. She returns it, leans into me, brings me into her with arms around my neck. I quiver from the thrill. A real connection, not a little peck or an "Aunt Minnie." It is sweet beyond sweet, tender beyond tender and lingering. Lusty heaven.

We kiss for a long time; her saliva tastes so good it makes me crazy.

With a deep sigh, she says, "I think you are wonderful, too."

We kiss some more, passionately. I graze around her face with my lips. I could eat this woman alive, I think.

"Jesus, what do we do now?" I whisper.

"Let's drive out of Telluride right now and never come back."

I am stunned by her suggestion. "Where can we go?" I ask.

"I don't know," she says breathlessly. "Anywhere. We can just go away. I don't like being married. I'll get a divorce and we can be together. Let's go now."

Stunned by her answer, I take a minute to absorb what she means. Leave Telluride? Give it all up? Become a vagrant—an absentee father?

"I can't. I've got kids and a business. And a wife." I hate my cowardice even as I say it. Instinctively, I know the price is too high to join her in this fantasy. I can't even think like this. My God, the price!

So I take her home to her husband.

I am a wreck. Going to bed with this fantastic woman is a real possibility. But after that, what? Her kisses are electrifying; the reflection of how I feel is the most exciting thing that has ever happened to me. Even parachuting. This is parachuting without acrophobia, without ever having to land. It is high-amperage adrenaline. Electricity. The sheer beauty of feeling for an incredible woman without reservation, without limits, is a new sensation where the sun suddenly rises in a different place and shines on a different country with a different language.

Sex is destiny. Somehow I will make love to this incredible young woman, and the idea twists the wires in my brain. I just have to do it without getting caught. Making love would be pure. Getting caught would be impure.

19

TÊTE-À-TÊTE RADIO

I'm at a citizens' meeting to plan the programs for the newly granted KOTO community radio license. All of the 20 people in the room know that they are undiscovered talents with huge potential simply waiting to be discovered. Each has finely tuned bathroom shower knowledge of their voice talent and what should be done with it. Each has a unique specialty that they are eager to share over the airwaves.

My specialty is talking to people—getting them to open up, share shocking confidences. I fantasize that I'm a male Rona Barrett, a gossip columnist with those special talents. But the organizer of this project—a boring, humorless baker—seizes the interviewing, conversational turf for himself, and I become a superfluous bystander.

As the meeting progresses, I notice the town's young doctor sitting in front of me. I lean over and whisper in his ear, "You know, you could save all of us a lotta pain, worry and medication. You could be the most important service on the entire radio schedule. You could be famous, even setting the tone for the big-time jocks out in LA or Albuquerque or Denver. Who knows where you could end up? You could be the morning jock who plays wake-up music and lets us choose the least contagious person to hang out with."

He turns to see if I am serious. "I'm a medical doctor," he says, "and very supportive of community health. A healthy community is a stable community, and this town can use some stability." He nods, agreeing with himself. Then he stares at me. "What's your idea?"

He waits patiently while I refine the show's title.

"Format a daily morning show and between songs, you can do a segment that would be a great service to us all. You can call it 'Who's Got What?'"

He harrumphs and turns away. The doctor does not take my suggestion.

The radio programming works as planned. Various citizens are assigned time slots where they play their favorite music. Taste in music is variable and some of it simply too awful to ponder. There are shows of reggae from the Rastafarians, mellow mood from old folk, disco from the cool set, an occasional polite Christian sermon from Brother Al and, of course, local news and the weather, snow conditions, town and county politics, and human-interest interviews.

Snorky has a radio show on KOTO that is going along swimmingly. It's mostly hard rock with long playtimes during which he does little except read *Playboy* and toke up with an occasional sweeping glance at the control board dials. Because the controls are designed by geniuses to be operated by idiots, tonight, the designers have hit their market.

Telephone call-in requests go unanswered. The only sign of anybody alive on the radio planet is the long-playing music, the DJ's station identification every half-hour, and perhaps an inane and inappropriate comment about something wholly detached from reality. It isn't the first time that a DJ has been stoned during his or her weekly gig. It happens often so Telluride thinks nothing of it.

But then a long-play record ends and the phonograph needle runs off the black platter and cuts to the inside where it goes shee ... shee ... shee ... shee ... shee ... again and again. It is puzzling. Where is the DJ? Where is the next song? Few things are as disturbing and tension-filled as dead air from the radio. For the listener, it is almost a criminal offense.

Then the town hears breathing, heavy breathing. Then some easy moans, rustling sounds, more moans but louder. Then groans, shee ... shee ... shee ... . More groans and panting, squeals.

And then a blood-curdling, glass-shattering, door-busting scream, and a man yells, "You son of a bitch!"

Then a different man's scream of surprise and fear: "No! NO!"

Then a gunshot explosion and sounds of things falling like pellets hitting the floor. Then fist thudding dull flesh and anger-filled groans.

A woman screams, "Get away! Stop ... stop ... stop! Stop it! Get out of here!" Desperate crying, slaps, unintelligible yelling. Then only shee ... shee ... shee ... .

Is this aural display real or radio drama?

It is real. Telluride's gentle folk are radio witnesses to an attempted murder.

It seems the DJ's studio guest is someone else's girlfriend. Her boyfriend hears her familiar orgiastic voice over the airwaves, grabs his shotgun and races to the station to catch Snorky and the wandering girlfriend on the floor *in flagrante delicto*.

Bursting into the control room, swearing, he pushes a 12-gauge shotgun against Snorky's temple. The instant before the DJ's head explodes, he throws up a protective arm, reflexively knocking the shotgun barrel toward the ceiling. The gun fires into the plaster ceiling, which falls in shattered bits down around all three.

The girlfriend screams and tosses Snorky off like a light blanket, jumps up and aims a fusillade of slaps and screams toward her boyfriend who, realizing he has almost murdered a man, grabs the girl, turns and runs for home.

Snorky pulls up his pants, runs his fingers through his hair ball to shake out the broken ceiling plaster and carefully queues up Dire Straits on the turntable.

20

THE KNOCK

The echo of pounding carpenters' hammers is a symptom of the changing society, luring people more interested in play than work, in sex than love and in drugs than morality. The mining town quickly gives way to a more interesting and adventuresome lifestyle.

I am standing in a new condominium unit belly to belly with Shirley. Our attraction, while suspected, is not yet public. Her husband has not acknowledged failure, even though she has rented a unit at the Lodge by trading out artwork. Home for me is strained and difficult. I will move out next week, rent a condo unit across the complex from Shirley's. But tonight, in the entire world, there is only her. It has been difficult to get together. Now is the first time we have been able to rendezvous for the stated purpose of lovemaking.

It makes me nuts seeing her every day. I watch her work while looking darling in her mattress-ticking coveralls. I want to taste her. I can't even look at her for too long or too intently. People will notice.

But tonight, it is all worth it—the waiting, the anticipation, the flow of warm feelings and frustrations. Tonight will be the payoff.

We kiss long and hard in the middle of her tiny apartment. I begin to undress her, slipping garments over her head and to the floor. As she is slowly revealed, her loveliness takes my breath away. I lead her to the bed and slide in beside her. Delicious.

A loud knock at the door sounds like someone exploded a hand grenade. We freeze. Passion drains away from me like a flushed toilet.

We gaze into each other's eyes. I put my hand over her mouth. We wait long seconds. I put my mouth close to her ear. "Who is it?"

"It has to be my husband. He's the only one who knows where to find me."

I look around for an escape route. We're on the second floor, 15 feet from the balcony to the ground. I will jump if I have to, but I sure as hell will break something. And I am stark naked. It is cold out there. Silently, deliberately, we ease out of bed and begin to dress in a studied, mechanical way. The knocking stops.

After some minutes, the phone rings. "Let it ring," I say.

She is already moving toward it. "It'll be my husband." She answers. In a few seconds, she nods the confirmation. "I was next door with some people from Texas," she says to the phone.

I whisper, "Keep him on until I get out of here."

If he had come into the parking lot, and it was only logical that he had, he had seen my Toyota Land Cruiser sitting in the frozen mud and ice patches. Since there is only one way out, all he has to do is wait for me. If he called from inside the lodge, I could collide with him at any time around any corner. Will he shoot me? Will he use a big pistol? Something that will blow my heart out in pieces and spread it all over the icy parking lot? I deserve that. It is unlikely he found a phone this time of night inside the lodge. The office is closed and there are only five or six permanent residents.

That's it. He has to be calling from town. I need to get to my vehicle and get the hell out of here. If I'm on the road, I have plausible deniability.

The freezing hallway is empty. My heart beats in my ears. I make myself walk casually to the stairway, down and out to the edge of the parking lot. My Toyota jeep is parked on the other side of the big, empty field. I look around the perimeter of willows and scrub trees to search for anyone suspicious. Nothing. I begin to trot, and then I pound hard across the frozen field. I can only run. I think I can feel the bullet slam into my chest, instantly expanding, tearing its way in deep, cutting off my breath, and punching the life out of me. My breath goes ragged. I snatch open the door and twist the key. The engine barks to life. I spin a U-turn and make it out to the street.

It is empty, no headlights anywhere.

"I can't live like this," I say aloud. My heart is beating from the adrenalin rush and my hands shake on the steering wheel. "But this is the first thing I've ever done worth dying for!"

21

BREAK THE BANK

I can tell when winter has hung around too long. When I walk to the post office and do not like anyone I meet, escape is required to relieve the depression.

The air hangs heavy above the town. Trapped wood and coal fire smoke floats 50 feet above the valley in still layers. Winters in Telluride are comparable to Anchorage, Alaska, with sunshine lasting about as long. The town turns blue, both in color and attitude. Every citizen gets a little bit insane, mentally trapped in the canyon.

The Jack Daniel's slides down smooth turning hot. Lily snorts and blinks his smallish eyes at the jolt of whiskey. The mountain wind whistles through the loose windows of the decaying house, singing its uncertain song and building a clean delta of snow from the door crack onto the scarred kitchen linoleum. He hands the square bottle to his roommate who tips it back, eyes closed. Lily opens the stove door, throws in a chunk of aspen and slams it shut. A puff of sweet smoke boils up through the room and spreads with the heat near the ceiling.

"Cold, George," Lily says, rubbing his hands together.

"Yep. It's a long winter. Never ends," George says, his front to the warmth, his hands out over the stove blessing it. "You know, right now there are people lying on the beach in Hawaii? You know that right now," he points with the liquor bottle, "there are women all over the beaches getting a tan on their naked little asses."

Lily looks up at George. In his mind, he can see tan rumps lined up like desert hills. "Yeah. I wish I wuz there. I wish we wuz there."

"You know, Lily, I'm pissed. I'm pissed off at being stuck here. I've been finishin' concrete in rotten weather for 10 years in this pissant town. I'm still broke. Broke! Everyone else made money. The real estate people made more money than God. The bankers made more money than them even."

Lily nods and takes the bottle. His mother named him Ralph William Tomlin, but the barflies call him Lily after an actress he vaguely resembles when he grins.

"The bankers ..." George trails off. He scratches in front, "... the goddamn bankers have made so much money off'n me. I don't know how much they've made off'n me. More than me, that's for sure. More than me."

"The bankers always make money," Lily says heartily. "They drive big cars and live up on the sunny side of the valley and they always make money," he says.

"Yeah. Sometimes I feel like going in there and getting some of my money back."

Lily laughs. "Hey, yeah ... wouldn't that be a hoot? Go get some of your money back." His eyes crinkle and his head bobs. He giggles. "That's a funny idea," he says.

Telluride's bank is a modern masonry building, an anomaly in the line of old frame structures. No criminal in his right mind would consider holding it up since there is only one way in and out of the town. But late winter can change desperate minds.

"I'm not jokin'. I want some of it back. I can get it back, you know .... I know how," George says flatly.

Lily pauses mid-drink. "How?" His eyes cling to George's across the hot column of the stove.

"I have a key."

"A key?"

"I poured concrete inside when they added on. I have a key to the back door."

"Fits?"

"Yep. I tried it during lunch. Went around to the back door during the lunch rush when everybody was out front on the teller line. It opened right up," George smiles.

"No shit?"

"No shit. Opened right up. They never changed the lock. It's the same lock that was there when I poured concrete in there. Same damned lock. Can you believe it? Same damned lock."

Lily tips the bottle up without taking his eyes from George. "Same damned lock. You'd think they would change the lock."

"They didn't." George turns to warm his backside. "I think it would be fair if we just went in there and took some of our money back, don't you?"

"How ya gonna do that?"

"Whaddaya mean 'you'? Aren't you coming along?"

Lily stares into the center of the larger man's back. "Come along? To rob a bank? I know people in the bank. They know me. They'll recognize me. They'll recognize you, too, ya know."

"No, they won't. We'll wear masks."

"Oh-h-h man, I don't know." Lily shakes his head slowly, "That's heavy. That's heavy." The stove pops as the softwood log catches and flares. Lily stares at the fluid fire glowing through the damper door.

"I thought you had the kinda balls it took to do things like this." George looks squarely at him. "I guess I was wrong."

Lily's eyes hold the live red spot. He sips at the bottle. He smiles at his friend. "I got the balls," he says firmly.

"Then let's do it. Let's hold the bastards up and take some of our money and go to Hawaii where it's warm. Besides that, they owe us. They sure owe me, anyway."

"They owe me, too," Lily says firmly. He tries to think of why they owe him but he can't think of anything. There is something though. "I don't forget it when people owe me," Lily says.

Two bundled figures trot along the white alley against the wind, the snow sticking to their hair, stinging their eyes and crunching like dry gravel underfoot. They huddle by the door; each shakes out a ski mask and pulls it on quickly, leaving only eyes showing. George pulls out a key on a string and fits it into the deadbolt of the steel door. Lily looks up and down the alley, then slides a sawed-off shotgun from under his dark coat and dangles it alongside his leg. The deadbolt slips easily, soundlessly, open. George opens the door and holds it against the up-canyon wind. Lily raises the shotgun and steps into the heat of the bank. George closes the door gently behind them.

Their breaths come short and quick. "There ain't nobody back here," Lily says softly.

George pushes the short double barrel out of his face with his forefinger. "Get the goddamn gun out of my face," he hisses. "You stay here. I'll go to the vault. Now dammit," George puts his face in Lily's, "don't shoot anybody."

Lily frowns. "I won't. I won't. Jeez, George if you think I'm gonna shoot somebody … . Jeez," he says under his breath.

George hunkers low and crabs between the gray worktables and accounting machinery toward the open vault door.

Lily watches him disappear inside. He thinks the door looks like the back of a big watch, just like the back of a big watch, where you can see the guts of it out in the open like that. You'd think they would keep the guts of a vault door covered with something that you can't see ins—

"May I help you?"

Lily jumps. Standing in the doorway of the workroom is a tiny graying woman, peering at him through thick glasses, her big teeth flashing.

Lily stands stock-still but tightens his grip on the weapon. He wonders where she came from. He didn't hear anything. "Hey," he says quietly toward the vault. "Hey—"

George's face pops around the corner of the big watch. When he sees the woman, his eyes fly wide.

The woman's voice scolds, "What are you doing here? You men don't belong in here." Bug-eyed, she looks straight at Lily.

Lily's gun begins to droop. It sags until it finally points at the floor in front of his toes. Lily looks down at it as if he and the shotgun have never been introduced. The killer weapon is suddenly a complete stranger. In silent, slow motion he turns, twists the doorknob, pushes the door against the wind, steps out, and closes it. The lock clicks.

He stands in the snow, entranced by the slowness of it all. It's snowing sideways. He expects George to be along soon … soon.

The door bursts open and swings to the stops. George gallops out of the bank and collides with Lily, spinning him like a top. Without slowing, he runs up the alley, tearing at his ski mask.

Lily trots after him, pulls at his mask with one hand and holds the gun inside his coat with the other.

At the end of the block, George spins right, his feet churn and slip. Between clapboard buildings, he peeks up and down the sidewalk of the winter street. It is empty except for the snowbank in the center pushed up by the plow. Lily trots up behind him out of breath. "Don't run," George says in a whisper. "Walk."

As the fire in the stove is coming back to life, Lily's shakes begin to die down with the help of Jack Daniel's. "Jeez, I just couldn't believe Maggiemay would just walk in there like that. I mean, here I am holding a goddamn sawed-off shotgun and Maggiemay just walks in there, just walks in there like she owns the place. Just like she owns the place." Lily shakes his head.

Blessing the stove, George says, "You didn't have to leave me in there. I'm in the friggin' vault and you leave. You just walk out. I couldn't believe it." He holds out his hand for the bottle. "I'm damned glad I wasn't in Nam with you."

"You said don't shoot anybody," Lily says defensively and holds the bottle. "I didn't shoot anybody. Besides, if you said to shoot somebody, I couldn't shoot Maggiemay. She is my mom's aunt's kid or somethin'. She's a second cousin or somethin'. I couldn't shoot her. She runs the Nugget Theater." Lily thinks a few seconds, then nods his head. "A banker maybe. I could shoot a banker."

George's voice takes a wire edge, "Well, it was dumb as hell to just leave. I'm in the friggin' vault and you just walk out. I'm in there and you just walk out and leave me." He blows a breath between his lips. "Besides, Maggiemay is a banker."

Lily shakes his head. "No she ain't. Jeez, I'm a local. I know who the banker is. The banker is Jimmy Langendorfer, the big cheese of the Elks Club. Maggiemay works up there in front makin' change for people. Jimmy Langendorfer ..."

George whirls and towers over Lily, punches his chest with a ragged fingernail. "Goddammit, Lily, she's a banker!" he shouts.

Lily cringes away and steps out through a curtain of linked beer can openers fashioned into hanging chains. He falls forward onto the bed with his boots on; the wool blanket prickles his face and smells vaguely of dog.

The white wind racing up the narrow canyon makes a loose roof-tin screech nervously. The fire flares and the draft makes the stove begin to breathe slow and labored like a fat man. George squeaks across the kitchen floor toward Lily.

"You know what?" George stops at the doorway and speaks through the chains. "You know what? There's a way to do it. We're gonna do it another way. You want to know how?"

Lily's voice is flat, "Jimmy Langendorfer is the banker."

"OK, he's the banker. Look, we're going to dig in. Hell, we used to work in the mine. We're going to mine our way in there underneath the vault from the old cafe next door. We'll break through after the bank closes Saturday noon. We'll have the whole damned weekend to go through all the safe boxes and everything." George sounds excited. A heavy gust sends seeds of flying snow peppering the frosted panes. "Well, what do you think?"

"Jeez, George, I don't know. I don't know if we should do that again. We damned near shot Maggiemay."

George snarls through his teeth, "Forget about goddamn Maggiemay." He takes a deep breath. "Jesus H. Christ, this is a good plan. A great plan. No guns, no daylight, lots of time ... ." He waits. "Maggiemay won't even know about it."

Lily hears George breathing heavily through the chains and wishes he wouldn't get so mad.

"And you know what else is in there?"

"What?"

"Coke."

"In the bank?"

"Yep. I know at least two dealers who keep their stash in there. How would you like to go to Hawaii with a backpack full of cash and a kilo of toot? Boy, you could get some women then, Lily. I mean they couldn't stay away from you. As soon as they found out you had nose candy ... ."

Lily can feel George nodding his head on the other side of the beer can opener chains. He thinks, cash and toot. Women. Jeez, women sure do like cash and toot. I've seen some real ugly guys get some good-looking women with toot. Us poor guys can't even get laid without toot.

On his knees beneath the bank, George cuddles a battery-driven drill in the crook of his arm and presses it upward into the bottom of the concrete vault. The drilling dust dribbles out of the hole and powders his glasses and the front of his wool sweater. His shoulders are hardwood planks urging the bit to drive straight and, with his head tipped back to get closer to his work, his forehead presses hard against the rough surface. He sweats from the effort.

After some minutes of cat-yowling sound, he backs the drill bit out carefully and his heart beats applause for holding the strenuous position for so long.

Lily shines a flashlight up the drill hole then pokes his finger in to the second knuckle. He thinks it's terrific the way you can take a battery drill and drill into concrete like that. Hard though, keeping the pressure on it over your head. "Damned dust gets in your eyes, don't it?" He shines the light onto George's face.

George's dusty glasses flash in the light. "How many times do I have to tell you?"

"Sorry," Lily says. "Jeez, I just forget."

Three months of weekend digging had brought them up under the concrete slab of the vault itself. The tunnel portal is a black hole in the old basement floor. It dips down several feet under the foundation of the abandoned building and dives deeper yet beneath the bank underpinnings.

The trapped air in the chamber under the vault stinks of sweat and propane gas from the lantern. It is always cool, and a breath-cloud punctuates each short stroke of the pick. The sounds are dull but, occasionally, the pick point will ring a rock squarely and sparks will comet by. Using a sawed off shovel, they fill a plastic bucket, then drag the full bucket down the tunnel floor for a dozen feet, under the foundations, then up to dump the dirt and rocks in the dark basement of the empty store. The pile of dirt and rock in the basement has grown taller than a man. Behind the mound, a rough wooden stairway leads up to a trap door in the floor. While they work, they keep the door locked from underneath.

Lily looks forward to weekends, working long nights with George in the dungeon. George is good at telling stories and he tells Lily stories about his home in eastern Oregon and growing up fly-fishing and poaching deer in the headlights of his pickup truck and balling girls out by the river and about his daddy beating the hell out of him and bar fights. He doesn't talk about Nam.

Lily never knew anyone so well. George would make up things they were going to do in Hawaii. He even pinned up a Hawaii picture he cut out of a travel magazine. It was a picture of a brown Hawaiian girl with a smooth navel the size of a dime and a big pink flower in her hair. George taped it up one night with silver tape in the kitchen right by the stove where they could look at it while they drank Jack Daniel's. *FLY UNITED TO HAWAII*, it says. He thinks, me and ol' George are gonna do it, too, soon as we get some of our money back. Ol' George is all right. Yep, jus all right.

"Hand me those," George points at hand tools carefully placed on a shelf cut into the dirt bank. Putting the chisel point in the hole at an angle, he swings powerfully with a fist-sized hammer. Sparks streak away from the point and concrete shards bullet across the dirt chamber. A chip the size of a half-dollar loses itself in the dirt. George swings and chips, each time a sliver of concrete or half a pebble fires away into the dirt. The dust hangs and swirls in the lantern light. Finally, his shoulders burning, he sags back to rest.

Lily scuttles quickly into George's place searching the working face with his light. "Terrific," he says. He puts his finger on a ribbed chunk of black steel rod with bits of white concrete stuck to it. "Hot damn! Here's a piece of rebar. We'll be cuttin' that soon. We'll bring that cuttin' torch in here and melt that sucker right outta there!"

George forces his chin onto his chest. It stretches his neck.

"We're almos' there, ol' buddy." Lily thinks, God I'll be glad to get outta this hole. It's been fun workin' with George though. When we get to Hawaii, we're gonna have some fun. It's been hard.

"We're almos' there, ol' buddy," Lily says again. "I'm gonna drag in the torch." He disappears into the black tunnel.

As he pops out of the hole by the dirt pile, he stops still as a statue. His eyes dart overhead. Footsteps. Hollow footsteps. They stop exactly over his head. There is silence for long seconds. He thinks, what's he doing up there? Is he looking at the trapdoor? Jeez, I hope he doesn't try the trapdoor.

Then he hears the lifting ring rattle. The door lifts up tight against the bottom latch. The ring rattles again as it drops back. The steps move quickly away toward the back of the building.

Like a rabbit, Lily races back through the burrow, twists gracefully under the foundations like an inverted high jumper. He whispers urgently, "There's somebody out there, George. There's somebody walkin' around up there."

"What are they doing? Can you tell?"

"Nah. He tried the trapdoor, then he left."

George drops out of sight down the tunnel; his boots scrape the dirt. Lily follows. In seconds, two sets of feet walk back and stop over the trapdoor. There is a hammering; the joists bounce and ancient coal powder streams from the bridging. They blink back the dust. There is a scuffle and wood cracks and howls and shatters and the trapdoor opens. Light floods the basement like a biblical event.

The two men drop out of sight as if gunshot. Retreating hastily back through the tunnel, Lily gets kicked in the face. Their panicky breaths fill the underground space. George reaches up and turns off the lantern's propane hiss and it begins to dim. They wait.

Scraping and heavy breathing comes from the tunnel. The afterglow of the lantern mantle is nearly out. A tense voice calls just feet away, "All right. Come out of there and come slowly. We have shotguns and we'll splatter your ass." The adrenalin in Lily's legs burn for action and his heart beats furiously; he can feel the throb behind his eyes.

A ray of light spears the darkness and lands on George's face. He squints and looks away.

"Is that you, George?" The tunnel voice holds the authority of God. "What the hell are you doing down here, George? Get your ass out of there and keep your hands where I can see 'em or you're dead meat."

"OK. Delbert, just take it easy. I'm coming. Just take it easy."

Lily sits in the darkness hardly breathing, staring at the tunnel. He listens to the voices through the tunnel but can't make them out.

Light reflects dimly down the tunnel and Delbert says evenly, "OK, Lily, come on out. It's over. Keep your hands where I can see 'em!"

Lily creeps toward the light until it fills his face and blinds him. He crawls out of the hole. A heavy foot between his shoulders smashes him into the dirt.

"On your face! Put your hands together behind your back!"

Cold metal encircles a wrist. With a yank that hurts his shoulder, his hand is pulled next to the other and the handcuffs close sounding like a large zipper. The bones in his wrists hurt. Gravel grinds into his cheek and he suddenly needs to pee.

George lies on his belly. Delbert and his partner stand over them, looking like evil giants in their bulky coats.

Delbert slips his pistol back into its holster, "You guys tripped the vibration alarm and you are in big trouble," he says easily. "Why are you doing this, Lily? This is a federal rap, man. This is a dumb idea."

George strains to look up into the cop's face. "No, it's a good idea. Getting caught is dumb. The idea's great."

Delbert looks down at Lily. "George is scum but why are you doing this?"

Lily closes his eyes and thinks hard. His mind is empty. With a mystical slowness, a thought begins to congeal out of the haze and take shape. It was just the idea of it, the fairness of it, the adventure and Hawaii and the coke and the hungry women that wouldn't leave him alone. And digging in the dark, moving dirt with ol' George.

In the angriest voice he can muster, Lily says, "The bankers owe me! It's my money, and I came to get some of it back."

22

HOJO IS GOD

The trip to Denver from Telluride is 335 miles over five mountain passes. With Crazy Shirley in the seat beside me, I drive it in two hours. Maybe it just seems like that.

In the Howard Johnson motel alongside the Valley Highway in south Denver, we make amazing love the whole night through, resting, talking, giggling and always touching. My heart just keeps flipping over from the excitement.

We have come to the city together, me to real estate school and she to printing school. Neither of us made it to our schools. Suddenly, we are children ecstatically carousing, touching and loving. It is a bounce-off-the-wall night. I have never loved anyone or anything so much. At dawn, my eyes click on like porch lights. I watch her sleep. She is indescribably gorgeous. Love is such a corny emotion. I love looking at her. I want to stay here just like this until I die, never to leave. There is a God and his name is HoJo. Thank you, HoJo, for giving me my first chance at real love.

I stare at the ceiling, a prestressed concrete structure with the popcorn finish that looks like fuzzy white mold growing. This ceiling personalized with tiny, shiny stars blown in at random is the most beautiful ceiling I have ever seen. My life will never be the same after this night. Even if this fling with Shirley turns out to be just that, a fling, my marriage of 14 years is over. It has been over for five years; it is now just a habit, not a relationship. It is nobody's fault. Growing apart is the fault line. We have both changed and now we have little in common except children and a house.

I know all about flings from my advertising days. Until now, I had kept them separated in my mind, carefully compartmentalized away from my family life, the actions never mixing with my business or family. Damaging my family was always out of the question. By tacit agreement, my spouse lived her life happily at home as mother and housewife. I lived my life happily as a hardworking business guy, photographer and production studio owner. To me, family was to be protected at all costs. My priority was to protect them from the silliness of the world and support them well. But now, after a night in paradise in a brown motel room with traffic noise leaking through the door, the thought of returning to my dull home life and workaday world is an absurdity, a distant, far country. Too far.

In the end, married love has gone stale. My spouse is a good woman. She has been a good wife, a fine mother, has given me plenty of room to grow and work and entrepreneur and take risks. But I have been emotionally neutral for years. Unending work stress does that to you. A long time being married does that. Insidious and gradual change does that. Denial does that. There have been few fights or even unpleasantness. No good-guy-bad-guy. On this sunny, cold February morning in a motel room by the freeway, my marriage ends. Life can never be the same. How am I going to stay moral after I've been to HoJo with the tastiest woman in the world?

23

THE A-TEAM

Some men of Telluride are draft dodgers and proud of it. Some came down from Canada where they avoided the Vietnam War. Some had connections that deferred them until the shooting was over. They often strut around as if they have beaten the game, laughing unselfconsciously when the subject of military service comes up.

"Yeah, I went to Canada and avoided all that war crap," one says with a broad smile. "Moved to Toronto—great place. Loved the Canadian women. Beautiful."

But you don't hear this kind of talk around the A-Team.

They are three Marines who returned from Nam with scary credentials; "17-cent-killers" the newspapers called their kind. Looking at them one can easily believe that they walked into the blind jungles of the forbidding countryside to kill the VC, hunt enemy snipers, to pull off "one-shot, one kill" missions. One shot cost the government 17 cents.

To the unobservant, they look like ordinary young men in great health. Underneath those good looks is the trained mind and muscle of killers. Stress wrinkles around their eyes make them look older than they are. There is a certainty in their step, a levelness to their stare. They look through you with an alcoholic gaze like a human target suitable only for killing. Women hang around them in the bar, pretty women.

The leader, Jack, lives with a beautiful heiress in her newly built luxury home on the flat expanse of Sunshine Mesa. The deck overlooks the fantastic geography of mesas and mountains stretching away to the horizon. It is a private place at the end of a dirt road on the edge of the mesa itself. At the end of the front deck, the mesa falls off rocky cliffs down to the river that ribbons along the canyon floor 800 feet below.

The trio laughs a lot, easily prodding and roughly harassing each other, but when a man outside their group tries to join in, they turn cold. Without saying a word, they become threatening, looking through the interloper and leaning in toward him.

Even though I had spent four years in the Navy, worked with and around men since I was a little kid, had grown up in a man's world without women, I avoid these men like rattlesnakes under a rock.

Standing in my usual corner of the Sheridan Bar, I can see the full length of the room and hear the conversations. I listen to these fearsome men discuss their lives, referring to their adventures in the jungles obliquely but talking openly about their sexual exploits.

Jack, the most handsome of the trio, is making a bet with his compatriots. "I'll give $50 to the first man to fuck a girl while riding the new Number 6 lift."

"I'm in," Arnold, the beefy one, says laughing.

"Me, too. Black or white?" Tim with the bull neck asks. They all laugh, their mirth mingling in the barroom.

I laugh with them.

Tim turns to me with icy eyes.

"What the fuck are you laughing at? You don't have the balls to do it," Tim says.

"You're right. I don't. I've got enough problems," I say as cheerily as I can and give them my best smile. My blood turns cold. "Well, you guys have a good one." I chug the last of my beer, slip off the bar stool and ease out to the street through the ornate doors.

Soon the gossip speeds around town that a couple was photographed having face-to-face sex on the way to the top of the ski mountain.

Jack sits on the Sunshine Mesa deck watching the sun scatter its blinding red rays over the blue La Sal Mountains way out on the horizon.

The veranda harbors two rocking chairs and a small table with a bag of weed and a pipe. A shotgun leans against the wall, lonesome in its thin, lethal profile.

Then Jack reaches back and picks up the shotgun. He puts the barrel in his mouth. Stretching his arm full-length, he presses the trigger with his thumb. He never hears the explosion that echoes back from the canyon walls.

A week later, in his rented bedroom in Placerville, Tim does the same thing.

Two weeks after that, the third good soldier, while sitting behind the wheel of his Jeep in Pueblo, follows his friends into the blind jungle of nothingness.

24

CRAZY SHIRLEY'S BARREL

Every car that passes delivers a small shot of fear, it's headlights a mortal threat. This is how men die at the hands of angry husbands, I think. Will Crazy Shirley and I be caught? Will she be caught? Will she show? Will she go with me? It is dark in this steep canyon 15 miles downstream from Telluride. I wait in Big Red, my VW Westphalia van. It is 10 o'clock, the time we agreed to meet at a wide pull-off by the Smokey Bear national forest sign.

All in all, it seems like love is an extra, useless appendage, like an arm growing out of the middle of your chest. It might be good for turning pages in a book when you are smoking a cigar with the left hand and sipping Glenfiddich with the right. But the rest of the time, it is terribly awkward. Nature makes a man want to stick part of his body inside another person's body. He becomes a sloshing, quivering bag of lust on the hunt for a cooperative target.

But love brings violence to the simple heart and upheaval to the clear mind. The distortions of emotion cause the lover to imagine weird things about someone who is barely known even if they have been sex partners for half a century. Why are we human beings stuck with something as useless as love? It isn't required for procreation. A lot of screwing and impregnation goes on without the bothersome interference of loving feelings. Lust works just as well and maybe better to ejaculate diversity into the gene pool. Did the Mongols ride those little shaggy horses out of the steppes with a need to fall in love to diversify their gene pool? No. They screwed any female of any age that they could chase down, and the devil take diversity. It is safe to say these midnight riders didn't worry much about pregnancy.

What causes a stable, even boring guy to comfortably drive along a well-marked road, staying in his own lane, driving under the speed limit, then suddenly find himself off the road at blindly speeding around a corn maze spinning the steering wheel lock to lock? Love is pain. What does it do? What does it help? Why does it unbalance me so?

The true Zen says that love just is.

One has to tolerate that eternal truth or feel shitty. I don't understand it at all. Like a dog, just flip me onto my back and rub my belly. I surrender.

After a time, she shows up in her little car. I am terrified. A few mumbled words through the open windows and we hold our breath. She follows my van for 50 miles and parks her car on a back street in Naturita where it is unlikely to be recognized. Escaping from Telluride and spouses isn't as easy as one might think.

She jumps into the VW camper and we run like thieves, jail-breakers without conscience, to rip off the hard-earned love of our spouses.

Paradox Valley is a red open wound in the earth's skin, the incision lined with vertical rock cliffs left by a collapsing salt dome. Paradoxically, the Dolores River flows across the canyon, not in it, out of a cut in one red rock wall, across the valley and through the other. On this night, there isn't a man-made light in sight. The brilliant moon floods the valley and when we stop at a roadside pullout, it is a wonderful and eerie world.

Shirley walks off the road, squats and takes a whiz behind a green trash barrel. I stand in the middle of an empty highway and peer at the canopy of stars and feel relief and happiness wash over my soul. God, I've done it. I have persuaded the most beautiful woman I've ever seen to run away with me, away from the guilt and the problems in Telluride. I don't know what tomorrow brings, but tonight I'm ecstatic, like a salmon swimming upstream to breed and then die.

Her dark shape trots up onto the pavement. "I love you, Shirley," I yell.

"And I love you." She smiles, her teeth showing ear to ear. In the moonlight so bright, I can see detail in the canyon walls: the desert floor, the desiccated trees and rabbitbrush, her face and the athletic outline of her body. We run up and down the middle of the empty highway swinging hands, pounding the pavement, laughing and hooting in the utter joy of being alive, even temporarily. We hug and hold on. Her body is warm in the coolness of midnight.

Shirley whispers, "This is a night to remember. This is craziness."

"Yes, I know. In celebration of craziness." We kiss passionately for a long time.

Deep down I know that in the future, this unmarked wide spot in the road in desiccated Paradox Valley will be known on my internal map as Shirley's Barrel: a power vortex in the universe. Whenever I drive by it on my way to Utah, I'll always remember the moon-flooded night when we ran up and down the highway like children ditching school, knowing life would never be the same again. I will relive the thrill of escape and the razor's cut of passion, the explosive release of primitive wild spirits trapped too long in the duty and honor of middle-class America.

I have gone to heaven. We struggle with our respective divorces. Hers goes rather easily; after all, what can a newly married couple build up in six months?

Mine is an agony in waiting. When it is over, I know I will be broke, bitter and if I weren't so in love with this woman, suicidal.

The town chooses up sides. The wives in town think I deserve whatever suffering comes my way up to, and including, testicle squeezing with red-hot pliers and a prolonged death rattle. The men think I am a brainless idiot following my pecker into disaster. I fight back valiantly by making love to Crazy Shirley as often, with as many variations, as possible. Living well is the best revenge and there ain't no living like a loving living.

Predictably, her parents live in full disapproval of our liaison. As hog farmers outside of Kokomo, Indiana, they are pillars of the church and the lifeblood of Middle America, where daughters grow up, have babies, a straight corporate husband, a suburban house, a clean Ford station wagon and eventually inherit the farm.

To escape the social heat and live a new life, we put the miles on Big Red, the Volkswagen Westphalia camper van that I bought for just such escape.

25

THE SEARCH FOR ABIGAIL DUFF

On a spectacular October day, Crazy Shirley's friend Abigail Duff, goes hiking on the ski area side of the Telluride valley. Night comes. She doesn't come home. Her boyfriend is frantic.

She could be lost, the most likely prospect since people from the flatlands often don't grasp the magnitude and the distances involved in the mountains. Everything looks so close, but a person standing on a hillside a half-mile away disappears.

Or she might be injured. Or dead. Or she just let the darkness catch her too far out to make it back to town. Overestimating stamina is a chronic mistake hikers make in this rough country and thin air.

The next morning, my buddy John and I jump on our dirt bikes to quickly search the obvious roads and trails. Perhaps she has broken an ankle and can't walk. We'll find her lying beside the trail, cold and in pain. One of us will stay with her, the other going for the mountain rescue team. If she has gone off the trail, it is possible that she will never be found. But that is unlikely. She will turn up somewhere.

In the slanting morning sun, we ride dangerously hard and fast for an hour, covering the ski area trails and roads within a three-hour walk from the south side of town.

The next day, a $10,000 reward is posted. Mountain-wise people search for the next month, hiking the most likely trails, taking known shortcuts through the trees, looking down avalanche chutes, looking for anything unusual, any clue. Nothing. Then it snows.

Competing theories float in the valley. Because she has straight dark hair parted in the middle, Charles Manson kidnapped her. Our local mystic has a vision of her looking over the town from a high place. Or she simply lost her bearings and walked the wrong way. Or she fell in the river and drowned.

In the mountains, the locals know the Grim Reaper is always near and death comes unexpectedly to the ignorant, the careless, the weak and the unprepared. Sometimes it is years before a lost body turns up. Sometimes never.

Abigail simply disappeared from the earth.

During the warmer days of spring, the snow begins to melt, especially under the sandstone cliffs that collect the heat of the afternoon sun. Spring skiing is here and two high school teenagers are catching their last fast run of the day. They schuss the hard-packed cat track, the access road from the top of the ski mountain down to town, and they race, their skis chattering on the icy surface of the road.

A hundred feet from the bottom, they spot a dark object like a big rock in the middle of the track. They check their speed and go around it.

They stop at the bottom near the lift station.

"Did you see that?" the taller one asks as he releases his bindings. "I thought it was a rock. But it was shaped exactly like a head. Eyes and everything."

"I saw that," his friend says. "And hair. It looked like a head with black hair looking up the trail."

"Yeah. It's the spookiest thing I've ever seen."

Abigail Duff returned to town six months after her disappearance.

While hiking last fall, she left the trail, took a shortcut through the trees and emerged on top of the red cliffs that hang above the town. She took off her hot hiking boots, tied the laces together and hung them in a bush. She sat down on loose rocks above the precipice and wiggled her toes. She looked at the toy town with the towering peaks above, the golden trees filtering the late afternoon sun. When she shifted around to ease her sitting, the small rocks beneath her began to roll. She started to slide down, dug in her bare feet till they hurt, but could not stop.

At the bottom of the 250-foot cliff, her body lodged in a deadfall, one leg above the fallen logs, the other below. In the winter, the animals burrowed under the snow and fed. When the snow melted in the spring, her head rolled down the avalanche chute and came to rest in the middle of the cat track.

It is the last day of ski season.

26

AVOIDING HOME

I am in nirvana. Living and loving Crazy Shirley makes me float through each day. The constant high that I feel when with her is a first for me, that feeling that anything is possible as long as we are together, nothing is beyond reach. It is a sustaining IV drip that takes me to a different mental state, a country I have never seen, with a capital named Euphoria—an insanity, a drug, an addiction.

Inside Telluride, it is a different story.

Our love affair is public knowledge. We are spotted on the main street of Durango, shopping, walking, talking and laughing together. We are discovered happily by Telluride's dedicated full-time gossip who can't get the painful word to my wife fast enough so that she can enjoy someone else's misery to spice up her unexciting and miserable life.

The people of the town think of themselves as an outlaw tribe—the Telluriders. The anarchists among them are delighted Shirley and I have violated the tribal laws. The tribal elders, on the other hand, are offended by our anti-social act and oppose us.

Much of it is gender bias. The men approve heartily because this older married man is now sleeping with a beautiful, young married woman. The women think we are horrible because an older married man with three children left his wife of 14 years for sex with a beautiful, young married woman.

The elders are right. In one night, I violated every quasi-moral rule I had ever made for myself:

1. Never dip your pen in company ink. (I did that.)

2. Never betray a friend. (Her husband was my good friend. I violated that.)
3. No married women. (I shot that in the head.)
4. Keep downtown life and family life separate. (Whoa.)

We both keep a brave face and hold our heads high when we walk the streets. We act as if what we are doing is the most normal thing in the world. Love is making me crazy. However, we are both carrying an overweight package of guilt; the fact that we are both married never leaves our minds.

So for us, town is a place to avoid. We travel. First we camp in beautiful spots around the Southwest, then to Texas and then California. Anywhere but home.

Big Red becomes our closest friend. The spare tire cover on the front of the van becomes a raised finger to the world. Shirley paints a big smiling sun with rainbow-colored rays that cause hippies in other vans to wave wildly at us when we meet on the highway. We wildly wave and grin back at them as they whiz by.

The vibe inside the van and Shirley's come-hither smell spices the self-contained, free life. Love overwhelms everything.

Often I ask her, "Will you marry me?"

"No," she answers with a smile.

"Good," I say.

And I mean it. There is nothing we can do that can make our oneness any better. Life and love are perfect. I know this can't last forever. Life is too fluid, too changeable and too temporary to count on anything. I dread the day when it will be over, when the arc of our love affair completes itself.

There is the age difference, the responsibility difference. I have kids; she doesn't. I have a business and people who depend on me; she doesn't. She is a young, beautiful woman with her life yet to be played out, and mine has already been set. She has a young disco nightlife to be danced away; I am past that. So this can't last until death do us part. It will last until the passage of time cools the passions and the end, bitter or sweet, inevitably comes.

27

HAMS

My Dutch friend arrives in town with a box of tools and a flat-faced Ford van and money he made smuggling hashish across the Khyber Pass between Afghanistan and Pakistan. He is such a fine wood craftsman from the Old World he has steady work. We drink together for entertainment and to conspire against the citizenry.

My offices are located next door to the drugstore, which has been closed for years. The store is an old building with an interior that is an artifact of the '50s.

Late one night, while staggering from one bar to the next, we notice that there are 10 young people putting the finishing interior touches on the space.

With a stroke of entertainment brilliance, we decide to show those late-night working folks a couple of pressed hams. We stand with our backs to the glass, drop our pants and press our naked buttocks flat against the plate-glass window. We knock on the glass and the workers' heads turn as one and then swivel quickly back to their paintbrushes. They don't laugh.

The next day I learn that the workers are teenagers from the Christian church camp in Ames.

28

CABORCA

The undersized engine of the VW van winds up tight in its labors, sounding hot and healthy. But underneath that healthy sound comes a more subtle noise, a ticking from somewhere down underneath the imagination. Crazy Shirley and I have left Telluride and driven out of Colorado as fast as the little engine will turn.

As we wheel down the wavy road in northern Mexico, the emptiness of the landscape is both welcome and frightening after spending the past six months in the mountain snows. The Sonoran Desert is a broken floor with spiky, gnarly scrub and stunted trees, poor and mean-spirited when crossed.

We slip out of the high country between two spring snowstorms. April is a difficult month in the mountains. It snows hard and long and deep, and the desert winds whip it into white smoke storms that spiral up through the trees. Telluride's spirit grays. Everything is gray, black or white—the mountains, the rivers and the meadows. And the people, they fight about everything. Small problems become issues for warfare. Homes become jail cells, and the most scenic main street in America turns into a cellblock. Meanwhile, it's spring in the low country, legitimate spring—beckoning, greening and soft with flowers and wind without teeth. In April, the nearest warm place with an ocean beach is Rocky Point, Mexico.

Daylight flees over the horizon. The night-black deepens, unpunctuated by lights of civilization. As we chase our headlights into the darkness, the ticking moves up from the imagination, into the subconscious, into the conscious. The click is here now; it is real.

If there is ever a place and time in the world I do not want to break down, it is here and now. Not with this fantastic woman, not on our great getaway from our exes, not on the Tryst-Of-The-Century, not out here in the wilds of northern Sonora. Every full turn of the rear wheels yields a snang-snang-snang sound that quickly approaches clank-clank-clank. My fear meter pegs.

At a place where two highways meet, the van takes control and refuses to go on. Her worn-out parts demand flatly, "We will stay here tonight." A road from the right dead-ends into our road 100 feet ahead forming wide shoulders that fall away steeply into arroyos. Big Red surrenders there in the T of the two roads, crippled and failed.

Breaking down in northern Mexico with its bandits, its unknown language and a gorgeous blonde available for the raping is more input than I want to deal with. Slowly, fear closes its damp palm around my heart and squeezes adrenaline down into my thighs.

A dump truck rolls up to the intersection and a dozen dark shapes jump down out of the back. It drives on, its untamed exhaust barks into the night sky. Dark, lumpy images walk toward us.

I look around for a light, for civilization, anything for protection. Seamless blackness. "God, Shirley, I wish I had a gun," I whisper. The men walk toward the van, more heard than seen. They talk in short bursts and grunts, low laughs. Then they walk by, barely glancing at us. Except for the last man who turns.

He speaks. He smiles and talks and points. I smile and smile and smile until my face hurts. I nod agreement. But I lie. I understand nothing.

Looking directly at the Mexican, I say, "Shirley, get the phrase book out and look up some way to tell this guy we need a mechanic." She flips pages for a minute or two. The Mexican worker babbles away. We agree to point at the offending rear end of the VW and nod together.

"It won't run anymore. It is broken. It will not move," I say slowly and clearly and shake my head. The Mexican smiles and nods and rambles as if we are having a real conversation.

"'Mechanica,' the word is 'mechanica,'" Shirley giggles.

I look at the Mexican. "I need a mechanica."

"Ah, mechanica," he says, his yellow teeth look threatening behind the smile but he babbles on, enjoying our company.

I point at him, then away down the road and then back at the van. "Here's five bucks. Go find me a mechanica and send him here."

He talks a bunch more with the bill in his hand. He nods his head, laughs and leaves; the blanket roll over his shoulder creates a hump on his back.

The quiet is eerie. The only sound is the engine cooling. The steel and aluminum muscles relax with tiny snaps and pops like electrical sparks.

I shiver. "Jesus, that scared me when those guys jumped out of that farm truck." The perspiration in my shirt is cooling.

"Me, too." Crazy Shirley throws down the phrase book and flashes a wall-to-wall smile. "I'm hungry."

During a dinner of canned soup and soda crackers, we replay the terror of the farm truck. Now that some plan of action is underway, we feel better. We wonder how many miles the Mexican farmhand will have to walk to find a mechanica. In Sonora, the home of lizards, bandits and millions of acres of struggling vegetation, who could guess? Quien sabe? It might be a day or two, but we have everything we require, mostly each other.

Since the first ecstatic night with Crazy Shirley in the Howard Johnson's motel room, I have never felt so devoid of the need of earthly possessions or so careless about my personal safety. She is the only thing in my life that matters. Being near her, around her, knowing where she is and what she is doing when she is out of sight, the chemical bond, how she smells and tastes and looks in the morning light is obsession and poetry, light spirit air and nervous beauty, soft and scary.

As we wash the dishes, three Mexicans—the *mechanicas*—walk up. With much talking, pointing and arm waving, they jack up the rear end. The best dressed of the trio, an older man, indicates he wants something from me. I shrug. I understand nothing. He makes a noise like an engine.

Studying the phrase book, Crazy Shirley says from inside, "I think he wants you to start it up."

I look into the man's eyes, reflecting dark brown from the interior van light. I point at my chest, "Vroom, vroom?"

He shakes his head no. He points to the van. "Vroom, vroom," he says.

The engine jumps to life. The jacked-up wheel spins with fits and makes loud, clanky and expensive grinding sounds.

They had brought three tools: a regular screwdriver, an 8-inch Crescent wrench and another Crescent wrench 3 feet long. Muttering, they set to work on the wheel. The older man directs the others and they place the yard-long wrench on the axle nut.

"Jesus, Shirley, this guy has a wrench on this wheel big enough to turn this van over." We laugh. The Mexicans laugh.

They putter around the wheel and peer up under the van's skirt with a flashlight, their heads close together forming a bouquet of automotive brains. Finally, the older Mexican chatters and shrugs at me.

"You can't fix it?" I ask.

He chatters and shakes his head and opens his hands like he's measuring a fish.

"You got to get parts? OK. When—*mañana*?" I am feeling better about speaking Spanish.

"*Si, si, mañana*." Then he talks some more and points to his wristwatch.

"*Mañana. Ocho*," I say.

The *mechanicas* will be back in the morning. Eight o'clock sharp.

Suddenly, it isn't quite so black. The stars sparkle and a warm breeze eases around through the intersection. What is adventure except handling the unexpected—and the elation of coping with it? Here we are in Mexico, away from the snow and mud of Telluride, the cellblock walls of the canyon, in the warm and spirit-filling desolation of the desert. And I'm with the only woman in the world I know I can spend the rest of my life with. Goddamn, I feel good.

We close the doors, pull the curtains, turn off the lights, fall together and make love. It is a regular thing, this heaven, and this *ménage à trois*: Big Red, Crazy Shirley and me.

The rooster starts about midnight. He starts crowing over by the right headlight. It sounds like someone dragging a rasp over the edge of a tin roof. His friend, in turn, crows for a minute or two and then passes the irritating baton to the rooster on his right, and he crows until his vocal cords tatter. Without stopping, the crowing circles the van, then back to the first rooster that started it all. You can tell it is he. He hits that ragged note at the end of each nocturnal insult.

For an hour, I lie there listening to the chicken chorus. Curious, I cautiously peek through the drawn curtains. Certainly I am hallucinating. I look out the other side.

In the softest of whispers, "Shirley? Are you awake?"

"What is it?" Her voice is tight.

"We're surrounded."

"By what? What's out there?"

"I'm not sure of what I'm seeing. You look and tell me."

In the slowest of motions, she pulls the curtain back and peers into the night.

"There are trucks out there. They're parked all around us. They're facing us with their fronts. Where are the drivers?"

"Beats the hell out of me. I didn't hear a thing. We're surrounded by Bimbo bread trucks."

"What reason could there be for surrounding us with a dozen delivery trucks?" I look again just to make sure they are there. They sure as hell are there.

In the morning, they are gone without a trace. Bright morning. When we open the curtains, we realize we are parked on the edge of a barrio. There are kids and dogs and women in flimsy dresses doing chores, gossiping and keeping a close eye on the neighborhood. And, of course, they stare at the van.

"Jesus, Shirley, there are women everywhere and I've just got to pee." Big Red doesn't have a potty.

"Me, too!" she says. "The hell with it. I'm going to go right over there." She jumps out carrying a little white flag of toilet paper, walks to the edge of the road, drops down like a frog and lets go. The neighborhood watches mesmerized. The neighborhood grins.

Well, I ain't goin' out there, I think. I dig around in the trash basket and come up with a Coca Cola can. If there is an advantage to being a man, it is the ability to maneuver in tight quarters. I fill it right up to the triangular hole in the top. With no place to throw it, I place the can of warm urine on the ground under the van, inside of the right front wheel.

The sun is brilliant and Shirley is beautiful. We chat happily over breakfast and plan for the repairs. She assumes the job of translating useful phrases out of the Spanish book that we will need for the *mechanica*. I study the VW manual for clues to our trouble. I understand little of what I read and curse myself for my ignorance.

A semitruck comes barking around the corner of the crossroad and, in a noisy and dusty display of highway disaster, runs down the embankment and rolls upside down in the ravine.

Shirley's eyes go wide. "What do we do now?"

"Don't worry about it," I say. "You just translate. There will be people along to help."

The driver clambers up over the edge of the road and emerges from the dust cloud, laughing hysterically and slatting his hat against his leg. More dust flies. Kids and grown-ups run from every direction. There are dogs and bicycles and old people surveying the big, dusty wreck, laughing and pointing. They cluster around the driver like a flock of birds, the men gathering close and the women standing back. To hoots and catcalls, the driver retells the disaster story to everyone who will listen.

From far away, a siren can be heard getting closer. It is a cop. He parks above the wreck and tries to direct traffic with much arm waving and whistle blowing. None of it works. He only snarls traffic more; traffic seizes and the scene takes on the air of a national holiday.

Our automotive messiah, the *mechanica*, arrives—a slim man in greasy coveralls. I expected to see an elaborate toolbox. He carries the same three tools as the men from the night before with the addition of a large Allen wrench and a rusty file. He slides under the van, pops out a minute later, sits on the ground and begins to file down the Allen wrench to fit.

None of this picture seems right to me.

"Jesus, Shirley, I don't like the feeling of this turkey working on my van." I make a command decision. "You stay here. Don't let him take anything apart. I'm going to find somebody. With all these people, this must be a larger town than it looks. If it is, then there must be a real *mechanica* somewhere."

Crazy Shirley frowns. "But what do I do if he starts to take the van apart?"

"I don't know. Show him your tits. Take off your clothes. Offer him your body—anything to keep him here, but not working, until I get back. It's possible that he could be our only hope."

She looks over at the dirty, skinny brown man patiently filing down the tool and grits her teeth.

"Look, don't worry about it. I'll be back in a few minutes," I say.

She looks worried.

Even worried, in the morning light, she is radiant. Her blue eyes sparkle and her oversized mouth turns up at the corners. Just the thought of someone, anyone, else with her makes my stomach roll over. "Just joking. Don't take anything off," I say.

She smiles weakly and goes back to translating phrases.

Among the crowd of wreck aficionados, a taxi driver stands propped against his rusty steed. He brightens instantly and opens the door for me.

"Take me to someone that speaks English."

The old engine grinds to life and we are off much faster than required, throwing rocks into the feet of the crowd. He turns around over the back seat driving casually with one hand. He speaks. I catch the word "Nogales."

"No. No Nogales. *Se habla Ingles, por favor.*"

"Nogales?"

"No Nogales. That's 100 miles away, goddammit. *Hombre Ingles?*"

He shrugs. We drive for another minute and stop in front of a small adobe house with a Volkswagen Safari parked among the yard cacti. The driver says some Spanish at me and I toss him a couple of bills without counting. I visualize Crazy Shirley easing out of her sweatshirt just about now to keep the *mechanica* from disassembling our home and salvation. He would slap his sainted mother for just a glimpse of those exquisite breasts. Any man would.

A short, gray-haired man answers my knock on the doorpost.

"Excuse me, sir, do you speak English?"

"Sure, what can a do for ya?" It's pure Texican. Relief flows over me like a warm shower on a cold morning.

"Boy, am I glad to find you. My van is broken down up where the two roads intersect. There is a man there trying to repair it but I am afraid he can't do it." I point at his little desert car. "Who do you have repair your VW?"

He speaks patiently, as if explaining to his grandchild, "I just take mine around the corner to the VW dealer. Jump in. I'll take you to see Juan."

The dealership has one car on the showroom floor; the salesman is also the *mechanica*. My savior explains my problem to Juan. Juan has a wrecker.

Riding back to Big Red and Crazy Shirley, I hold my breath, expecting to see either Big Red's parts laid out all over the ground or the doors shut with Crazy Shirley and the *mechanica* inside. But when we arrive, everything is status quo. The *mechanica* is still filing the wrench to fit, the wreck crowd is bigger and noisier than ever, and Crazy Shirley still has her shirt on.

Shirley smiles relief. "You aren't going to believe this but another big truck came along and tried to pull the first truck out of there, and it rolled over, too. Now there are two trucks down in there. Everybody got another free show."

There is more laughing from the gaggle of watchers gathered above the trucks.

Backing the wrecker up to the van becomes the new center of attention. As Juan attaches the chains and lifts the van's rear end up like a kitty in heat, 20 brown kids gather round the front of the vehicle. They joke and laugh and point through the windshield and ogle Crazy Shirley and me about to ride off backward into the dust.

"Be sure to hold the steering wheel straight," Juan says. As I hold the steering wheel, the kids crowd in around the windshield, their brown faces just inches away from ours. They giggle and jostle each other and glance down expectantly under the car as if waiting for something.

"Oh, Jesus, Shirley, don't laugh," I say. "I think they are going after the pop can."

"What pop can?"

"The one I whizzed in. I set it under the van."

There were several expectant moments and then the van begins to move. A scuffle breaks out. Up comes the Coke can of urine on a platform of quick brown hands. It floats upward into the air seemingly loose, airborne. It drifts between upwardly stretched hands and fingers. The tallest of the urchins finally gains partial control of the prize, and stretching his body and neck tall, puts it to his mouth and drinks deeply, his face to the sky, his eyes closed. Another hand jerks it away from him mid-swallow. He sprays a shower of yellow liquid over the smaller children. Now the second kid has a mouthful; he spits violently and throws the can into the dirt. Through the windshield, the children, some laughing uproariously and others angry, grow smaller and finally disappear in the dust cloud.

We ride backward through the Mexican town of Caborca, hooked onto the wrecker fanny to fanny like mating stinkbugs. The natives of Caborca sit on their porches and grin and wave. They love us.

I love us, too. I know that for better or worse, in and out of adventures, Crazy Shirley will be with me always.

29

JULY 4

Telluride is overflowing with July 4 revelers. There is no place to park, and black-vested bikers crowd the main street. Their cycles are backed into the curb at an angle, taking up a whole block. They stand around in the street, drink beers and look mean.

The safety meeting between the motorcycle gang leaders and the marshal's department had gone well, finishing in an agreement: You biker bosses keep your people in line and we, the cops, won't bother you. A handshake seals it.

Mostly, the agreement holds up. Oh, there is the drunk who flips his three-wheeler going too fast down the main street; the rumored rape in the park; and lots of drugs flowing, including heroin. We find needles.

I work the microphone in the sound truck and watch the crowd swirl around our vehicle. In a small town overfull with people and vehicles, it is hard to tell what is happening. It is confusing. It feels dangerous.

Each year, the day's events kick off at 6 o'clock in the morning with a bone-rattling dynamite blast, the "Miners Alarm." The echoes rumble back and forth between the canyon walls. Since the 1880s, the Fourth of July Parade brings every drunk white man and Indian, every hell-raiser within driving distance, up from the desert and down from the hills. People are on the roofs of the buildings in order to get a good look at the parade and the forgiving nature of the town's entertainment that has drawn them here.

In the old days, there were rock drilling contests for competing miners, tugs-of-war, ore loading contests, blackjack gambling and fistfights.

The school kids hang off the old fire engine that rattles around winding the siren. The Whistlers go by: volunteer firemen who are stripped to the waist, big, painted lipstick mouths around their navels and plastic eyelashes above their nipples, ears sticking out the sides of their chests, their arms, heads and shoulders stuffed up into a huge hat with a 4-foot brim. They march along sucking their fat stomachs in and out to the rhythm of a whistled tune from the loudspeakers.

There are the usual suspects: the dancing groups of scantily clad women with pretty bodies, the radio station DJs, the veterans in uniform, the kids' ski team, this year's heroes of wholly forgettable events, the old-timers in old cars, politicians, flags and bunting, kids on bikes, babies pulled in red wagons, the antique Plymouth ambulance with a weak siren and old flashing red lights, and embarrassed dogs dressed in baby clothes, hanging their heads in shame. The Queen of the Fourth, adorned in her prom dress, and the King, wearing a cardboard crown, ride on the trunk of a shiny Chrysler convertible. The sheriff's car flashes red lights behind the cowgirls on horses that bring up the parade's end; the crap managers push barrels on wheels and sweep up after the horses.

The mood changes after the parade and as the day wears on, for no apparent reason, men are suddenly angry. People run across the tops of the shaky, old two-story buildings that have been drying out for 80 years. Kids set off fireworks over the street from the tops of the fragile wood-frame structures.

The firemen drink steadily to keep their buzz going. The bars are packed belly to belly and back to back with tourists, cowboys, miners, skiers, carpenters, bikers, easy and difficult women, and kids running in and out the front door, squeezing through and between the adults' legs. The noise is deafening.

The whole main business block will flame up if a fire gets started in the cheek-by-jowl structures. The firemen are all drunk and there is no way they can fight a fire. There are spectators everywhere, some sure to get hurt or die in the conflagration.

There are reports of fights, and bikers roar up and down the street dodging pedestrians and dogs. We are one step away from mayhem.

This mining town tradition has outlived its fun, I think. The visitors have changed and the Telluride Fourth is now a violent playground populated by disrespectful outsiders with an "anything goes" attitude. The temporary cops brought in for this special occasion are helpless against the angry crowds. This holiday is dangerous to the town and its citizens. Civilized fun has turned into anarchy.

At the next town council meeting, I complain bitterly about sponsoring such a frightening event. "Somebody is gonna get killed here! Do we have to burn down the town in order to stop this?" I say with great passion.

The old guard says, "The Telluride Fourth is a historic event and cannot be changed after 90 years of tradition!"

"That's bullshit!" I answer.

After a reasonable cooling-off period, the council reverses course and decides that the 1976 Fourth, celebrating the 200th anniversary of the Declaration of Independence, will be a nonevent closed to outsiders. I am hugely relieved.

Approaching the next Fourth, the old guard works hard to extract their revenge for my killjoy position on this traditional event. As usual, they hold a public election for the King and Queen who will sit in the back of an open convertible and lead the parade.

After the votes are counted, I start borrowing appropriate parade clothes: pink tights, purple women's panties with ruffles worn outside, a see-through top, and an old lady's round dust cap with lace brim. I become a vision in pink, purple and lace.

As the white Chrysler leads the parade, I stand and give the twisty but elegant Queen's wave to whistles, yells, hoots of laughter and middle fingers from the crowd of locals on the sidewalks.

The angry citizens had elected me both King *AND* Queen.

30
DESERT

There is no glorious spring in the high Rockies. Whoever coined that famous phrase never lived through a high-country spring where one day it is white and nearly sterile winter and the next day it's water and mud mixed with dog shit and nameless, unidentifiable detritus—corruption frozen hard beginning to thaw, trash that the winter snows have hidden for months well out of sight of the next, brilliant summer.

But summer is invigorating, heavenly. Sixty days of nirvana, physically and spiritually enriching. In deep summer there is no place on earth like the sparkling high Rockies.

After Mexico, Crazy Shirley and I move in together. We live in a cheap rental house located as far away from our angry exes as possible—three blocks. Telluride has ostracized us.

The summary ostracism did more to push us together than anything else. In the public mind, I quickly slide from pillar of the community to pervert. We become a nation of two and we travel at every opportunity, as much to escape the agony of public guilt as for love and adventure.

On the road, home troubles seem to fade to a tolerable level, but I am trapped and can see no way out. I worry about my children. I'm going broke from several directions. Every road into the future is barricaded; going back is unthinkable; going ahead is disastrous. Circumstances will overwhelm us and there will be a train wreck. It is only a matter of time.

My love for Shirley is insane, clinically, certifiably crazy. She is everything I have ever wanted as if my wanting makes any difference. She fits some genetic imprint, some message so primitive and buried I can't understand it. And I don't want to, knowing that even if I define the problem, I can't solve it; a solution is unattainable. Serious, bone-deep love has never happened to me before. In a sense, I am a 40-year-old virgin. At the cellular level, I am both aflame and terrified.

Everyone around us, the innocents in the game—her husband, my wife, friends and ex-friends on both sides—just know it has to be sex: this round, little egoist having a body fling with the Big Ten cheerleader from Purdue. That is true. Desperately, terminally true. But there are times when I am so in love I weep, bursting into tears over my good fortune and my terror at being a slave to life out of control. It is a sickness, but we laugh every day. Every day. We work together and scheme together and hold hands and touch and smile and silently giggle into each other's eyes. The insanity can't be helped, can't be slowed and can't be stopped. It is a chemical bond between us.

Over the years, I had cheated death several times—in the Navy, in construction, in business. I never saw anything worth dying for until Crazy Shirley. Suddenly, I know how people murder in the heat of passion and now understand everything about life and love, of living with a single mate until death and the ancient tribal instincts of protecting a loved one.

I learned two things out of the Mexico near-disaster. One: do not leave oneself unprotected, and two: learn about the inner workings of Volkswagen vans.

I buy a .45 automatic pistol and set of metric tools with a book, *The Idiot's Guide to Volkswagen*. I take the engine out of the van and carry it into the kitchen. For a month, I disassemble and reassemble it. I fiddle with it, feel the bolt holes and look into the hot guts of German engineering. Brown puddles of oil foul the linoleum floor. When the engine goes back in, jacked up under the fat skirts of the bus, she runs perfectly. Every winter for the next three years, I will rebuild Big Red's heart and soul. Out of sheer gratitude, she will never fail us again.

Out in the deserts of the Southwest, we explore little known Anasazi ruins in side canyons and beat down gravel roads and sand tracks through the Indian reservations. We cook in the red sand and hike through the sage. In Big Red, we lie in the cool desert nights, making love, talking quietly and touching while the ancient Indian ghosts watch enviously and applaud.

We run naked among the light brown rounded rocks of the Waterpocket Fold in Utah and retrace the Outlaw Trail. On Comb Ridge, we make love in sight of the highway; our suntanned bodies perfectly blending with the color and form of the round rock ribs of Mother Earth, camouflaged from the cars that pass unseeing just yards away. We lie in the sun, the sand warm against our haunches, and discuss the inevitable erosion of relationships, those moments made sweeter knowing that somehow we will be overtaken by circumstance and this bliss will pass. With luck, that ending is far off, perhaps even a lifetime away.

The desert sun paints the sand, the standing rocks and us with sundown gold. There is nothing closer to nature than lying nude in the desert, except perhaps drowning in a storm-tossed ocean. There is time to fill in the holes about one's lover, to answer those strange lingering questions that flit though the mind while alone.

"Do your folks go to church?" I ask.

"Yes. They are good, God-fearing Methodists," she replies, gently picking at a tiny cactus thorn in her hand. "How about you? Have you ever gone to church?"

"I did when I was a ward of the court. The foster parents in the home I was assigned to were heavy-duty Christians. They belonged to a Holy Roller church, speaking in tongues and dancing in the spirit and all that."

"What was it like? Did you believe in it?"

"I was a teenager. I was there because people told me to go ..." I laughed, "... and get saved."

"Did you?"

"Well, one night during a revival meeting, in the middle of shouts and amens and hallelujahs and arm waving, the visiting revival preacher yelled at me and 50 other grievous sinners that we were really the pond scum of the earth and deserved to burn in the everlasting fires of hell unless we came forward to the altar and confess our sins, open our hearts and let the Lord Jesus in to forgive our sick, sad souls. The preacher yelled that I was the Devil's spawn because of my secret sins: that I cussed, used the Lord's name in vain; that I lied about why I was in the home; fantasized about sin; had dirty thoughts by conjuring sexual images of naked women. Back then I got erections eight times a day. Certainly I was the bastard child of Adolph Hitler, the worst of the worst, and a sexual deviate. Looking back on it now, the worst sin I ever committed was running away from my dad to save myself.

"Sooooo ... I found myself shuffling down the aisle with a bunch of other losers who didn't deserve Jesus' blessing either. But the preacher said that because Jesus was such a good guy, if I prayed hard enough and put no other gods before him (by the way, I didn't know there were other gods), Jesus would write us a new lease and we could start clean—be born again, as it were."

Shirley lay on her back, her body honey-colored tan without lines. I studied the fetching curves of her thighs, the rise of her smooth belly and the gentle mound of her womanhood, the pubes a good, honest Midwestern brown, the innocent hair of a country girl.

"So what happened?"

"Well, I get to the altar, a flower-carpeted platform with two steps. You kneeled on the first step and put your elbows on the second step, clasped your hands together, raised your face to the fluorescent lights, closed your eyes and did your best to look holy and needy at the same time.

"An old guy came out of the crowd, kneeled beside me and put his sweaty, righteous hand on my shoulder and began to pray for me real loud. 'Oh, Lord Jesus, take this young man, Jeremy, to your bosom and forgive him his sins and point him in the name of righteousness down the road of believing in You.'

"And, Shirley, I prayed hard ... damned hard ... goddamn hard ... . Nothing happened. Didn't feel the spirit of the Lord, I didn't feel freed or see Jesus or feel better about myself."

Shirley looks at me accusingly.

"And then, Jesus shows up! And I get a good look at Him. He doesn't look anything like his picture hanging above the altar: blond hair and blue eyes and white robes and all. He's dressed in a cotton muumuu printed with giant hibiscus blooms. He is short with black, curly hair, olive skin and a black beard. And he smiles at me. A front tooth is missing, which gives his speech a little hiss. He speaks to me: 'Come walk with me on the Pathway of Righteousness, Jeremy, and I will give you everlasting life.'

"'Jerry,' I correct him quietly.

"I decided that if he was talking to some guy named Jeremy, then he must not be talking to me. I raised my head and looked down the row of kneelers. The man getting saved next to me was really into it; I could tell by the rapturous look on his raised face. I tap him on the shoulder. His eyes fly open like he was expecting to see someone else. He looks disappointed to see me.

"'Excuse me. I'm sorry to bother you, but what is your name?'

"'My name is Jeremy and I am being saved by our Lord and Loving Redeemer.' He claps his hands together; his face flushes and his eyes snap shut.

"'Is that your real name? Jeremy?'

"His eyes pop open and he searchingly peers into mine. He challenges me, 'Is there something wrong with that?'

"'No, no. I like the name.'

"'That's good.' A long pause. He whispers, 'You're not a queer, are you?'

"'I don't think so,' I say seriously.

"'How do you know?'

"'Because when I jack off, I think about girls' titties.'

"'Oh.' His eyes click shut, and he collapses back into his saving posture, his head droops and he resumes the charade.

"I've got it now. Jesus has us confused. He's not talking to me. He's saving the man next to me.

"Then Jesus abandons my salvation, maybe shifting his focus to the guy next to me where it belongs. I shrug and return to the job at hand: trying to save my worthless soul.

"Quietly, still on my knees, my hands clasped, my fingers entwined, faking being saved, the only picture that forms in my mind was me, Jerry, my correct name, out behind the church playing with Jackie Bobenski's erect little pink nipples. I instantly get hard."

Shirley rolls over and laughs into the blanket. Her laughter makes me feel better than anything I had ever felt in church.

For me, the desert is a retreat. All of the distractions of civilization and worries of home are gone and I'm left with a clean slate upon which to write new thoughts and ideas, to see new art in the rocks that change with each sunlit minute. A continuously morphing scene, now in shadow, now in sun, marks the passing of the warm day and the counterpoint of the cool night.

We stand on the edge of a mesa in the bright moon and we can see 100 miles across Monument Valley, across the Navajo Nation, all the way to Black Mesa, through the 1,000-foot sandstone skyscrapers that make the valley into a moonlit lithoscape. One thousand feet below are the sinuous curves of the goosenecks of the San Juan River. For us, Muley Point is a private overlook. Few people discover this place out on the very edge of a mesa. The auto trail zigzags up the face of the cliff and squeezes the car dangerously close to the drop-off. Here is a private heaven. For now, on this incredible night, Crazy Shirley and I own it.

In this place seldom seen even by God, we get the giggles about some cosmic joke and listen to the wind play Big Red's three notes. When the wind hits 10 knots, something on the van near the front, a piece of sheet metal or a hole in the frame, warbles flutelike the same three musical notes, rising and falling with the wind gusts. Big Red feels good about being one of us and sings our song.

The coyotes yip musically and lope in a panting pack toward some happy destination, feeding each other gag lines with perfectly timed hoots of happiness. We listen and track them, bearing down on the van from upwind; they are unable to smell Big Red's chronic oil leak or the happy humans sharing their empty, exotic domain. At the first hint of Big Red and us, their conversation cuts off like a tape recording. Silence. The three notes play on. With the woman-child, I live a childhood I had never known in any lifetime.

31
WFO

I think the guy is surely dead. All I see are two feet sticking out from under a pile of racing motorcycles. I think I might save his life. It is the manly world of motorcycle racing and this is my very first race. Here is a golden opportunity to save the life of a luckless racer. Unexpected nobility springs from my heart right in the heat of competition.

As seems to be my mission, I throw my motorcycle into the dirt alongside the track and run to pull the crashed bikes off those feet kicking in the dust. A man I have never seen before, tall and dirty, jumps up and, without a word, stands up his bike, viciously kicks it alive and rides off leaving a rooster tail of dirt clods, small adobe missiles leave little red bruises in my cheek. I swear I'll never again stop for a fallen racer. Screw 'em.

How does a man get so dumb? Only with practice. Some months before, I had seen a motocross race in Grand Junction and was appalled that any sane human being would get on a motorized vehicle that can't stand up by itself. What was the purpose of riding hell-for-leather just to finish ahead of other men of equal stupidity? But all that rampant testosterone got my macho up. While I hate being predictable, within a few weeks I purchase a motorcycle just like the studies of divorced men said I would. Shirley is my beautiful pit tootsie.

On my first trip down to the hilly race track in Montrose, I take my small Yamaha enduro bike that I used to putt around town on, pump up the tires real hard, set up the suspension real hard and bounce my kidneys out on the back side of the course. Painful.

In the great tradition of America, any problem can be solved if you throw enough money at it. I realize that the only way to race well is to buy a full-out racing motorcycle.

A trip down to the motorcycle dealer secures a modest racing machine for an immodest price, and I learn that car dealers are saintly compared to motorcycle dealers.

The bike is a screamer. It doesn't go terribly fast but faster than my limited courage will allow. It makes a lot of noise, so much that the neighbors complain of falling soufflés each Saturday morning when I tune my bomb, revving it until windows rattle. It is yellow, built in Czechoslovakia and has a transmission you can shift without a clutch. Hot. Much hotter than me, I would learn.

On race day, we load the trailer with tools, gasoline, oilcans and motorcycle and pull the whole cortege to the track in the barren adobe hills outside of Montrose. The track is a hilly trail laid out around junk tires in a barren, windy wasteland. The butterflies had started at bedtime the night before. By race time, my stomach is in full rebellion against the coming punishment. It anticipates agony as if the impending events were death by lethal injection.

At the race start, my knees shake. My stomach turns over like a winter lake, but my smile is confidently fraudulent. I line up with the rest of the racing children and their 16 machines. Behind the starting barrier, a piece of surgical tubing is stretched tautly at eye level. Very fitting, I think. We can always use the starting barrier as a tourniquet if required. When the flag drops, the tubing zips by my eyes and the clear Montrose air and the quiet desert setting becomes a living hell. Dust and roar and exhaust fumes all combine to blank out any reality except the fiery, filthy confusion of the start. I am the epicenter of this oil smoke Hades, blind, scared and unwilling to die for something as simple as winning a motorcycle race in a no-name place in western Colorado.

At speed, the ranks of bikes that started side by side are squeezed down to one lane. That causes much handlebar banging and many awkward wrecks with bikes falling, wheels spinning in the air and bodies mixed in. That's when I attempt to save the man's life. On the first turn, a rider goes down, and bikes stack up on top of him. My victim is under them somewhere. Frantically pulling motorcycles off him, I sacrifice my place in the race to save his life. He isn't dead yet. Whoever he is, he still owes me.

I race my heart out against the teenagers. They never tire and they never get hurt. The 15-year-olds ride the course, busting berms and taking crashes that would leave a 37-year-old man for dead. They heal while still on the ground, jump up as if stung by a bumblebee and ride off at WFO—Wide Fucking Open, the only throttle setting they know. They never look back to see what unlucky hand of circumstance has brought them crashing to dusty earth.

It is a religious experience. I have never seen people recover so quickly from death

As the season races on, I take lessons from the best motorcyclist in my world, Billy Boyd, a simple but skilled mechanic from Norwood. Billy had been a world-class racer with Team Bultaco, the Spanish manufacturer. While racing flat track, he strained himself through a fence and now carries enough metal in his body to make the airport security people crazy. He can make a screaming motorcycle do impossible tricks. He is humble, he is good, and I admire him. He made me walk the track, learn the fastest lines through the turns and taught me how to use the berms.

I feel stronger and stronger. I ride harder and faster. Then my day comes. At the awards presentation, I step up to the trophy table and the officials hand me my prize. After thousands of dollars, a year of racing, practicing with Billy, dying with the teenagers, reading books and learning to shift in the air while blinded by dust, managing fear in the gangbuster starts, cracked ribs and a broken hand, I have finally done it. It is the only trophy I will ever win racing: a 4-inch tall tiny bike statue topped in sleazy-cheap gold plate. I have finally finished in the money. Sixth.

Preparing for the next race on Saturday, I go to the garage to tune up my bomb. It is gone. I look carefully around the garage. Yep, it is definitely gone. Stolen, I think. Some thief stole my motorcycle! And I was starting to win, too, set to be the oldest motocross champion in Colorado!

In a few days, I get a phone call from Chicago. My buddies Burt Richmond and Chicky Baruffi, who was the Illinois State Enduro Champion, had stolen my bike, trailered it to Chicago and sold it. "To keep you from killing yourself!" they say.

It is a lowdown trick, stealing a man's racing machine. I liked riding WFO, but down deep, I am relieved. But if I had kept on racing, I could have been a contender. Perhaps the oldest motorcycle champion in the entire world.

Billy's advice stuck. He taught me a lesson I would always remember and live by. Looking off to the horizon and the white peaks of the San Juan Range, he rubs his metal elbow and harkens back to when he raced professionally: "If you follow the man in front of you, the best you can ever finish is second. So, pick your own line and ride your own race."

Somehow, it justifies Crazy Shirley and me. WFO.

32

CRAZY SHIRLEY'S SHIRTS

There isn't a real estate buyer within 300 miles, thanks to the Saudis' oil embargo. Telluride is shut down; there are few cars on the street, and the ski freaks are trying to commit suicide by jumping off the curb. Nothing is moving. The nation is in shock. And so am I.

This October, the golden glow of the aspen leaves fade, leaving the gray tracery of limbs. The weather is cooling quickly. The sky is graying, and the locals are already dragging files along their ski edges and watching the weather in the Sea of Cortez where the big storms slide up to dump snow on the Southern Rockies.

While being broke is not new to me, this time it is critical. Shirley and I live in a cold, old house with a coal stove that stinks up the place. The $150-a-month rent is already nine months behind. I call the landlord in Midland, Texas: "Dick, I am so broke I can't pay attention. But I promise you I will pay you when I get some money."

Food is running low and my confusion is locked in place.

When Shirley lived at the Telluride Lodge, she painted signs in exchange for apartment rent, so she is recognized as the sign painter in town. She has a monopoly.

A softball team asks her to print its sponsor's name on T-shirts. She delivers professional-looking, silk-screened shirts rather than the sleazy iron-on numbers and names. The whole league is envious, so all the teams want to advertise their sponsors' slogans.

Seeing their enthusiasm for becoming walking advertisements, it dawns on me that someday, as a regular thing, people will wear T-shirts with printed graphics on them. As an experiment, we could try to sell some. So we print two dozen shirts with a graphic of a terrified cartoon character on skis pointed straight down the mountain with the caption *I Survived the Telluride Plunge.*

Skiing the front face of the mountain is a mark of bravery or stupidity, depending on whether one views it before or after the event.

The Plunge falls 3,000 feet in less than two ungroomed, mogul-filled miles down a narrowing alley hemmed in by thick trees on each side and peppered with stumps and downed timber and several vertical headwalls. As it increases in steepness, it decreases in fun.

It is a challenge few skiers can meet. Many expert skiers are humbled on the front side of the Telluride mountain and discover too late that it is a real mountain, not a slope.

It is deceptive from the top: It looks easier than it will turn out to be. At 10,500 feet, the jumping off spot, known as Joint Point, slopes away into a rather gentle, wide mogul field. Skiers see the whole town of Telluride between their ski tips while they toke up.

But deceptively, 200 yards below Joint Point, it becomes a steeper and narrower mogul chute. That's where it begins to close the trap and the happy ski adventure changes to vertical fear. The problem becomes how to escape—how to get back to reasonable pitches and get back to having fun. The duped skiers stare longingly up toward Joint Point where they had toked up a few minutes before. It has disappeared, replaced by a clear and breathtakingly cold sky. They can't climb back up; it is too far. It would take hours. Nor can they swallow their fear of dying a tumbling, out-of-control, airborne death if they keep skiing down into the unseen pitches to become forever lost in oblivion.

Further down, the run turns into an alleyway with 60- to 80-degree pitches of challenge so narrow skiers cannot traverse. In some places, the steepness makes it appear the mountain tucks back under itself. They try to peer over the vertical 10-foot-high mogul faces and their butts pucker.

Here, stopped by burning muscles and steaming anger, they stand at the edge of the trees. The tears start to flow, and many fine black diamond Aspen and Vail skiers quit, remove their skis and post-hole down the final pitches, skis and poles in one hand, the other hand outstretched to the uphill face to steady themselves.

After an hour, they arrive at the bottom of the mountain, exhausted, humbled, raw ankles skinned and burning from brick hard ski boots, sweating all the way back to their car in the parking lot, swearing at the miserableness of this day.

In their car, they whisper, "I'm never coming back to this fucking place."

The *I Survived the Telluride Plunge* shirts sell out in one day. We get an order for 10 dozen more.

Thus is born Crazy Shirley's Shirts, a business that will carry us for two economically grim years. We buy T-shirt stock by the truckload, often filling the living room floor to ceiling with boxes of shirts.

Early on, the burning production question arises: How do we print one wet color on top of a different wet color and keep it all lined up and in register?

Our ink supplier tells us of a big silk-screen operation in Denver that prints four-color shirts for the Denver Broncos, so off we go to find this mystical place.

The steps to the street entrance lead up to a big painted door. The chances of simply walking in and requesting a technical briefing on its business secrets seems a bit of a reach. We park in the alley behind the industrial building.

The alley door is wide open with a sign on the brick wall that reads "Employees Only."

"Shirley, let's go take a look. When we go in, you stay behind me."

"Are you sure?" she drops her chin and her eyes widen.

"Of course I'm not sure."

A man stands behind a printing machine loading one white shirt at a time onto a platen. A silk-screen frame with the correct color of ink comes around on a horizontal wheel with a silk-screen frame at each compass quadrant. When rotated, each screen is dropped onto the stationary shirt, the squeegee pulled, flowing the ink to print one of the four colors in register.

The operator glances up but doesn't acknowledge us.

"That's the secret," I whisper, nodding toward the printing wheel.

It is all rather simple and in a minute or two, I memorize how it is designed. Two minutes later, three angry men quickly wind their way through the machines and hover over us, looking very big and very pissed off.

The obvious boss yells, "What the HELL are you doing in here?"

I give him my biggest smile. "We came to talk to your order department and then I saw all this machinery through the open door and it looked interesting."

In a voice, high-pitched, tight and threatening, he thrust his face into mine.

"Bullshit! If you don't leave now, RIGHT NOW, you'll wish you had. You are TRESPASSING on our property!"

I look into the six glaring eyeballs pasted in three flushed faces, their anger radiating over me, raising the heated smell of their sweat.

Slowly I begin to back up and herd Shirley backward with my body. I splay my open palms fully extended in pleading supplication like an Arab rug merchant.

"Jesus, I'm so sorry to have come uninvited," I say in my sincerest tone.

Creeping backward, I say, "I had no idea I was trespassing. Again, I'm so sorry ..." letting some fear inflect my voice.

On construction jobs since I was 5 years old, I grew up with roughnecks and barroom fighters. I didn't have a mother; my father was a prizefighter and I had hung around jobs with him as a child. I had learned in his rough and tumble man's world that to avoid trouble, act a little afraid and walk away. It keeps one's face unscarred.

We back out the door, turn around and walk to Big Red. I drive around the corner, park at the curb, find a notebook and begin to sketch the printing carousel we had seen.

"I was terrified in there. Weren't you?" Shirley says.

"Not really. Concerned? Yes, but I assumed that they were more bluster than attack. Usually men bluster before they attack. I learned that from my old man. Those guys were still in the bluster phase. The easiest way to win a fight is to back off. They knew that if they hit me, the cops would be the next people they talked to, even if we were trespassing. Which we were."

I chuckle. Shirley giggles. "Besides, I've been pounded by an expert."

"Really? Who?"

"Oh, my old man. He was a boxer."

"So, did he beat you?"

"Yes. Knocked me cold once."

She peers out through the bug-spattered windshield into the sunshine. She is quiet.

Then, "What did your mother do about that? Couldn't she stop him?"

"I grew up without a mother."

"You did? How'd that happen?"

"I grew up in a man's world and I'd just as soon not talk about it."

Back home, we build a duplicate of the printing wheel out of scrap materials and a bicycle wheel. After considerable adjustment, we are on our way. We sell every shirt we can print, even the mistakes. By the thousands.

Much like L.L. Nunn's alternating current, our four-color silk-screen T-shirts come to Telluride ahead of their time.

As we learn and perfect our silk-screen technology, orders for posters follow. So Shirley answers the request from the promoters to design the first and second Telluride Jazz Festival posters and the second Telluride Film Festival poster. As each silk-screen print is a handmade original, they disappear quickly from the store windows, stolen by collectors of such memorabilia.

33

SAFE HOUSE

Telluride is the perfect government safe house. The CIA or the FBI furnishes money and a new identity, if you need one. The community furnishes everything else required to keep the witness or political refugee alive, well and hidden. How many? Who are they? There is no way to tell in a place where nameless people show up and disappear weekly, using their cover as tourists. Visitors with accents and dubious backgrounds easily hide in plain sight. When a local asks where a person is from, a cursory answer is enough to satisfy us. We never check for truth.

Sometimes they start businesses. The original promoter of a music festival is a personable Czech, married with a child, who lives in town for a couple of years and then mysteriously disappears without a trace or a forwarding address. As do others. We know them by their first names.

I wonder if the local cops know who they are. Probably not; they can't keep a secret that big. Everybody knows everything about everybody except for a few people like the festival promoter. These mysterious folk come and go like ghost ships that leave no wake.

34

SAILING

To live many lives, you must die many times.

Almost symbolically, I sell out the residue of my Denver advertising photographer life—my precious Hasselblad cameras. They are the last hangover from that life—the married, middle-class striving one, the stress filled, capitalistic, advertising and hustling one.

Big Red is tired. Something over 100,000 miles had dulled her sharpness. When I sell her, I hold back a tear. I flash on the Italian kid that sold it to me and understand his grief completely. I mourn that freedom fantasy.

My new life comes equipped with a Dodge window van that has a huge engine and automatic everything. With cruise control, you can race up a mountain feeling truly sorry for the VW owners who grind along in third gear, absorbing the bad vibes of the drivers lined up behind. The new life also brings along Miss Laid, a 16-foot O'Day sailboat. The van is two-tone blue, and so are the boat and trailer. Crazy Shirley calls it our "Ken and Barbie Go to the Beach Kit."

Since I have never sailed a boat before, we drive to San Diego to learn how. That's when we have a serious run-in with the U.S. Navy.

The plan goes like this: We will go to Shelter Island or one of the yacht marinas, hire an instructor (probably tall and tan and blond) and learn how to sail. I will bone up with a little sailing instruction book I have bought so as not to be thought a total fool. Together we will become proficient in a day or two and then we will go racing and likely win.

On the road to San Diego, I study the boat nomenclature and sailing techniques every waking minute. On arrival, we are in a foreign port. The atmosphere surrounding sailboats is more polished, arrogant and self-congratulatory than we are used to, even in Telluride. Big-mountain skiers think they are the elite. Skiers are peons with psoriasis compared to the self-importance of recreational sailors.

At the Harbor Island Marina, I wander along the redwood decks and look up into the multilevel architecture and posh shops selling stuff for boats I do not understand. At the yacht brokerage office, there is an oh-so-tasteful sign hinting at the possibility of sailing instruction for hire. Boats for sale in the photos are large and expensive. I peer through a window at a tall, tan, blond sailing instructor who looks just like I knew he would.

I watch him surreptitiously, pretending to look through the Yellow Pages of the pay phone by the window. On top of being beautiful, he is cool. Very yachtie cool.

"Screw him," I think. "I won't let that asshole anywhere near my boat. Or Crazy Shirley." I find her in the clothing store, picking over the T-shirts.

"Shirley, I have decided that we can do this without any help from these people. They just get involved with big boats. We have a little boat."

"OK. So what do we do now?"

"The first thing we are going to do is go over to the public boat ramp and just practice taking the boat off the trailer and putting it in the water. That couldn't be too hard."

The public ramp on Saturday morning is a Roman circus. There are moms and pops and all the kids are attempting to get every kind of waterborne conveyance imaginable into the water without losing the car and trailer.

We watch the melee for a while, trying to get a feeling of how this is done. We get in line behind a guy with a wife, a hot speedboat and a new Mercedes. He looks serious, every inch a lawyer-skipper. He gets out of the car and the wife slides behind the wheel. Obviously they have done this before. She backs down the serrated concrete ramp; he directs her with tight hand signals to back ... back ... back. The trailer enters the water; the boat floats free of the cradle. He whistles for her to stop. She does, sharply. The offshore breeze that drifts toward the rocky breakwater catches the boat, and it floats away from the trailer, away from the ramp.

All ramp activity stops. All eyes turn to the drifting speedboat. The man howls like an injured animal, something otherworldly, and runs up and down the ramp. The boat drifts farther out toward the rocks. He calls his wife a dumb bitch. Bystanders laugh. She flushes.

As she looks at the drifting boat over her shoulder, her foot eases off the brake and the trailer now slowly disappears from sight. The baby blue Mercedes creeps back, the water inches up over the perfectly painted and waxed wheels. The onlookers hold their collective breaths. The exhaust pipe goes under and the soft whisper of the motor becomes a saltwater gargle.

Fifty feet away, the man shifts his eyes off his loose asset drifting irrevocably toward rocky destruction to his semi-submerged car. He starts screaming at the wife. The scream sounds like something between an elk bugling and a baby strangling.

The onlookers convulse in laughter. The wife hits the brake; the water flows into the rear doors of the car, filling the back seat. She goes white, shifts to forward and kills the engine. The husband's attention snaps between the boat and the car. His head flips back and forth like a tennis judge.

Another boat comes in through the breakwater, sees the dilemma and heads the loose boat off the rocks.

Now very tense, the man opens the door, hauls the wife out onto the concrete, starts the car and spins it up onto the dry pavement, the saltwater draining out of the rear door panels, bumpers and wheels.

The public ramp returns to its normal state of chaos. I nod to a man hanging over the railing. He smiles and I smile back.

"Man, that's something. Did you ever see that before?"

"Oh hell, yes," he says. "I come out here every Saturday and Sunday morning to watch this. This is the best show in town."

"It is more fun than television, I suppose," I say.

"Let me tell you something," he says. A serious mood steps in. "The boating public is the biggest collection of fools and dimwits I have ever seen. It is a wonder more of them don't drown."

"No kidding. They really are a stupid bunch," I say.

I take my van and boat out of line and park in the lot.

"Shirley, I ain't putting our boat in the water until that fellow over there by the fence leaves."

She looks quizzically at me. "Why not?"

"Because he is a smartass. It's time for lunch anyway. Can't sail on an empty stomach."

Smart Ass finally leaves.

We back the boat into the water without event and tie it off to the floating dock. I am very proud. The members of the boating public are indeed very stupid if they cannot do this without losing their toys.

Heartened by the ease of entry into the wonderful world of the rich man's sport, I decide that the next obvious move would be to motor out of the lagoon into the big bay where there is lots more room. A close reading of the sailing book makes it appear that hoisting the sails might be complicated and will take some space. But when the sails do fill, the boat will take off like a zebra, and from then on, it's simply a matter of driving and holding on.

The little green Sears outboard starts on the second pull. As we pass through the breakwater into San Diego Bay, the wind feels stronger than at the dock. Only later would I learn how wind turns water into waves if not protected by a high ridgeline.

We motor out into the open bay; Shirley takes over the outboard to steer. I pull out the sail bags for hoisting just like the book says.

"Shirley, just hold us steady. Don't do anything fancy. I'll hoist the sails."

"I don't know how to do this. I've never even been in a boat before," she says.

"Don't worry. I'll tell you what to do. Just hold 'er straight into the wind."

The jib comes out of its bag folded. I snap it on to the forestay. As soon as it is released, the wind catches it from behind and flips it into the water. The sheets, the attached lines that control the sail, trail aft and wrap around the propeller. The engine stalls instantly.

Both of us look into the water, not actually believing this day can end so quickly.

Stepping on her feet, I push over the top of Shirley to get to the motor.

I hang over the stern and struggle to unwind the lines from around the propeller.

As the boat drifts, I say, "Shirley, help me get the sail and those lines back in the boat."

With both of us in the bow, I lean over her shoulder and help pull the sail back aboard. Shirley takes the tiller again.

Since the jib is a mess, I scrap that part of the plan and start work hoisting the main sail. Theoretically, the sail feeds up a slot in the mast. I am happy that, attached to the mast, this time there is no way this sail can blow overboard.

As we drift along, I feed the sail up the slot. The wind is building. The sail resists in the slot and starts to flog, snapping wildly. It seizes about a third of the way up the mast.

Using both hands to clear the sail in the track, I drop the halyard, the line that hoists the sail. It flies away in the wind looking like a lazy snake standing out from the top of the mast. I swear like the sailor I'm not.

"Goddammit, Shirley, hold the bow into the wind! I can't get this sail up unless you hold the front into the wind."

I look back at her; she is white, looking past me in horror. I look up past the flogging sail into a great gray wall.

Shirley stammers, "Is that boat moving?"

"Boat? Boat? That's not a boat! It's a goddamn ship!"

A hundred yards away bearing down on our tiny craft is a U.S. Navy Destroyer Tender the size of an average skyscraper, steaming into the bay at four knots. If they had to, and if they were lucky, they could stop in a mile of water. The bow wave from the ship's forefoot forms a threatening, lethal smile.

"Turn away! Turn back, Shirley!" I scream into the wind. She throws the tiller over hard and holds it. Our boat turns but now we are drifting backward, downwind, under the bows of the giant gray ship.

Shirley's voice trembles, "What do we do now?"

"I don't know what's wrong." The noise is frightful. The wind howls; the sails slat and flog and crack in the gusts. The huge ship engines turn into rolling thunder and her bow-wave crashes.

Sailors' faces appear over the lifelines 40 feet above us. They laugh uproariously, slap each other's backs and hover over the lifelines to watch our terror. As we drift underneath the overhanging bow of the giant ship, her sides are so close we can see the hull rivets and the texture of the haze gray paint.

The bow-wave catches us, lays us sharply over in the trough, but the boat recovers nicely. The wind dies. The big ship blocks the wind. In a minute, the overhanging stern passes us and the strong wind returns in steady, implacable force.

"Shirley, the next time I tell you to turn, TURN, goddammit!"

"I did turn. I did turn." Tears well up in her eyes, then they flow.

"OK, OK. We don't have time for that now."

I return to struggling with the main sail. It is now firmly hung up in the mast slot and will go neither up nor down. It flogs in the wind trying to tear itself apart. The boom trails out to leeward, the end dragging in the water. The halyard that had been streaming out from the masthead now has taken some wraps around a stay. I stand tiptoe trying to release the line from the sail head. The shackle is frozen. The sail is seized in position.

Shirley speaks calmly, almost spiritually, "We are going to go up on the beach."

"What beach?" I don't look down from fighting with the shackle.

"That beach."

At first I do not believe what I see, but there it is: Fifty feet away is the sand with waves and trash bobbing around.

"Not the beach, Shirley!" I scream. "Not the goddamn beach, Shirley! Don't drive us onto the beach, Shirley! Oh goddammit!"

I jump into the cold waves.

My feet find the bottom. I stand up to my shoulders in the cold water, holding my new sailboat off the ground. It bucks and jumps, slapping the waves with the broad hand of its fiberglass bottom, fighting to get to solid ground.

Shirley's eyes are wide. She sits holding the tiller, the other hand on the gunwale. "What do we do now?"

"The hell with sailing." The cold water is draining me fast. "Start the engine. When the engine starts, I'll jump back in, and we will call it a day." I am working hard to be a captain in this emergency.

She bends over the engine and the little piston fires on the second pull. Thank God for Sears & Roebuck and its masterful engineering, I think.

Suddenly a helicopter swoops in overhead, its rotors wapwapwaping. A loudspeaker clicks on. A heavenly voice with a Southern twang falls down on us: "Do y'all need assistance?"

Shirley looks at me, pleading. "Do we need assistance?" she repeats.

Angrily I say, "Hell no! Ain't no Navy Airman son of a bitch gonna save me. Tell 'em to go away."

She looks up into the angel rotating above us and shakes her head vigorously and waves them away. The helicopter does not move.

"OK, Shirley, when I turn the bow away from the beach and give you the signal, gun it. If I miss getting in, come back and get me and we will try again."

I push the boat against the wind. The bow comes around slowly and on signal, Shirley turns up the throttle. I hang onto the gunwale and with an arm-breaking effort, finally roll over the gunwale into the sole of the cockpit.

The wash of saltwater I bring in with my clothes runs aft under Shirley's shoes and out the drains. I shiver.

"Let's go home."

She looks past me, over the bow toward the other side of the bay from whence we had come.

Lying in the cockpit, I calculate we have been underway for something like 10 minutes. In that time, we have fouled a prop, fouled both sails, avoided a fatal collision with a Navy ship, run aground and been under surveillance from the North Island Naval Air Station Security. Not a bad day, all in all. I begin to giggle. Shirley begins to cry.

I hate to see her cry. "Come on, honey. We survived, didn't we?"

Under the tears, her face takes on resolve. She speaks in a flat voice. She looks at me dead in the eye and in a calm voice says, "I will never go sailing with you again. You are a fool."

"Wait, give me a chance, darling. Something went wrong here. I don't know what it is but when I find out, I'll cure it. By tomorrow, we'll be good. Just don't sweat it."

She shakes her head and doesn't look at me. "You want to know what I think?"

"What?"

"I don't think the centerboard was down."

I look at the short centerboard rope, the pennant, still in the same position as it was on the trailer.

"Nah, that's wrong. When the boat comes off the trailer, the centerboard drops down by itself. Besides, you didn't read the book. How the hell do you know?"

"Because we just blew across the whole of San Diego Bay like a leaf in the wind. We couldn't steer. We couldn't do anything!" She doesn't look at me. "We just blew across there. You are a damned fool. I'm not sailing with you anymore."

I pick up the centerboard rope and pull. The centerboard falls out of the trunk with a resounding and satisfying thunk, and the underwater resistance steadies the boat's motion against the waves, now solid in the water and answering her rudder. Even cold, I feel the embarrassment heat my face.

At dinner in a classy restaurant, we laugh uncontrollably over the replays.

They ask us to leave. We do.

In the motel, we make love and sleep. Both are delicious.

35

CARPINTERIA

I once ran into a welder from Carpinteria, California. He said, "Nothing ever happens in Carpinteria." And that is the kind of town it is. One of those California bedroom communities joined at the hip with all the other towns by the asphalt sutures of the freeway system. Sunday mornings are deathly quiet.

Sambo's Restaurant exhales grill-grease smoke over the freeway. We ease into the empty parking lot and I buy a Sunday newspaper from the box.

After a breakfast of salt and fat, the coffee lets me know that the time is nigh for the morning constitutional.

"I'll be back," I say to Shirley.

Grabbing the business section of the *LA Times*, I retire to the restroom.

Sitting in the stall, I light my pipe, a handmade work of art with a hugely carved briar bowl. The custom-mixed tobacco smoke boils up out of the stall and the hearty aroma instantly fills the tiled room. Reading the latest gloomy economic forecast, I hear the outer door open.

Without a thought, I glance up as a pair of thin ankles in black strappy heels walks by and enters the next cubicle. Settling back into the depressing article, the image of the high-heeled pumps clicking on the tile floor comes floating back. I ignore it and go back to reading. A clear image of the black pumps with the thin straps wrapping thin ankles returns in three dimensions.

What the hell would a woman be doing in the men's restroom? I think. Well, this is California. Anything can happen in California. It can be a thin line between men and women in California. With that conflict resolved, I go back to the financial news. I relight my pipe; the smoke blue-billows up to the ceiling. The image of the black spikes returns. I looked at the partition to my left. There hangs a stainless steel box with a caption embossed into the shiny steel: "Napkin Dispenser."

I note that I have never seen a napkin dispenser in the men's room before. Must be a new thing. All trends start in California. What the hell. I return to the paper.

What possible use—what possible use can men make of napkins away from the breakfast table even in California? I wonder.

The realization starts slowly, way in the back of my mind, underneath the compulsion to keep reading the news of coming disasters on Wall Street. It creeps forward on hands and knees and finally stands up. My focus sharpens and confusion falls away.

Suddenly there is no doubt about it. I am lounging around, working on my morning constitutional, smoking the world's biggest, smokiest pipe and reading the *LA Times* in Sambo's near the freeway in Carpentaria, California, hanging out in the women's restroom.

In this quiet town, this can be a big offense. These are straight folk. They don't brook perverts that hang around women's restrooms smoking up the place with handmade pipes.

"... caught reading the business section ... obviously a cover story," the cops would say. "Yes sir, we caught one of them Colorado mountain freakos down at the Sambo's. Judge gave him 60 days for indecent exposure. Don't know what happened to his cute little girlfriend. You would think a guy with a cute little girlfriend that has a great ass like that would be happy. But is he? Hell no. He's got to hang out in the ladies' toilet. And my daughter works there, too. Creepy bastard. Last time I saw his girl, she was climbing up into the cab of this big Kenworth diesel loaded with artichokes. And with this great big smile. She had a smile from here to here. Serves that perverted bastard right."

I begin to hyperventilate. The pipe goes out. Should I wait for the woman in the black straps to leave? Should I just sit tight and wait for a break in the traffic?

This situation calls for calm leadership. I'll stay cool and wait until the woman leaves, casually pull up my pants, hitch my belt, fold my paper and walk out like I own the franchise. That's how a real urban commando would handle this.

What happens if another woman comes in? Am I going to wait for her, too? And then another? On Sunday morning, all those women do is drink coffee and talk about their stupid men. The cafe is full of females dressed in their Sunday best, yakking endlessly. It'll be a steady stream of 'em. Jesus! I'm trapped like a rat.

A rustle of clothes, then the outer door creaks closed as my intimate neighbor leaves. Quietly and ever so slowly, I stand up, pull up my pants and buckle my belt, tuck the paper under my arm and bolt out of the stall like I am being chased by a hundred Amazons. At that moment, the outside door squeals open and a lady dressed for church spies me. Her surprised eyes flare into mine.

Without breaking stride, I brush by her, "You're in the wrong room, ma'am." I ram through the door directly opposite into the men's room. I catch my breath. I hear high heels click in the hallway and mumbling. I sit, relight my pipe and resume reading the business section.

The cops in Carpinteria are a bunch of straight rednecks.

36
CHANGES

Crazy Shirley goes to visit her girlfriend in Denver and escape the confines of the tight valley. She needs a break. Printing T-shirts day after day is a tiring enterprise, and I happily send her off to have a good time and get refreshed.

After a week, I drive down to the airport to pick her up. As soon as I see her emerge from the gate, I know something has happened. Even from across the terminal, her vibe has changed. She looks different—pinched, tired and guarded. I have never seen her like this.

We kiss but it is perfunctory, not warm and caring, not promising as they usually are.

"What's wrong?" I ask. This is not like her. This is a different person than the one I had known for three years, slept with, made love to several hundred times, lived with, always touched tenderly. Since the beginning I had felt a spiritual connection, the kind one reads about but never believes is true.

"Nothing's wrong. I'm just tired, I think."

We go to bed early, but she isn't interested in making love.

In the night, I hear sniffles, then smothered crying.

"For God's sake, what's wrong?" I ask softly.

She says after a time, "Oh, I'm just miserable."

"Why?"

"Because I'm in love with two people!"

"Me and who else?"

"A guy I met before, when I was student teaching in Florida."

"What brings all of this back now?"

"I saw him in Denver. He flew out to visit me. He loves me and wants to take me back to Pittsburgh to live with him and get married."

She cries harder for a while. "I don't know what to do."

My stomach rolls over. My vision of the world narrows. Is this it? Is this the end? Is it the end of the purity of our relationship where we swore to be faithful as if we were married?

Dread overwhelms me, but I have to ask, "Have you slept with this guy?"

She sobs for long minutes while the question hangs on the ceiling. Finally, she whispers, "Yes."

I go to the bathroom and throw up in the toilet.

37
END OF 3/4 TIME

The Navajo Reservation in northern New Mexico is the Appalachia of the West. Driving through the stark land where the noble savages drink themselves to death, the sun catches the broken bottle shards that sparkle along shoulders of the roads marking the torture of an unfortunate race in an unfortunate place.

We had crisscrossed the reservation many times, happily visualizing some new adventure together, always together. Crazy Shirley is the first woman I ever anticipated living with always, growing old with her. On the first high ridgeline south of Shiprock, under lead-gray skies, Crazy Shirley tells me she is going away—not for a visit, but for good. She needs to return to the Great American Middle Class, 40-hour weeks, career and the institution of marriage with a corporate type. In Pittsburgh with a Xerox salesman. A frigging Xerox salesman! In Pittsburgh! These were all parentally approved activities, of course.

Driving music, our favorite Jimmy Buffett tape, is playing, "Living and Dying in 3/4 Time." My heart hurts. God, it has been three incredible years.

I know I will be lonely for months, maybe years, maybe forever. There is only one copy of Crazy Shirley. There is only one love like this. What will I do with all this love?

It has not been right between us since the sailing adventures. I knew she had seen another lover. It was a disaster for me. I decided I would good vibe that adventure right out of her life.

Everyone says that love conquers all. Enough love and good vibes will win.

Angry, I yank the tape cartridge out of the deck and fling it across the desert. It climbs on the wind, sails higher against the dark gray sky, spins upward in a wind gust, then suddenly it tips over and plummets down out of sight into the red dirt behind us.

Like Crazy Shirley and me.

38

ART SHOW

Friday afternoon brings me to the art show opening. It has been a difficult week, and I am relieved it is Friday. I, along with 200 other locals and visitors, have been invited to the opening, but invitations are a formality as anyone can walk in and usually do. The show is an interesting cross section of the town. The local artists are a fascinating lot, ranging from the housewife-cum-watercolorist to the professional painter. On this late afternoon there are seven artists represented, all locals, all hovering around their works like vultures over carrion. Their attitudes are solicitous or arrogant or embarrassed. Shows are the worst time for an artist, having been removed from the warm comfort of their creativity and reduced to having to sell their precious creations in broad daylight. Regardless of the quality, each artist feels a twinge of pain when the art is gone from his or her life; a child kidnapped, never to be returned. Because of the loss, they are driven to breed again, conceive and birth new work only to watch it disappear in exchange for filthy lucre. It becomes a speeded up version of life, the preservation of personal visions of historical greatness like van Gogh or Delacroix or Matisse.

The show is held in a low, brick, corner building on the shady side of the main street in a long, narrow, high-windowed room, one wall cleaned to the brick, the other wall plastered white. Lights show on the hanging works.

I hello my way into the room and take a quick walk around to get the flavor of the art. The good work usually goes fast, and I always make a quick tour to be sure there isn't a sleeper, a spectacular artwork that some other buyer might beat me to. Some of the art is good, but at this show there is nothing special, mostly the usual paintings and watercolors of local scenes created for the tourists to decorate their homes in Tucson or Chicago.

Making a passing dip at the punch bowl I wander over to talk to Joan England, a colorist who uses large patches of brilliant colors to produce sharp impressionist paintings. Her work is very decorative. She has an animal manner—lean, sharp-featured, quick mind, and she is a communist. She has studied art in Spain and it shows.

I go for the cheese dip and look over the groups that form around the various pieces of art like chickens feeding. I hear a laugh I know only too well. It is the photographer, a wild and friendly sort, married to the woman DingDong and I made scream in the toilet. The photographer works in black and white, photographing scenics around the area. He is good, not great, but his enthusiasm is contagious. He ekes out a living. Other people laugh listening to him laugh. He is talking to Spencer Glidden, the gay potter.

"Now there's a combo," I think.

I feel someone beside me and turn to face a fat woman with a mustache. She is so altogether unlovely that I avoid being around her whenever possible. She has me penned in.

"Hiya, Jerry," she coos.

"Hi, Gwen. How are you doin' today?"

"I'm doing fine. Did you see my work? It is the best I've done, I believe. They have more to communicate because I am maturing, both as an artist and as a woman," she says proudly.

Maturing ain't the word for what you're doing, baby, I think. You are going to be the Telluride entry in the Rose Parade, the mustachioed float from the high Rockies.

She has me by the arm, shepherding me from one childish drawing to the next. Each has a free verse explanation of the art and what it means in the larger scheme of life.

"What do you think?" she asks anxiously, looking steadily at me for a hint of opinion.

"I think your work is wonderful. It's not my style, Gwen. I'm not into heavy art. I like lightweight stuff, cartoons. But yours is beautiful. Keep it up."

"Oh thanks," she gushes. "I do respect your opinion, being a regular buyer and all."

But among her watercolors hangs a credible picture of sand dunes, beautiful in their female curves, repeating tan images drifting away toward snow-covered mountains. An image of Shirley's lovely tan body in desert colors flashes through my mind, round and warm, the warmth in this picture, but real, alive, smooth, yielding and available.

We are interrupted by John, who grasps my arm and bodily tugs me through the room out of the reach of the heavily padded Miss Gwen Silver.

"Thanks, John. I thought I was gonna die," I say dramatically. "She's embarrassing to be around. How're your drawings selling?"

"Good, good," John says nodding. "It's a good crowd and the people have money to spend after a good ski season."

We fall silent, watching the crowd circulate, listening to the comments and sipping the spiked punch. We both find ourselves watching Lou Steele. He is holding court for two little gray-haired ladies. He expounds on the historic meaning of art and how he fits into the whole history of art since the Lascaux cave paintings.

"That asshole is at it again, John." I shake my head. This is a scene played at every show Lou Steele attends. He is clean-shaven, 37 or so, it's hard to tell. He hikes and hunts, and in the summer runs the 18-mile footrace across the mountains from Ouray. He is an excellent physical specimen, over 6 feet with a precise painting technique but no imagination and little design sense. He is a plodding technician. His subjects are broken-down mine buildings and mountain scenes beautifully executed, but without flair.

"Not only is he a pain in the ass, his pictures stink," John says with malice. "He thinks he's the world's expert on the Old Masters and the drawing techniques of Big Mike of the Sistine Chapel. He tried to convince me I should be painting with egg whites. I told him to kiss my egg whites."

"John, you're downright testy today," I giggle at my friend's show of temper. "I thought you guys were buddies, being fellow artists together here."

John flashes an angry look at me, shaking his head, and says softly, "Screw you." He falls silent for a moment, then, "The last time we were together at the artists group meeting, working to set up a show, he was telling us about the famous forgers of the world. He is a friggin' idiot. If I didn't need the money, I wouldn't be showing in the same town as that egotistical phony."

John's ire is rising again.

"Hell, John, it takes all kinds here in paradise. Why don't you take some painting lessons from him?"

"Screw you again."

The art show is turning into a party. There will be a series of parties growing out of this starter, but first there is a duty. An appearance must be made at the Sheridan Bar. It isn't by formal agreement or social expectation; it is just something that is done each Friday afternoon. The week isn't complete without showing up.

In groups of three or four the crowd begins to wander to the opposite end of town and the newly restored Sheridan Hotel. It is a historic structure, rather plain but well proportioned, and it does have a real history attached. It had been the finest hotel between somewhere and nowhere, the extremes differed with the storyteller. It was the elegant statement of the town. William Jennings Bryan gave his Cross of Gold speech from a roughly built platform in front of this building, the men listening in the street, each wearing a gentleman's hat, while the ladies watched from the narrow high windows above.

The bar occupies half the first floor. Two large windows open onto the street, the name decoratively gilded across the plate glass. This afternoon people are wall to wall; some stand out front on the sidewalk.

I ease in with two tourist women and look around. It is smoky and jammed with businesspeople, government workers, skiers and the usual hangers-on. The music is loud, and people are shouting to be heard, or stand, talking close, heads nodding, a glance from the corner of an eye, a smile. Willie Nelson is singing "Georgia on My Mind" at the amplified top of his strident voice. There is the ongoing sexual play of adults, a smile, a proposition, a refusal, a giggle, a blush. It is all a stage play, the lines rehearsed and ever the same; only the players are different. Tonight's line copied last night's line, spoken by a different person but still the same line.

Customers are standing two deep around the bar, waving at the bartender like commodity floor brokers in the Chicago pits. It is a flurry of activity, a melting pot of every political and personal point of view in the town. For the newcomers, it is wonderfully exciting. For the locals, the Sheridan Bar is just the bar down the street where one drinks shoulder to shoulder with both friend and enemy.

It is a great room. It tries so hard to be elegant, but it is like an aging hooker—still knowledgeable, still able to deliver satisfaction but with small frays in the elegant dress of the room. The silver-embossed tin ceiling is the genuine article. The mirrors are add-ons installed by set designers for a western movie. They are set at a sharp angle around the top of a large walnut back bar that reflects the heads of the drinkers. The mahogany back bar is impressive. Installed in 1883, it is stacked with bottles. The back-mirrors double the size of the room and return a darkened reflection of the drinkers.

The Sheridan had been rougher in the earlier days. The miners and the pioneers had physical clashes in the place. The new people are more civilized. They don't feel as physical about things; they are more settled, not as wild. They don't punch; they discuss. Giving way to a more physically civilized clientele, the bar is usually noisy but peaceful now, and laughter prevails. The miners are mostly gone, and the fist-fighters of the early days have left or married or committed suicide.

I visited the Sheridan for the first time in the early '50s.

Shooting varmints—coyotes, marmots and prairie dogs— was my old man's favorite pastime, and he indulged it at every opportunity. In southwestern Colorado, varmints lived where people weren't. That's where we hunted.

We made our way across Dallas Divide and into the San Miguel Canyon along a rough gravel road that twisted from Ridgway to Placerville to Telluride to Dolores. For a time, coming down Leopard Creek Canyon, we drove alongside a funny-looking train, obviously hand-built, silver, its single car pulled by a gas engine that idled down the canyon grade.

Looking for a bite to eat in this dusty little nowhere town trapped in a box canyon, we entered an old brick hotel, tattered, paint trim beaten by weather. The café was in the back, and we entered a room of gloom. When my eyes adjusted to the darkness, I could see the booths and tables were separated by big mine timbers holding up strings of tiny glowing lights akin to Christmas lights but dimmer. Do they use these kinds of lights in the real mines? I wondered.

Why would anybody live so deep in the mountains except to dig for money in a dark hole?

I was there again in 1964. The San Juan Mountains were alive with color. Aspen trees in great blankets smothered the hillsides, wandered through canyons, flashing bright yellow, standing together as separate families along the streambeds, shivering together with the slightest breeze.

The place looked unchanged in 13 years. The mountains were the same: same black alpine presence overbearing the valley, same mine works at the end of the box canyon, same carefully drawn waterfalls against the canyon walls, same trees, same huge, gray tailings pond, same empty, cracked and potholed main street, same beat up and collapsing buildings. Nothing on the street moved that July day.

The high peaks were painted with alpenglow, the warm golden light that inhales the canyon shadows. I walked into the Sheridan Hotel. It smelled of age and neglect, old varnish, dirty carpets, stale beer and years of lung-toasting tobacco smoke.

At the mahogany counter, a droopy sign in purple crayon instructed:

Pick a room.
Take a key.
See me in the morning.
Mgr.

I saw no reason to even have a key. The place was as quiet as an early morning brothel. Walking up the foot-weathered stairs to the second floor, I picked a room overlooking the main street. The street was empty; the potholed pavement disappeared up canyon into some trees and down canyon it disappeared around a curve.

Out on the broken sidewalk in this deserted town, I walked slowly up canyon toward the mine. I stopped by light from an open door. A stone bank building with light pouring onto the sidewalk surprised me. Inside, a rotund farmer in overalls stood behind a roulette wheel. He mumbled; it spun, chips flashed down on numbers. Behind him was a chuck-a-luck cage and card games; the click of chips and laughter and curses floated outside.

It didn't take me long to understand the width, breadth and depth of the town. Except for these points of light, it felt empty, dead, soulless, aged, an old woman without hope working day to day to pass uninteresting time until death.

Back in my room, I laid on the saggy bed with my clothes on. In the bar downstairs, smoky and dim, a few people could be seen through the smoke only in outline, dancing to Herman's Hermits' song "Henry the Eighth, I Am."

As the only upbeat tune in the playlist of old sad songs, the phantom dancers downstairs played Herman 10, 20, 30 times, over and over. The sound invaded my room; the bass notes vibrated the floor. The drumbeat lasted until midnight. Then it went quiet and I slept.

The morning opened bright, the sun high over the ridge to the south, the rays reaching the main street holding promise of a snappy, crystalline day. I returned to the lobby desk and behind it was an actual human being.

"Goomornin,'" he said.

"What do I owe you for the excellent room?"

"What room did you take?

"101," I said.

"That's one of our better rooms," he didn't look at me. "That's three dollars and a half."

Friday afternoon at the Sheridan is a delightful place to watch the people of Telluride perform their weekend mating dance.

In recognition of the thousands of dollars I've spent here, I raise my forefinger. Without comment, I get my gin and tonic quickly from my neighbor, the bartender.

I back up against the wall behind a group of skiers engaged in their predictable conversation. If the crowd were dressed in cowboy clothes instead of rags and Patagonia, this would be a western movie scene.

39

CRAZY SHIRLEY LEAVES

Her announcement in the Shiprock desert broke my heart, but I am determined not to show it to anyone. Somehow I will rise above this cataclysmic event. The thought that I would be separated from my love-drug scares me.

I know it will take a long time to get over Crazy Shirley and all the memories of good times, adventures, sharing and the unstoppable passion I have for her.

Fighting and losing this forest fire of emotion leaves me empty, aching.

Yet my head knows that for her, it is the right thing to do: to allow her to move on with her life, to set her free to be what she needs to be, to seize her place in the universe, to mark out her space, to become fully realized, to become an adult. So I can listen to my heart that hurts at the thought or to my head that won't allow me to try to change her mind. But, God, it hurts.

As she starts packing her little orange Beetle, my life sinks lower and lower. I can see her driving along with her two cats on an eastbound highway.

The engine valves haven't been adjusted in months on the small, air-cooled engine, so I pop the valve covers and adjust the clearances to the proper specifications and overhaul the carburetor so that it runs cleanly. Then it is ready to roll away from me toward Shirley's new destination in life.

Dry-eyed, she kisses me warmly and, without words, slams the car door. The engine hums as the packed little orange

Beetle makes a U-turn and all my love, my entire life, my future, disappear down valley.

Back in the kitchen, I hold back tears. I am numb. It has been three years of heaven and one year of hell lived in fear that this would happen.

In the classic love story:

Boy finds Girl.
Boy loses Girl.
Boy finds Girl again.
They live happily ever after.

But the real story is:

Boy finds Girl.
Boy falls obsessively in love.
Girl falls in love with different Boy.
Girl leaves to marry different Boy.
Girl never returns.
The end.
Boy hurts.

"She'll be back," I say aloud. "She'll be back. How will she find someone that loves her as much as I do?"

Nobody answers.

40

WATER

A 30-below night is tough on high country real estate.

This blue-cold February night sports a full moon and the valley is fully lit. The snow bounces the moon glow in every direction, and each detail of the town is revealed in near daylight.

She has been gone for a month. Everywhere I look I see her face. I am miserable. She is making love to another man. Is she doing the same things with him that she did with me? Is she making the same sounds at orgasm? Imagining it makes the tears flow. I have to stop thinking about her to regain my sanity. I know that. Nights have become long battles to quiet my mind. Without thinking, I slide my hand to where her sleeping body lay and find it gone. Loneliness washes over me like a flooded stream and drowns me.

But she'll be back. Our love is too strong to go wasting. How can she stay away from the belly laughs we had every day? And bed—how can she stay away from our sexual addiction? Our expertise?

When I look out my window, the town appears as a movie set evenly illuminated by a giant broad light source covered with a blue gel. There is not a yellow light to be seen anywhere. The town looks abandoned, but it isn't.

The electric power is out everywhere. In this temperature, the buildings cool fast. The water pipes in my properties and the properties I manage are in danger of freezing hard, expanding, bursting, spraying water throughout the building. The flood will freeze at night, thawing in the daytime and spraying the house again and refreezing on top of last night's ice. In a week, the layers will fill a house with tons of hard ice turning it into a "Dr. Zhivago" ice palace. The pipes burst in different places and the sprays open in different places. Water flows across kitchen floors and down stairways that turn into icefalls. After freezing, buildings must be closed until warm spring temperatures thaw them out.

And the people? They must move to other houses until spring when they return home to repair a wholesale disaster: collapsed ceilings, hanging icicle spears, floors warped, carpets and furniture ruined. And always fights with insurance companies. Floods aren't covered by insurance, only water from above, which means damage from rain and hail. When your house floods, then freezes, you are on your own. Since housing is always short in town, it is likely you will have to leave town to find new digs for the winter.

My fury at the power company builds slowly. It is their job to keep the power flowing to this remote place, and tonight, it has let us down. Is a generator down? Is the grid down? Is a flying saucer sucking power from the transmission line through a straw made of exotic metals? How long will the blackout last? Who knows?

Now is the worst possible time to drop the electrical load. Frigid night, ski season, overbooked hotels, drunks on the street. A car rolls along with yellow headlights, a rude intrusion into this sparkling greeting card scene.

Occasionally there is a flashlight. Car lights throw a glow behind a building. People gather in bundled-up groups trying to decide what to do or if there is anything that they can do. Out at the mine, a generator kicks in at the Pandora Mill, and it lights up.

I watch for a long time. From my front window, I can see the full length of Colorado Avenue and up canyon to the white walls of the peaks. From my rear window, I can see down canyon. Not a single alternating current electric light is glowing anywhere.

It is ridiculous to rely on hydroelectric plants that are miles away and use transmission lines vulnerable to avalanches, rock falls and high-altitude lightning strikes.

Screw the power company—I'll build my own power company. There is a 660-foot waterfall at Keystone Hill 3 miles away at the west end of the valley. There is power in falling water. I'll figure out how to build my own little electrical generation company, sell electricity to the town, and we will be self-sufficient. This opportunity is a major blow for freedom.

I can envision a penstock that crosses over the highway into Telluride. It is painted in big, bold Helvetica letters on the silver pipe: VASS HYDRO. Everyone who enters the town will know that name. I can even sponsor a softball team if I want. Talk about seizing a market! America—what a country!

"Hey, Zebra."

He answers with a laugh since I am the only person who calls him that. It's an old joke between us.

"Hey Vass, how you doin', brother?"

"Perfect." The phone connection crackles and pops as it often does in cold mountain air. "Hey Z, I'm so pissed off I can't stand it. The power went off last night for four hours. It was 30 below, the town was full, and everyone's property was in danger and those power assholes didn't even apologize in the morning. So, I'm going to build my own power company. Tons of water flow around here that can be turned into electricity, and I intend to use it."

Z laughs.

I plunge on, "You were an oil company land man dealing in leases, mineral rights and all that stuff. Do you know how to file on water rights for hydroelectric use?"

"Jesus, I don't know how you come up with this stuff. My partner and I have filed applications with the feds on a number of hydroelectric sites in Colorado. There is a group called FERC, the Federal Energy Regulatory Commission, that grants licenses to entrepreneurs that allow them to build small-head hydroelectric plants. They also stipulate wheeling privileges on a must-take basis."

"What's that mean—wheeling?"

"It means that you can hook up to the nearest power transmission line no matter who owns it. The power company must allow you to hook on, and they have to transmit the power along their lines to wherever you sell the power. That's called 'wheeling' in the power business."

"Oh." A long pause. "I think there is a transmission line within 500 yards of the site I have in mind. That'd be good."

Once hooked up to the existing transmission line, it's less than 4 miles of wheeling into town. Telluride will obviously buy the power, perhaps even for a little more than they pay now. They are all ecofreaks. Hydroelectric power and hippie hair go together like mom and pop. They'll buy anything that smacks of organic. I can't lose.

"Well, Z, ya wanna do a hydro deal in Telluride, City of Mystery and Intrigue?" I ask.

"Hell yeah," he says. "We surveyed two sites around there already and have plans in our files. Come on over to Denver and let's see if we can do a deal."

I explain about routing the penstock along the side of the mountain and the pressure it would generate when it turned the water straight down to a turbine.

"That oughta chew up some fish and newts," he laughs.

So the 10-megawatt Vass Hydro is painlessly born. Perhaps too painlessly.

In Denver, I meet with my new partners and the discussions go well, chased with a bottle of bourbon and lots of laughing and rude jokes. Z's partner, John Skelton, a geologist and lawyer, is brilliant. And he knows a lot about water, so much so that he has rewritten parts of Colorado water law by the bright light of his incandescent ideas, a stunning piece of new thinking about old laws. Every water lawyer in the state is envious; water law has been holy writ since the state was founded, untouchable by mere mortals, and yet Skelton saw water law in a different light.

In the early days of the West, men murdered each other for access to water. Water is money, the flowing blood of life of every Westerner, horned toad, hawk, tree and weed, the resource without which the western third of the United States would be desiccated rock and sand like the Saudi desert, barren of everything, even hope.

Because the founders of the state felt that keeping people from killing each other was fairly important, the State of Colorado wrote water law into its 1876 constitution. Very unusual.

The law holds that all water is public property and available for the use of the people. To obtain the right to use some, however, water must be diverted and applied to beneficial use. Water rights were originally allocated on a "first in time, first in right" priority basis; the first rancher to find and use a water hole or stream had the right to water all his cattle until their fill. Then the next rancher in line could fill up his cattle, and so on down the line until the water ran out, or somebody got shot.

Today, one claims specific volumes of water, usually measured in cubic feet per second. Every teaspoon of water in the West is overclaimed by three or four times.

And thus, I entered the water game, a naif, an innocent, a stupid.

In 1890, L.L. Nunn, a local lawyer and investor, with the help of Nikola Tesla and George Westinghouse, built the first alternating current power plant in the United States 4 miles southwest of Telluride. It sits right below the Ophir Loop at the bottom of a cliff on the Lake Fork of the San Miguel River. The installation included 3 miles of transmission line to power the Gold King mine near Alta Lakes and, a short time later, into Telluride to power the streetlights. Telluride became known as the City of Lights because it was the first town in the country to be lighted with alternating current streetlights.

This construction created a big fight between the founder of General Electric, Thomas Edison, a direct current power promoter, and L.L. Nunn's side who promoted alternating current.

Alternating current can be transmitted over long distances at a fraction of the cost with little loss of power. Direct current can be usefully transmitted for only one mile with high maintenance costs. So Nunn won locally, and alternating current power generation caught on and revolutionized the electrical systems of the world.

His partner, Nikola Tesla, a Serbian who invented all kinds of electrical stuff, including the alternating current generator and the wireless radio, helped bring that newfangled alternating current power source into Telluride.

Later, after his Telluride successes, L.L. Nunn built the power station on the Canadian side of Niagara Falls.

Z and Skelton, my new partners, had already scouted and surveyed two hydroelectric sites: one directly above Ames on Howard's Fork and the other on the San Miguel River at the Keystone Hill site. After negotiating with them, I land total ownership of the Keystone site and half ownership in the Ames site.

After the FERC permit gets issued, I will be the happy proprietor of the largest solely owned hydroelectric site in the United States. Keystone will be my beautiful baby. This project will make me famous, alongside the pioneers of the 1880s.

In a 30-minute hearing with little fuss, the water court judge grants me water rights for nonconsumptive use of all the flow in the San Miguel River.

To stake a water claim, one has to physically, and in real time, drive a stake into the spot where the water flow will be diverted from the main stream into a pipe that funnels it to a generator. With my brother as the official witness, I gather up two stout wooden stakes and a hammer and stumble off through the bushes to strike my blow for electrical independence. Now this is an adventure, plowing through the underbrush to the edge of a mountain river to do something that has never been done before. I am the first.

The river's edge is gravel. The water flows fast and clear in the channel, leaves eddies and white tendrils over the half submerged rocks and gaily muscles its way toward its destination down valley. To capture the power of the river, I'll reroute it here above the waterfall and herd it into a penstock, the pipe that runs for a half-mile along the mountainside then turns 90 degrees downward. The water's full weight will plunge riotously straight down the fall line 600 feet into my power plant to violently collide with turbine blades that spin a generator and then escape back into its original streambed. Now, all those little H_2O molecules are happy again after a thrill-filled Disneyland ride that doesn't consume a drop.

My brother and I step out on the riverbank and walk downstream a few yards to the top of the near-vertical drop-off. The raucous river disappears down and away over truck-sized boulders into the unseen bottom of the canyon.

To our surprise, hidden underneath the overhanging bushes, we discover a head gate already there, a heavily built structure as big as a one-car garage built of 1-foot thick, square-cut timbers.

I turn to my brother, "I think L.L. Nunn beat us to this site."

"Does that mean we can't claim it?"

"Nah, he's been dead for 50 years. Or maybe this was a diversion for the hydraulic miners who worked this place in the 1880s. They used high-pressure water cannons, called monitors, to wash down the mountain side and placer mine out the gold. But even back then the government made them stop. Too destructive. Killed the mountain. Clogged the river. It was a mess even for those folk who had little concern for how they made money.

"See how that big hillside is washed away there, where you can see the raw rock and gravel? Those are the guts of the terminal moraine that dams this valley. It's where the glacier stopped and melted. All that rock you see here came from up canyon someplace carried down here by the glacier."

I hold the stake in front of the heavy head gate and my brother swings the hammer. Vass Hydro's claim sinks through the sand and gravel, the water swirls around the wood and my fortune is pregnant with the seminal seed of L.L. Nunn.

Like every government program, people are lined up for FERC permits, and my application is only one of many standing in line behind them. I find that many big, rich companies are vying for these permits in this rush for water gold. It becomes obvious that my odds are zero of getting a FERC permit to develop my babies.

On the phone, Z says, "If you can get sponsorship from a municipal government, you can jump to the head of the line in front of all those big firms. Do you know where you can get a government sponsor?"

"You bet I do. The town will trip over its own feet to sponsor this!"

In the town council meeting, a yes vote takes less than 10 minutes. I receive the sponsorship of the Town of Telluride. My application speeds to the top of the list.

Two months later, the feds issue me a permit to build the Keystone hydroelectric plant. I have beaten the big boys. Vass Hydro lives!

The day I receive my official letter granting me the permit, the sheriff walks into my office and hands me a notice naming my partners and me in a lawsuit for $2 million in damages. People I don't even know are suing me.

The tall buildings of downtown Denver show through the floor-to-ceiling windows. I sense this meeting in the lawyer's conference room may not go well. I have spent my life carefully avoiding governments and lawyers. They both represent trouble or at least extra, unpaid work.

My partners and I sit at a huge walnut table. Across from us, the men suing and their attorney. The lawyer is an asshole; I can tell by looking at him. He is everything I dislike. He is smarter than me. He is taller than me. He looks tougher than me, but I am sure I can put him down with one solid punch to the solar plexus. He is the ultimate smart Jewish lawyer. He scares me. I hate him.

"Mr. Vass, what do you know about the contractual agreements my clients, Messieurs Gantjos and Tollett, have with you and your partners?"

"I have no contractual agreement with them. I have never heard of your clients or have any knowledge about their involvement. My partnership is with Mr. Skelton and Mr. Zaring, not those men."

Actually, I had heard about Skelton's other partners. He often complains about what pricks they are, but I'm not going to admit to anything.

"Do you know that they are partners of John Skelton and funded the land surveys, planning and blueprints of the sites you now claim to own?"

"No, sir. I have no knowledge of that." His eyes bore into me and it is irritating. I refuse to be intimidated by this hired gun. If I am going down, I'm going to take him with me.

I say, "I know that when one seagull gets a hunk of bread, all the other seagulls perform aerial tricks to steal it from him," I add. "I think that is what is happening here. You are the aerial trick in the room."

The lawyer bristles. His chin drops and his head squares up on his shoulders. He stares at me hard.

"I am a straight businessman," I continue. "I don't cheat in order to win. I don't know anything about this legal matter other than I came by my FERC permits and water rights fairly. I don't know why I am being sued. I resent being brought into this. I do not belong here." I feel my voice rise along with my anger.

"You and your people are trying to steal my deal after I have done all the hard work. You are a bunch of claim jumpers."

Mangling Shakespeare, the lawyer says with a sneer in his voice, "Thou doest protest too much, sir!"

He turns away from me and addresses my partners who answer calmly and businesslike, like adults should. After a half hour of discussion with them, he turns back to me and says, "We can settle this if you sign over your rights to my clients. Or we can meet in court. It's up to you."

"You crooks can go fuck yourselves. I'll see your clients in court. I'm gonna stick their lawsuit right up their litigious asses. In addition, I'm gonna sue you for harassment and report you to the bar association. I ain't takin' any more cheap shit off a jerk-off, big city lawyer."

Back out in the street, I shake with anger. My partners laugh at my performance with the lawyer.

The fight is on. While in Denver, I hand the best litigators in town a check for $25,000 to start preparing my defense and countersuit.

I'm screwed. Even if I win in court, my legal costs will make the deal unprofitable.

When extracting electricity from water, what you see is what you get. Production is totally controlled by the amount of flowing water and the height from which it falls. Power plants, poles and transmission lines, and turbines custom designed for each site are all fixed costs, a given amount of money with no opportunities to find windfall profits or savings. There is no business magic a developer can bring to this deal that can sweeten it.

Except for one condition: The FERC permit allows electricity to sell on a formula based on the avoided extraction costs and current prices of fossil fuels—coal and oil. If prices go up, inflation will make the extraction costs rise, ergo, one can charge more for electricity.

My numbers are based on oil at $40 a barrel, which has risen dramatically from Saudi's $2 a barrel. Our country is in a panic. Inflation is rampant. Gasoline lines stretch around the block and up the street. There are gas pump fistfights. Oil prices keep climbing; some say it can go as high as $100 a barrel. If it does, my $10 million hydro project will pay off in four years. I'll be in clover. Talk about being on the right side of God and country!

Gossip holds that a manager from San Miguel Power Company has said, "If he gets this plant built and hooks onto us, I will suck his dick on the courthouse steps."

To perform this nasty act, he will have to drive miles into town while I, with my camera, will need only to cross the street.

If no one believes I can do this project, then that is all the more reason to make it work. I hate to be underestimated. I will wheel electricity to Telluride within a year. Vass Hydro will be a modern historic step. The citizens will love me. I might run for the House of Representatives based on sharing my talent and vision with my friends and neighbors.

So I work along, researching, learning about power generation and the transmission business, and carefully watching the price of oil, cheered that it is holding firm around the $40 mark.

Then, in one day, oil prices fall out of bed. Americans are driving less; the Saudis have a change of heart and loosen their grip on the supply. Oil prices sag back to $20 a barrel.

And just like that, Vass Hydro becomes just another vaporous daydream. There is no way to profit from an electric plant at these oil prices. It can't pay. It is a loser all the way around. I stop paying my lawyers, fold my plans, permits and water rights and stuff them into a cardboard box, and kick it under the desk.

Disappointment hovers over me like a mist. Messieurs Gantjos and Tollett have won, the asshole lawyer has won, but they have won a worthless property.

Vass Hydro becomes my embarrassment. I mope for a while. My only consolation is that at the height of my winning, I had not been arrogant enough to turn the power company manager's challenge into a big-money bet where the winner gets a blow job. I would have welched on that wager.

All I have left from the adventure is a stack of bumper stickers:

41

GULF STREAM

My plan is quite simple: I will sail from Fort Lauderdale to the Bahamas using the northerly flow of the Gulf Stream to boost the boat along to sort of slingshot across. When the winds are favorable, out of the south, it's a romp. The wind and water both help the boat make her way. In the right conditions, even a small boat can make up to 10 knots over the bottom. And that is what we, the boat and I, are doing, using everything to the boat's advantage.

A 23-foot plastic lake boat with a retractable centerboard isn't a deep ocean vessel. It is too light, less than a ton; the keel is too small, and that makes the boat tender, hard to hold on course in big waves. She yaws badly when overpowered by too much wind or too much sail. She will lie down on her leeward gunwale, turn into the eye of the wind and hang there, in irons the sailors call it—sails slack, stopped in the water, her sails flogging noisily.

Now the rainbow-colored spinnaker bellies out like an oversized brassiere cupping a pendulous breast, tautly pulling me into the largest river in the world. My little sailboat moves quickly, near her hull speed of six knots, toward West End on Grand Bahama Island. I plan a night entrance into the boat channel 65 miles away. It has a green light entrance marker that is easy to see. The sailing guide says so. I am single-handing, so I have to trust the sailing guide.

My Gulf Stream crossing starts perfectly. With the wind at my back, it is a classic spinnaker sail out of Fort Lauderdale. I blow north with the current along the beach, empty in the morning light, too early for yesterday's toasty-red tourists to muster for today's sun wars. The sea state will change radically if the southerly wind clocks around to the north and stacks the water up into sharp-sided hills.

I steer away east, pinpoint a chart position from landmarks on the beach and plot a straight-line course. I roll the tiller slightly and adjust the sheets, easing the lines around the winch heads and cleat them.

A quick Gulf Stream crossing and I will be in the Bahamas where I can duck behind islands out of the rough seas that go with powerful wind. And so far this morning, it is going better than planned. I hadn't expected a southeasterly wind quite this strong.

The wind builds slowly and steadily. I lower the big bra cup, the thin nylon sliding around on deck, until I jam it into its sail bag and drop it down the forward hatch. I replace it with a standard jib, which, if the wind is building, I won't have to change again unless it gets really rough. In big wind, changing headsails on this small boat can be life-threatening. Even on my buddy, Bob Callard's boat, which is six times heavier and a real stiff New England deep-water craft, changing a headsail in big wind gets dicey.

I have made this crossing twice on Bob's boat. He is my mentor. He is an engineer and technically skilled. He has sailed the Great Lakes since he was a kid and has lots of sea time. And he understands everything. I have worked with him to prepare for this cruise, but I am sure there are gaps in my knowledge because sometimes when teaching, Bob makes poor assumptions about my sailing knowledge. And like a fool, my ego lets him. When I make mistakes, Bob just smiles slyly out of his gray beard. That smile makes me crazy, embarrassing me in my ignorance. To avoid that chiding smile, I won't admit my ignorance so I don't learn things I should know.

Teachers occupy a special place in my brain. While I was a D student in high school, the Navy taught me to pay attention because in that seagoing world, dangerous situations were called mankillers. It is easy to die from inattention. So I paid attention to Callard and sailed with him in my head. I learned from him that there were mankillers out here. I talked to him often in my mind, asking him questions, listening to his answers. Mentors are those one calls on for advice when in trouble or lost or confused or scared. But here and now, I don't need Callard. I don't want to talk to him. I will make this crossing alone, one man in a small boat.

The boat, Street Hustler, and I sail briskly through the morning. In the early afternoon, the wind shifts from the south around to the west across my port beam. That worries me. While it is giving me a lift now, what if the wind continues to clock around north? The wind from the north would push the north-flowing stream into hills and then mountains. If it does, this could be a nasty trip.

I lounge in the cockpit and drink a bottle of beer and nibble Cheetos.

This isn't a lake in Colorado or protected San Diego Bay. Out here in the deep blue transparent currents, I feel like a real sailor, plying the same ocean river the Spaniards used to ship home blood-soaked Indian gold and silver from Peru in clunky, heavy, slow four-masters. The Spanish Main is a deep and totally impersonal river. Now friendly with 2-foot swells, it can become a deadly maelstrom in minutes. There is no estimating the number of lives the Gulf Stream has stolen. Thousands? Hundreds of thousands? Millions?

Out here, when you drown, your body turns to shark turds that float off toward New England, by Newfoundland, south of

Greenland, by Ireland and then west of Europe. That's the theory. There is no reason to believe that a drowned body floats more than a few miles before it becomes a shark's serendipitous sweet and tender breakfast. Only last week a fisherman cut a shark's belly open to find a man's partially digested foot still laced into a new white Nike running shoe. The sea isn't malevolent by nature; it's simply uncaring, neutral, minding neither cause nor effect. A sailor deals with the sea's changeable personalities as they come. As in few other places on earth, a man must take care of himself out here. I like that bargain.

It is nearly dark. And then, out of the northwest, the black clouds fly in low and fast like vaporous fighter planes that strafe the tops off the waves. This is no place to take a knockdown where wind gusts knock a boat over and wind pressure holds the sail flat, the boat's bottom to the wind. Held down too long, the sea floods in—first the cockpit, then the cabin. Then it sinks. Every boat in the world is fighting to get to the bottom. I don't want to help this one.

I shorten the mainsail to the first set of reef points, raise a smaller jib, and the small boat stands up straighter, rides better. Her weather-helm, the pressure on the tiller, eases; she steers almost without rudder assistance. The boat is balanced between the steering and the sail trim.

The dead-reckoning course I've laid out on the chart is, at best, a guess. Computing time and distance is easy but when you add in the big river's wandering current and leeway, the sideslip of the boat and the *laissez faire* attitude of the sailor, it's impossible to pencil-point a chart and say, "This is my exact location." I have no need for an exact location anyway. An error of 1 or 2 miles is close enough for me. But if I sail north of my target, my next stop will be Ireland.

The wind against the current begins to stack the sea into 6-foot hillocks that crest, break, fall apart and drop into nothing. The boat bobs onto and then over the white tops, sometimes dropping dramatically into the hole beyond. Each plunge leaves my stomach in the air until it too falls into a pool of nausea.

It is dark, an impenetrable blackness, as dark as the real world gets. The boat has only one battery and my weak running lights reflect off the fast, foamy water. Occasionally, the highlight of a wave flashes as it breaks a few feet away.

The compass light glows red; the rolling, wandering, rotating ball perfectly projects the boats motion in miniature. A wave of fear comes over me. The red light turns into a smear. Tears. I cry. Something is wrong with Crazy Shirley. I feel it. I know it. What is wrong in her life? Is she in danger? Is she hurt? I can't think about that. It is too painful. The thought of her leaves an empty feeling. Hollow.

I read a dozen books about single-handed sailing, fine stories about the great sailors like Joshua Slocum, an alarm clock his only navigational instrument. The round-the-world boys all had self-steering gear. I too need a way to rest, so after spending hours researching and designing, I build a self-steering rig with surgical tubing attached to a tiny sail attached to a windward shroud. It doesn't work very well. It will keep the vessel on course for a minute, but when a bigger puff comes, the boat wanders off, rounds up into irons, and stops, rolling in the troughs of each new wave, the sail flopping around fecklessly.

Sea motion excites the little hairs in the middle ear to a state of erection that is hardwired to the stomach. I steer with my foot, and it takes four or five minutes to calculate and draw my estimated position on the chart. Within a minute of taking my eyes off the horizon my stomach rebels and I toss it all, flash what is left of the Cheetos and beer into the cockpit sole where they mix with saltwater and swirl back and forth with each wave like little yellow buoys around my feet. Callard enters my mind.

We have been at sea for 12 hours. By rough estimate, we are 20 miles west of West End, Bahamas, and maybe a touch high to the course line. Which means if we are where I guess we are, it will be at least another three hours, perhaps longer, before I can find land and rest. Maybe I ought to steer a little more to the east, maybe even dead east. My estimated time to West End was 10 hours.

I don't see how we can be south of the course. With a 20-knot wind on my nose and a 4-knot current pushing north, we are doing all right. I don't want to stay too far south. It makes Grand Bahama a lee shore. If the wind keeps blowing from the north, it will be a lee shore anyway. Sailboats work well if there is plenty of sea room. A lee shore is the sailor's biggest fear, the fear of being driven downwind onto the beach by a strong, inexorable, merciless wind, getting tumbled in the surf, the mast breaking, the boat rolling over and over, reduced to a beaten fiberglass hulk in the rocks and foam. A lee shore makes for big adventure. I am confident we will avoid that; Callard is confident, too.

Around midnight, the waves are falling into themselves from 10 feet. The cresting caps break above my little boat and spit off spray that flies away downwind like parade confetti. She slides into the troughs with a shiver. Then the wind pressure drops and she stands up, slowly climbs out of the hole, catches the wind again, heels over hard and, with power on, climbs the next hill only to skid away into a new trough. She yields to the growling wind like a featherweight boxer. She is doing fine, but her captain is tired and seasick. Beating around in a tiny boat is like being trapped in a paint mixer.

I try to focus on the chart with the straight pencil line drawn from Fort Lauderdale to West End. I gag down my nausea. I feel frustrated and while my head doesn't want to hear it, I know in my heart the course line now means nothing. A real line would look more like a snake's trail in the New Mexico sand heading off to God knows where.

The wind shifts more to the north. It pushes up building-sized stacks of black water. There is no way to tell where I am.

"I think I'm lost," I say to my phantom companion, Callard. "I think I'm 5 miles out of West End but, to be honest, I don't know if I am north or south of the channel entry. I think it's over there to starboard somewhere. If it is, we should see lights in the east soon."

Callard doesn't answer. For what seems like a long time, I peer east into velvet blackness. I'm not sure at first but then, a couple of waves later, I am sure. Indeed, there is one tiny flickering light quickly covered by waves.

"A light!" I yell. "Callard, there's a goddamn light!"

It could be another boat, but that is unlikely. Only fools like me are caught out in this weather. All the smart sailors are tied up to solid land, drinking gin and tonic and caressing the round fannies of beautifully tan, bikini-clad airline stewardesses (euphemistically called "crew" in this part of the world), telling tall tales of the sea. Yo-ho-ho, and a bottle of rum! Fifteen men on a dead man's chest … . Men talking to ships and all that rot.

"Head toward that light!" I bark. Just giving a command to Callard's face makes me feel better.

The light grows steadily stronger. "Hey, Callard, that light has to be West End." Now that a landfall is in sight, I feel better about life generally.

"Steer for the light," I command, "then we'll follow the beach line to the channel entrance. Callard, my man, we've got it made."

He smiles broadly. "A hell of a piece of navigation," he says.

I feel great. We have done it. Against wind and wave, we have navigated across one of the most unpredictable and dangerous stretches of water in the hemisphere and found the port we were looking for. And in a Clorox-bottle boat. I don't mind that he didn't say "Sir." He should have; I am the captain.

The light hides from us intermittently behind the waves. In some minutes, we climb out on top of a wave. The light is nearer. As we close, the light quickly separates into a group of individual lights. I think I can see people moving in front of the lights, occasionally blinking their brightness through the spray.

"I think it's a motel," I say. "See the outdoor room lights? It's a beach motel on West End, that's what it is. Steer right at it."

We seem to be closing fast, faster than usual. Each wave brings us noticeably closer to the motel. It is now large enough that I am scanning to take in the length of it. Somehow, it seems very close, too close too soon.

Then the motel moves, actually moves, the room lights roll a bit from side to side. The motel speeds toward us. Then I see green and red lights on each end of the motel and a white light way up on the roof. Recognition of death comes sparkling like a ball of St. Elmo's fire. It electrifies my mind and sends a shock to my vocal cords.

I scream over the noise, ''It's a ship! It's a big fuckin' ship! It's right on us! Collision! Collision! Tack! Tack!'' My voice goes hoarse. The backs of my legs go hot. We are on a collision course. Our weak running lights are mostly under water. They can't see us. We stand no chance in a collision. Our paper-thin craft will be flattened like prairie dog roadkill.

"Tack! Goddammit, tack!" I yell to Callard.

I throw the helm over and fumble for the masthead strobe light switch, a bright flasher on the tip of the mast that lights up the waves around us. As we come into the eye of the wind, we nearly stop. The jib backs full, wraps against the mast, and the boat heels dangerously over. Equipment falls noisily from a storage locker into the cabin sole. With backed sails, the boat is trying hard to sail in a circle. I release the jib sheet and the sail flogs, pops and cracks until I harden it and the boat stands up and regains her footing. Suddenly we are pinpointed in a powerful spotlight. I click on the radio and flip to the ship-to-ship channel.

"Spotlight? This is yacht Street Hustler. Over," my voice quivers in the mike and I hate it.

"Yeeeaaah, Street Hustler, what the hell are you doin'?" His voice sounds stressed through the static, his first word drawn out, almost a yodel.

"We're trying to stay alive. We have reversed course away from you." As we ride high on a wave, the spotlight floods into the cockpit. My fingers squeeze tighter around the teak tiller, and I lean forward as if to coax our little craft to go faster.

I thought about what Callard would do. Callard wouldn't be lost. Callard is never lost or even confused. He always knows what to do. And he is never afraid. I look around the boat as if there is some solution to my problem I have overlooked. I glance at the chart with the phony straight pencil line. I can see Callard with that goddamn grin making fun of me. I swallow hard. I click on the mike. "Spotlight, could you give me a magnetic course and distance to West End, please?"

"Yeeeaaah. Stand by, Street Hustler," the radio says. The spotlight goes out, and we are again in blackness.

The huge oceangoing tug brushes by so closely we lift on her bow wave, and we hear the diesel exhausts over the raging wind. I look up at her sides and see how steadily she rides with a slow, stately roll. All her crew is dry and warm. I am cold and wet and scared and shaking.

The radio hisses on, "Yeeeaaah ... your course to West End is one zero five magnetic, 18 miles."

"Thank you for your assistance. We really appreciate it," I say as sincerely as I can.

"Yeeeaaah ... . Good luck." There is a touch of sarcasm in the radio's voice.

"Callard, we are way the hell out here. I wonder how we got way the hell out here ... waaaay the hell out here?"

"I told you to stay south of the course," Callard says without feeling.

I apologize, "It was a lee shore. I wanted to stay away from the lee friggin' shore."

On the chart, I shakily draw a new course line to West End and step off the distance with dividers. My hand shakes and it takes me three tries to get the dividers to stick into the chart paper. We are 20 miles north of where we should be. I see Callard grin again. It is annoying.

And I see another problem: The narrow channel entrance is open to the north. In this northern blow, it is a lee shore with 30 knots or better of wind and crashing surf. With high boat speed, even with bare poles, there will be no way to slow down and no margin for error. If we miss the channel, we will most certainly end up rolling in the huge surf and aground.

Just to get to the channel entrance we have to navigate a slim gut of a pass a half-mile wide between a small rocky islet to the north and Grand Bahama's beach to the south.

Should we go in there? If no, we will have to turn and run south along the big island another three hours to find shelter. Exhaustion owns me. This is a tough prospect. The little boat bobs around on the heavy waves like a light bulb. It beats and abrades my body to raw exhaustion. And I am hung over from the adrenaline rush from the near-death collision with the tug.

What would Callard do? He is in Miami at the dock at Dinner Key, living it up, looking cool and tan and salty, sitting on the fantail of his blue-water boat, telling sea stories to the rich yachties who listen enraptured.

I can hear him telling his story. With a big smile and a far-off look, he leans back with his glass of vintage chardonnay and says, "We had the choice of going into this blind pass in a norther or turning south to a nice, safe harbor 30 miles away at Freeport. But I decided that we would risk the West End channel." The yachties ooh and aah. Callard shrugs his heavily muscled shoulders and lifts his bushy eyebrows. "Well, a guru once told me that one day you are alive and then, you're not," he says and sips his wine. Nods and big smiles all around.

If he can do it, so can I. "OK, Callard, I'm goin' in. Inside the pass, there should be enough water to turn around and come out. The entrance to the boat channel is supposed to have a green marker light right there at the entrance. If we see the light, we'll sorta sneak up and take a look at the entrance. If it's too dangerous, we'll tack back out."

"Hey, we're doin' great," I say. "I'll just steer between the rocks and the beach, and we'll do fine."

"Whatever you say," Callard doesn't sound convinced.

The new course puts the wind on our port beam, an ideal point of sail, and the boat settles nicely into sliding down this trough and climbing up onto that crest. Digging around, I find some dry crackers to help settle the nausea. During our violent turn out from under the tug, we shipped water into the cabin and it sloshes around in the sole of the boat and mixes with bread slices that have fallen into the water and scoot around like inedible little barges. I am too tired to talk or even think. I just hunker down out of the spray and listen to the wind howl in the rigging and the nearby crash of waves as they collapse on themselves.

Entering West End proves to be tight. It is a mean place in a norther. I decide to drop the storm jib and go under mainsail only. It reduces our power, but there are fewer potential foul-ups handling one sail. Without the jib, the boat can't beat upwind as well but it is more manageable in tight quarters. Dropping the jib means I have to go forward into the leaping, crashing world of water and wildness. I watch for a while to see if a wave pattern exists. There is none. I buckle on a chest safety harness with a safety line.

"Don't fall over the side," Callard whispers, "or you'll die, and nobody will ever know."

"I ain't gonna die," I say weakly.

I crawl up out of the security of the cockpit and inch myself along the high side of the boat. Halfway forward, I snap my harness line onto a lifeline. The boat pitches high, high on a wave, then plunges down into a black pit, falling weightlessly. I float in the air, clear of the deck. The bow crashes into the water, and I slam down. The saltwater stings my eyes as a wave breaks over me. I feel the boat round up slightly. I release the jib halyard and the sail goes limp, then flogs wildly, snapping and cracking. The lines flail like wild snakes; the jib's steel shackle whips around trying for my eyes, trying hard to blind me. On my knees, I reach up and frantically pull down the sailcloth, hand over hand, and pile it on the deck inside the lifelines. I roll onto the stack of wet nylon and push it up against the lifeline netting. Each time the boat plunges into an abyss, the bow wash breaks over me. In a minute, I am tired, and my breath is short.

Callard's face comes up and says, "You should have done this before it got so dangerous." I tie off the sail so it can't be swept overboard in a wave. "I know, I know ..." I say as I crawl back into the safety of the cockpit and shiver. Callard grins. I steer back to the course and trim the main.

This time the lights of West End are real. The red lights hang high on an antenna on the point of the big island. I confirm it on the chart. As the boat and I enter the thin pass, I can see waves break over the low and rocky islet upwind, a threatening white line of disaster. I enter shallower water, and the waves moderate a bit behind the rocky outcrop but the wind still howls, screeching in the shrouds.

I keep my eyes peeled to starboard for a green channel light on the land.

We sail tentatively, feeling our way into the pass as the wind drives us deeper into the trap. With each yard of water, it is harder to extricate ourselves, and we become more committed to the surf line.

And here, close aboard the port side, is a rocky little island to the north. The waves crash and break high, the spray flies far downwind into the pass.

"Can you see anything, Callard? The chart shows that the boat channel is a mile or so in beyond that antenna. We're there, and we're about outta deep water." We strain for a ray of light ashore, any light.

"I can't see any light at all. I think we ought to get out of here. We've got white water here and there both," I point to the big island and then the rocky shoal. The narrowing pass shows white water ahead of us. "We should tack while there's still room."

"Nah," Callard says. "We better jibe out, keep the wind behind us. We're on a lee shore. We don't want to lose power in a tack. Watch the boom when it flies over, jibe-o-duck!"

I push the tiller over with my knee. The little boat stands up straight as the pressure eases off her centerboard. The wind catches the sail backward, then the boom swings violently across the cockpit with a crash. The shock vibrates through the boat and twangs the rigging. Now we are barely outside the combers. Breaking crests mark the line where the incoming waves feel the ground and stand up, building until they crash onto themselves spilling tons of water to the bottom, relentlessly pummeling everything to destruction.

"Dammit, Callard! The wind has shifted a bit. I can't beat away from the beach!"

I sheet in the main sail hard and struggle to get the boat to head up, away from the breaker line. Without the jib, she doesn't respond. It is too late. I look windward into the face of the disaster approaching above us—a wall of water climbing, steepening, darkening, curling, boiling, breaking at the crest, white teeth gnashing viciously. Under my breath, I say matter-of-factly, "Hold on, Callard, we're gonna roll."

The big wave slaps the boat hard, black water breaks over her cabin, twists Street Hustler onto her beam-ends, her mast horizontal, the tip nearly touching the water. She surfs sideways down the wave wall. I look back at the rudder now clear of the water. We are out of control, at the mercy of the breaker sliding us to the rocks with a killing impact. Equipment falls inside the cabin. I can hear things squeal and break. I stand mesmerized, my feet on the low side of the cockpit, which is in the water, and my hands strain the upper lifeline. Saltwater floods over the edge of the cockpit like a dam spillway. I am just a passenger now, and I watch the setup for sinking in horrified fascination. She slides sideways, trembles down the face of the wave, feels like she wants to give up and roll over like a fat woman, fill with water and sink.

For the first time in 30 years, forgotten words of the Navy hymn come back to me: *Eternal Father strong to save, Whose arm hath bound the restless wave, Who bidd'st the mighty ocean deep* ... .

But she hesitates, hangs there undecided. Then her keel weight overwhelms her, and she decides not to roll. She lazily stands up, black water rushes off the deck and sheets overboard, races along the toe rail and out her scuppers. She rounds up into irons, points into the wind, pauses and shakes herself like a wet dog. Then she falls off the wind and starts sailing again as if nothing happened. The saltwater swirls out of the cockpit, shedding weight. *Its own appointed limits keep; Oh, hear us when we cry to Thee, For those in peril on the sea!*

The wind shifts back. I can now gain distance away from the deadly teeth of the breaker line.

"I thought for a second we were going for a swim," Callard says in a laughing voice.

"Damn close, damn close ..." is all I can say. My hands shake.

By pinching the wind, we carefully work our way along a few yards outside the breaker line and around the point into the deep, black, bumpy ocean. Open water, however rough, never felt so good.

"You went in too far didn't you?" Callard chides. "You were late on your decision, weren't you, and you trusted the Bahamian navigation markers, didn't you?"

"Yeah, goddammit, I did," I whisper.

"You forgot that for 200 years, the Bahamian people made their living by moving navigation markers and luring ships aground, then stripping the beached vessels bare. They call it 'wracking.'"

"Yeah, I did. I forgot that."

In the small hours of the morning, inside the Freeport commercial harbor, I tie up opposite a cruise ship at the dock so high one can barely see the tip of Street Hustler's mast.

I wake up near noon, then stop by the harbormaster's office to pay my dock fee. Inside his plain little office, the winter sun slants across a blackboard with columns drawn on it. The headings say,

SHIP NAME/HOME PORT/ LENGTH/CAPTAIN
SS Norway—Oslo—1,035 feet—Capt. Svensen

The next line says,
SV Street Hustler—Telluride—23 feet—Capt. Vass

I stare at my name chalked on the blackboard and chuckle at the contrast.

Callard's face comes up. He shakes his head. "You're a dangerous man to sail with," he says sadly.

The wind is calm and the little boat is silent, resting.

I sit on my bunk with a bottle of bourbon, uncork it and take a hot slug.

Crazy Shirley comes back in a rush, assaulting me with that empty, aching feeling. I lost her in San Diego on that near-disaster. That was the beginning of the end. I am amazed that I was so stupid. It could have ended up badly, but I remember how hard we laughed when it was over and getting kicked out of the restaurant. I thought it was a great adventure. She didn't. Jeez, I miss her.

From nowhere Callard says, "Why are you still fretting about her? Why don't you forget her? Don't you think it is time to grow up and be a man? Us men are supposed to spread our seed as far and wide as possible. Women are like buses: a different one comes along every few minutes."

"I know," I say sadly and shake my head. "But she comes to me through the airwaves. There is only one of her."

"It's time for you to move on," he whispers. "A messy passage, wasn't it? You almost killed yourself—twice."

"Seriously, Bob, this is the second stupidest thing I have ever done."

42

HOPE

The phone rings in the night. It's her. She cries and I cry with her.

"I'm so unhappy," she whimpers. "Can I come home?"

My heart leaps. "Of course. I can't wait."

The thought of recovering our former ecstasy, of not being lonely, of sliding my hand over to where she lies, to find her there eases my soul, but not completely.

Could we ever be the same? She had spent time with another man, played with him, fucked him, perhaps many times. Is he better than me? Does he make her come more than me? Is his unit bigger? Does he love her as much as I do? He couldn't. It's not possible. It makes me crazy to think about them.

But she is coming home now. She's had her fling. Deep down, I knew love would win.

Within a week, she calls and says she is out of his house. We meet in a hotel near the airport and immediately go to bed. But she isn't the same. The time she spent with her lover is a translucent curtain hung between us. We are almost together in our minds but not quite. She is different now.

Her time at home lasts a month. It is awkward for us both. The affection is still there, but the trust and the laughs aren't.

Early one morning, she throws her clothes in the car and hurriedly leaves. She drives away after a perfunctory goodbye kiss.

I am, by turns, both angry and depressed. To hell with her, I think. He can have her. I can't spend my life agonizing over her. I am going to forget her and get on with my empty life. I must be content with being self-contained and alone.

Alone isn't the same thing as loneliness. Alone is a state of being. Loneliness is a state of mind, I think, like I know what I am talking about.

I am instantly lonely.

43

THE PERSONAL AD

When I leave town for a short trip, I am a respected pillar of the community and one of two Goldwater Republicans in the county. When I return, I am disgraced, set upon by two men of ill temper, and branded "'Bubba'—as befits a hack writer," they say.

A day later, seeing an opening to expand on the prank, the slandering conspirators refine the name to "Bubba Ram Vass" after the real guru, Baba Ram Dass.

I am assigned the poor-white-trash-Louisiana-bayou-levee-walking-coon-hunter name by mean-spirited and small-minded locals named Buck Lowe and Jim Bedford.

My options are limited: I can fight the idea, be a sore loser and never live it down, or I can accept the inevitable and play into the name and eventually it will go away.

But it doesn't go away. Within two weeks, it becomes Telluride's town joke.

So it sticks. Even the editor of the newspaper refers to me as Bubba Ram Vass. The choice between my obscure Christian name and this new heathen name seduces me.

Bubba becomes an inside joke and test of town citizenship. Visitors call me Jerry. The locals call me Bubba; they know I am a phony, but they still ask me for free spiritual advice. And just like the local preacher, I make shit up to fit the occasion, hiding the bad news, expanding on the good news. I even have pretty women approach me and ask if they can become a follower—a "Bliss Ninnie."

I say, "You bet your sweet ass, baby cakes! With all humility I welcome you into my spiritual kingdom." I hold my hands above them and say, "Bless you, my child." They seem happy with this.

Roll me over and call me Bubba Ram Vass. Better a phony guru and town joke than remain a nameless nobody forever.

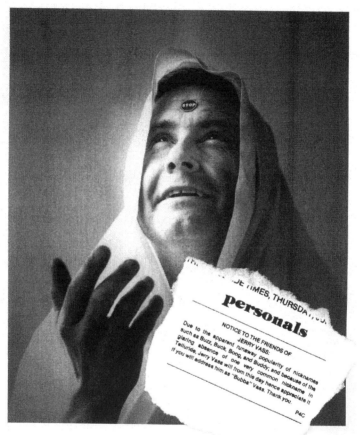

Photo by Bruce Macintire

BUBBA RAM VASS
Mahesh Nebbish Rocky Mountain High Yoga
The Best Zen Master in San Miguel County
Mediocre Advice at Discount Prices

44

THE MUSHROOM OPTION

I've never seen dollars stack up so quickly as with water rights in the West.

While losing in the hydroelectric project, winning in water court and spending time with my smart partners, I began to appreciate the extreme value of water rights in Colorado.

Water rights are severable rights much like gold and mineral rights, which means that they can be separated and transferred from the land across which they flow or exist. They can be owned separate from the land.

We think of water as flowing from our kitchen faucet or running in a ditch or stream. Under Colorado law, there are different classifications of water. The most obvious is tributary or surface water: streams, lakes, rivers, snowmelt, rain—the clear liquid that one sees with one's eyes.

The second classification is, predictably, nontributary water, that is groundwater that does not flow into an existing tributary within 100 years. Ancient water creeps along deep underground or doesn't creep at all but remains in place forever like water in a bucket, stored and still. And there are storage rights in natural reservoirs, which, in some situations, can have high value.

My genius lawyer-geologist partner, Skelton, using his blazing imagination, finds a hole in the law and files for rights on 73 nontributary sites in the Rockies. These sites are high valleys dammed by terminal moraines; rock and gravel dumped when glaciers melted, and water filled in behind the natural dam, making a lake beneath the existing valley floor.

Drilling down to the trapped water and pumping it into the nearest streambed allows water to flow downstream to the most likely buyer—a big city with a water shortage. Under the current law, the naturally trapped water can be tapped by the owner of the rights and sold downstream as far away as Los Angeles. In this case, the rights to the 73 sites are worth $1.2 billion (with a B!) when sold.

So here I am, along with my partners, a defendant in a lawsuit. Even though the hydroelectric properties are now worthless, the lawsuits are still in place, and I am broke. But, there is a difference between broke and being bankrupt. Broke is something I can cure; the Big BK means I am out of business and out of Telluride—the end of the road for Bubba.

In the middle dark of a worried and pillow-beating night, I have an idea and I glimpse sunlight at midnight. I leap out of bed and begin to dance naked in the dark, flailing my arms and legs and loudly singing, "I can see clearly now, the rain is gone. I can see all obstacles in my way ... ."

I have this stroke of pure genius.

On the drive to Denver, my heart lightens. Bankruptcy seems a bit more remote.

In his cheap little office building on Denver's west side, I ask Skelton, "Why don't you sell me an option on those water rights? I'll go out and sell the option on the rights, take a little bit for brokerage and the rest to settle the lawsuit with the assholes from the East, and split what is left over between us partners. They're happy, our partnership is happy, I'm happy. What'll you take for an option on the 73 sites?"

"Oh, I don't know. How much have you got?" His sideways smile knows the answer.

"Nada. Nothing. I don't have two nickels to rub together. But I'll give you a check for $10,000. Don't cash it. It's no good. Cash it when the sale goes through."

With that, Bruce, a friend and coworker who is smart and very funny, and I jump into my van with a signed option contract and a brown grocery bag full of psilocybin mushrooms, feeling that the world is a wonderful place. We zoom off into the soft, optimistic day to make our fortune. Guaranteed.

We start out cold sober for this is a serious endeavor, not one to fool around with. We know we are perfectly capable of blowing it, so we bring some shrooms along to mellow us out, sharpen our senses, give us good humor, make us smile and shorten the miles.

Our destination is Penn Square Bank in Oklahoma City and, if that doesn't work, then on to St. Louis and Bruce's old boss for another try.

Penn Square Bank is the lender of choice for many of the oil and gas people in Oklahoma. We have the name of Bob Callard's son, Jeff, inside the bank who can steer us to the high rollers with both the money and a speculative nature to buy my option for $1.2 billion in water rights. The price for my option contract is only $600,000 cash.

We roll along watching the prairie pass, cruising along the Interstate treadmill, telling jokes, discussing locals we know and the craziness they inhabit.

Oklahoma City is no particular place, some high-rise buildings and gracious-plenty suburbs sprouting from a flat plain blanketed by a cloudless sky.

Driving into the Penn Square Mall, a shopping center populated by the predictable retail stores, we look for the bank: three-story marble columns, impressive aspect, big brass doors, Roman letters that yell (but in a classy voice) "BANK."

We can't find it. I stop alongside a man in the parking lot and ask him where the bank is located.

He points, "I think it's right over there, next to the beauty salon. In that little setback."

He's right. We park and walk over by the beauty salon to a regular glass door with small gold leafed words: Penn Square Bank.

I look at Bruce and he lifts his eyebrows.

"Maybe this is the back door." I'm puzzled.

We step back outside and look left, then right at the line of stores to see if we have made a mistake. A well-dressed man walks toward us.

"Excuse me, sir, is this the entrance to Penn Square Bank?"

"Yes, it is. It doesn't look like much does it?" he asks with a slight smile. "It's one of the biggest banks in town, however. There's a drive-thru window on the other side of the building so the housewives don't have to get out of their BMWs."

Inside is a small foyer with a stairway going down. Nothing else. No teller line. No furniture. No signs. Nothing. We descend with a bit of trepidation. Who are these people?

We step out of the stairway into a basement lit almost to the brightness of daylight. A receptionist sitting at a modest wooden desk flashes us a big smile. To her right is a fluorescent-lighted hallway lined with doors that disappear into the distance, perhaps 100 yards long. There isn't a hint of sunlight anywhere.

"Hi," I say. "We were given the name of a man, Jeff Callard, who we are supposed to see."

"Yes, sir. Jeff is our reservoir engineer. Did you have an appointment?"

"No, ma'am."

She punches the phone, speaks one sentence and says, "He'll be right up."

We introduce ourselves and follow him to his office, a geologist's workspace—maps on the wall, graphs, notices stuck up with pushpins.

"Jeff, we were given your name as someone who could help us do a water deal," I say.

"Deals are what we do here every day. What's your deal about?" He leans over a big table, his elbows crinkling the maps on top.

"We have an option on $1.2 billion worth of water rights in Colorado," I continue. "It has 73 storage sites: natural reservoirs that can be drilled and the water sold downstream. We have the engineering and surveys in place, and each site can be inspected. They are in mountain valleys, so the easiest way to see them will be by helicopter.

"We understand that you lend to oil and gas prospects, and we thought that water rights traded as a mineral might be of interest to some of your clients. It's not that different from what many of your clients are doing now. The option price is $600,000. How is Oklahoma doing these days?"

I stop. I've said enough.

Jeff takes a deep breath. "It's going nuts. Oil and gas keep going up. This morning, it was over $39 a barrel. We think it is going to $70. Here's a graph of our projections," he points to a graph on the wall. The price line climbs steadily at a 45-degree angle. "Everyone in the business is making real money."

"So how do you guys work with your clients?"

"We lend them money based on the oil they have in the ground. Within the last year, we have become the largest bank in Oklahoma," he says with a touch of pride. "We have $2 billion out now, and the president says that is just the start. When oil goes to $70 or even $100, we can double up on everything—loans, collateral, participations, everything. Every bank from Chicago to Seattle wants a piece of our loan action."

He stands up, big shoulders, wrestler's body. "If it has resources in the ground and it requires drilling, that's right up our alley. I'll talk to some of our people. Perhaps we can create a loan using the water as collateral. Let me take a few minutes and gather up some guys on the loan committee, and you can explain it to them."

I look at Bruce. He is smiling. I lift my eyebrows that say it looks like we may get somewhere here. He nods.

Jeff returns. "I can't get them together right now; they are all busy. So if you guys agree, we can meet for dinner and talk about it."

We meet at a super-cool, high-rent restaurant, upstairs away from the busy areas, six of us men at a circular table. Over drinks, the conversation goes well. All three men from the loan committee seem eager to finance the deal for an existing client, naming this potential buyer or that one, nodding, murmuring agreements.

They are straight guys in their mid-20s in ill-fitting dark suits, white shirts from JC Penney; lean animals with healthy, polished skin, good haircuts, clear eyes, nice teeth; young churchgoers on their way up in the world and playing the part of important bankers. Bruce and I play it that way, smiling a lot, nodding agreements, fully attentive to every word they say, never taking our eyes off them. Who has the most influence? Who is the natural leader here? Who can pull the trigger and take it upstairs with total confidence and defend the decision? What will I need to do to persuade these three guys to sponsor the deal?

We order drinks around. In time, the waiter arrives with his pad at the ready.

I say, "On your menu you have mushroom soup. We'll have six mushroom soups. We'll order the main courses later."

Bruce looks at me hard. Several banker eyebrows go up, too.

The mushroom soups arrive in large, flat bowls beautifully spaced around the white linen tablecloth.

I pull out my brown bag of magic mushrooms and walk around the table and crumble pieces of the dry happy-fungus to float on the tan surface of each man's bowl like a happy little navy.

"You'll like this," I say with a laugh. "This is really good stuff."

Bruce's eyes go real wide.

Within a half hour, we are all laughing uproariously at bad jokes and we cannot possibly be closer friends. As we stagger out of the restaurant, a banker has his arm over my shoulder and another has his over Bruce's. I know my deal is done.

The rest of the evening is a nightclub kaleidoscope blur of neon lights, marionette bodies dancing in slow motion to unrecognizable music, drums thumping a backbeat to uncontrollable laughter. We lose the bankers somewhere along the way; they go home to their wives and kids.

Bruce shouts over the music, "We have to go! We don't belong here. These are all college kids!"

I make my eyes focus on the dark, flailing bodies. Crazy Shirley's tight little butt dancing in the Roma rushes back. God I loved that ass. Still do. Every man's dream. I miss that ass and everything attached to it. I'm empty again. How do I get over her? She lives with me.

Bruce is right. We need to leave.

On the backside of the parking lot, we find the van. We just sit in the front seats looking out the windshield at the colors and listening to the psilocybin thrum in our heads.

Just beyond the windshield, men exchange blows in slow motion, the thud of fist on flesh, their faces red with anger. There is blood and finally, at least what seems like a year later, the bloody kid picks himself off the pavement and stumbles away held up by a girl in a short skirt.

"Bruce, I think it's time to go home," I say. "We've got a deal with Penn Square. From this point on, it's just housekeeping. We can do it all by fax."

He stares at me with a faraway look in his eyes. "I think so, too. I called my wife from the club, and she said she was going to divorce me because she thinks I lied and told her this was a business trip. The background noise told her something different." He sighs deeply. "She's very angry."

"She needs some shrooms," I say.

"This isn't funny," he says.

At daylight, we start back toward home.

As my faculties make their stumbling return, jubilation floods my body. My money problems are solved, and the shadow of bankruptcy is pushed away by the bright glow of money from Penn Square Bank. I can continue to live a good life with a pure and generous heart, breathing the clear mountain air with all my friends. Life is good. My heart soars. Talk about making lemonade from a bucket of lemons. If it had gone the other way, it could have been real bad. Bubba, you are good. The Penn Square people can see over the horizon, see the magnificent potential of water in the West. They are visionaries like you, my good man.

A week later the Sunday *Denver Post* runs a tall headline and a long article in the business section:

OKLAHOMA BANK FAILS—
BIGGEST FTC TAKEOVER IN HISTORY

Two Billion Dollar fraud involves Chicago's Continental Bank and Washington's SeaFirst, both in danger of failure. Penn Square Bank of Oklahoma City, located in the basement of a strip shopping mall, famous for making oil and gas loans on shaky collateral, was taken over by the Federal Trade Commission on Friday night and will reopen on Monday morning under the name of Dissolution Bank of Oklahoma.

I sit in my office and ponder. Well, Bubba, you have the touch. You've done it again—snatched defeat from the jaws of victory. How in hell can you make a whole bank fail? It's your genius. It's your ego, that's how, you dumb bastard. The Dissolution Bank of Oklahoma just dissolved you.

45

CANDYMAN

Inside Sid King's dirty-book store on East Colfax Avenue in Denver, I carefully peruse the stock. I'm not exactly sure what package I am looking for. In use, the contents look like large, shiny ball bearings.

I finally spot the package among lines and stacks of adult toys. "Ben Wa Balls" it says on the plain white box.

A middle-aged man emerges from a booth in the back and walks quickly by without raising his eyes from the floor.

I am buying this item as a gift for a friend, a married woman. She confides she is not happy with her husband and their sterile sex life and wants something she can do herself. I suggest an ancient toy that helped working women get through their day. It is said that Japanese girls, bored at their silk looms, would rock all day with these orbs inside.

A few days later I am walking to the post office when I see a woman out of the corner of my eye crossing the main street on course to intercept me.

She whispers without breaking step, "I hear you bring things from Denver."

"Occasionally," I say. "What do you need?"

"What do you charge?"

"I don't charge anything for the transportation. You pay what the package is marked. It's a favor for my friends. There ain't a sex toy within 100 miles of here, so I bring them in as a favor."

"Would you bring something in for me?"

"Of course. I'm going over next week. Whaddaya want?"

And that's how Bubba Ram became the Candyman, the sex toy importer of Telluride.

On every trip after that, to fill orders, I stop by Sid King's on my way back to the box canyon with sex toys littering my car's back seat.

46

SPANISH FLIES

Mosquitoes bring one quickly into a visceral rage, that floating hostility that one has so carefully cultivated and hidden over the years.

I am a veteran of the Mosquito Wars of Mexico. I just got caught up in it. I was an innocent, really. When the rage came upon me, I could not control it. I dealt out death with a sure and unerring aim and a conviction that was, to be frank, frightening.

I trailer my little sailboat down to San Carlos, Sonora, to sail on the Sea of Cortez. A fabled body of water, it is clear blue and transparent, necklaced with white surf that slams onto the shallow beaches and raw, vertical desert rock. One of the great fisheries of the world, it is the ideal world for whales, porpoises and other slithery critters.

Wandering around the primitive little settlement of adobe houses, I strike up a conversation with two young women who sit in front of their camping tent. Casually, and with no agenda other than the company, I invite them to go sailing that afternoon. Glances pass between them, a nod.

"My boat is named Street Hustler. I will leave in an hour or so for an afternoon sail. If you would like to ride along, just show up."

More nods.

They show up. In a half-hour, we clear the headland and sail into open, azure water. It is a perfect sailing day, 12 knots of wind, a beam reach, the boat moves comfortably, gently, slapping the waves that occasionally show a white cap. We murmur along a couple of miles from the beach. Pure pleasure.

As with any pair of young women, there is a pretty one and a not-so-pretty one. The prettier, in her early 20s, a dishwater blonde with a nice body, has a good vibe and bright brown eyes. The other is bulky, rather seedy with stringy hair. Not unpleasant but without grace of limb or attitude. And she drinks vodka. Straight. From the bottle. Indelicately tipping the bottle back and slugging it like a lumberjack.

I have a couple of slugs myself. After all, it is a perfect day— sunny and gentle on the spirit, the only boat on the ocean, no threatening weather, just puffy clouds hanging out to the horizon.

I lean back in the cockpit and ask Miss Vodka if she would like to steer. She takes the tiller. "Just hold the boat straight and you'll do fine," I say.

Miss Blonde reclines on the cabin roof in her bikini. She is tan. We talk about Mexico and her college courses and what she will do after she passes the bar.

As a single guy with a refined taste in women and as an ex-photographer, I like this young woman but have little interest beyond appreciating the smooth aesthetic of her athletic body.

"Do you mind if I take off my top?" she asks.

I smile. "Of course not. Make yourself at home."

Her breasts are tan all over. Those bumps have great shape. Perky. She's obviously spent time under Ol' Sol sans bra and is comfortable without it. She then stands and crawls up into the belly of the mainsail where the bottom meets the boom and leaves a hollow that just fits a slim, reclining female body.

So there we are, drifting along with a mostly naked woman laying in the belly of the sail, a vodka-swilling woman steering, and the captain fully in control of himself, the boat and the situation. Life is good.

It goes peacefully for a half-hour or so. I gaze absently forward to the southern horizon and then focus on something strange there. It looks like a soaker hose laid across the horizon—a kind of fog all the way across, a solid line of mist that stops a short way above the water line. Is this too much booze? Am I imagining things? Seeing things? Can't be. It is a clear desert day. I can see forever. Yet here is this watery veil hanging in the air moving toward us and closing fast.

I crab to the foredeck and stand holding onto a shroud. Out of the mist come animals, wild animals, swimming shoulder to shoulder as far as the eye can see, left and right. A single rank of hundreds of porpoises playing in the perfection of the day. They come directly at us; the line separates around the boat, closes ranks at the stern and keeps going. Six to eight feet long, they leap alternately, smiling and laughing, ogling us as they clear the water by the boat. The soaker hose spray and froth move with them and then diminish behind us toward the northern horizon.

I lie in the cockpit and watch them march out of sight, tirelessly leaping and shimmering in synch. Moving jewelry.

In my laziness, I do not see the wind shift coming; I feel it. A jibe. Vodka steers off and a strong puff fills the mainsail from the wrong side. The boom swings dangerously and slams across the cockpit and across Vodka. The mast shudders and shrouds twang; the boat jumps as if startled. The naked blonde launches out of the belly of the sail, or rather where the belly used to be. She slingshots into the sea, flails through the air and splashes into the sea 10 feet from the boat. We sail away from her surprisingly fast.

Fear seizes me by the throat.

"Oh God! Oh God! Oh God!"

While small sailboats appear to be slow, making only five knots, a 23-foot boat travels 40 feet in five seconds. A person over the side is out of reach in 10 quickened heartbeats.

I had practiced man-overboard drills with a floating life jacket just for the drill of it, killing time during boring times on the water. The drills never felt real, just a way to pass the day. There was never the remotest thought that I would have a real person go over the side.

And now I have a woman in the water. Frantic, I throw everything that floats over the side: cockpit cushions, life jackets, foam cooler, everything. The sea looks like a yard sale. She is on the surface and swims for the floats. With the sails backed, filled from the wrong side, the boat now out of balance crabs in the water, moves away, heels steeply, opens more distance.

I shoulder Vodka aside, grab the tiller and yell, "Point at her with your hand. Keep pointing at her."

Vodka looks blankly at me.

"Can you see her?" I ask.

"Yes."

"Then point at her, goddammit!"

Vodka's hand slowly rises and points in the general direction of the swimmer whose head lifts and falls from view in the waves.

I seize the tiller and throw the rudder over to bring the boat through the eye of the wind to get the boat back to sailing.

The blonde screams, "Oh God, save me! Save me! God, save me! Please, save me!" She screams and squeals and makes terrified animal sounds.

Sweet Jesus, at least she can swim! Relief.

We slowly circle and close downwind of her. I let the sails luff, reach down, grab her arms and with strength created by stark fear, lift her clear of the water and onto the deck. She pants, fear floats in her eyes, her body glistens like a newly landed fish.

"Oh, thank you, thank you, thank you ...," she murmurs and slumps onto her arm. And then she cries softly.

Looking down at her, I resolve to never again give the tiller to a bad-looking woman who drinks vodka like water from the bottle.

At the dock, the women wander off into the sunset, one totters from vodka, the other from an adrenalin hangover.

As usual, my van is parked for the night in the middle of a vast dirt parking lot near the boat dock. There isn't another car or human in sight. It is hot, in the '90s. Lots of stars, no moon. Dark, dark, dark and hot, hot, hot. Sleeping nude, for comfort, of course.

And then it starts. Subtle at first, a subliminal buzz, going away, no, coming this way. Wait—flying parallel to my dozing body, certainly not threatening. Quiet. Waiting. Breathing quietly now. Waiting. Nothing. No sound at all. He has landed somewhere up by the steering wheel.

Aha! Here he comes. No, this is a different sound, lower. He either had a tuneup or it is a different mosquito. No, there are two mosquitoes. The hell with it. They can only do two bites. I can stand two bites. To sleep. To sleep. Settling down now. Have made peace with fear of bites. Look how big I am and how little they are. What's to be afraid of? A little blood. No sweat. If life never gets any worse than this, I have it made.

As I relax, the pointy nose of a Mexican mosquito penetrates my jugular and quickly inhales a pint of blood before the reflexive pain enters my brain. I cannot stop the blow; I can't even slow it. I hit myself in the throat and nearly pass out. Hanging over the side of the bed, I try to regain my breath. My throat is in spasm. I know I am turning blue in the blackness.

Fortunately, there is no one here to comment on how stupid I am. I flash on why I am single after all these years. Without being asked, women will tell you how retarded you are for slapping yourself out of bed. If one were here now, I would never hear the end of it.

In my throat, the bile comes up in place of the spasm—the purest anger, hot, killing anger. I lay there staring into the black and listen to the crescendo of mosquito wings that threaten my soul. Quietly, I hunt around for the TIME Magazine I know is over there by the spare tire. I find it and without turning on the light, roll it into an instrument of death, a solid cylinder that will wreak such havoc on wiry mosquito bodies that El Diablo himself will yearn to intervene.

I flick on the only electric light within a square mile. There are mosquitoes everywhere. They fly like dozens of attack helicopters, darting black bodies, hovering, lusting for me like starving men leering at a pork chop.

With a primal scream of vengeance, I turn into a killing propeller, the magazine a weapon of choice and revenge. Stark naked, I lunge and plunge up and down the length of the van, sweating and swearing, bare buttocks and my boys flashing intimately in the overhead light. In this backward and remote place, it is man against insect, the evolved against the primitive, intellect against instinct.

For an hour, I stalk and swat, dark bodies litter the bedsheet, and I revel in the bloodbath. Smears on the windows become trophies and I laugh insanely, smashing the bugs with all my strength, shattering, smearing impacts. The van shakes and resounds with revenge. Kill after kill after kill. Finally, nothing moves. I love it. Triumphant, I turn out the light. There is no sound. No wings, no buzz, no threat. My eyes slowly adjust back to the dark, dark night.

Standing feet from my back window, a Mexican family—mom, pop and a kid in an overlarge policeman's hat that sags down over his ears—cover their mouths, stifling convulsive laughter, heads thrown back, bodies shaking, faces to the twinkling stars.

Exhausted, I lay in the dark conjuring all the things that could have gone wrong when the girl launched overboard. Luckily for both of us, she could swim. What if she couldn't? I was trapped on a sailboat with a drunk who was sublimely ignorant of sailing or boats or emergencies or any other damned thing. What could I do? Jump in? If I had, how would we get the boat back to pick us up? If I didn't, should I just watch her drown in the glass-clear water, her blonde hair trailing, languidly waving, and sinking slowly out of sight to become shark food?

A knock on the side of the van rouses me.

I sit up with the thought that I am going to kick that little Mexican's ass, big cop hat and all.

Squinting into the darkness, I can see it is Miss Blonde. I slide the door open and she climbs in.

She smells fresh in the heat. "Hi. I'm here to thank you for coming back."

"Well, you're welcome. I wasn't about to sail off and leave a pretty girl swimming in the Sea of Cortez. I might have left your friend, though," I grin. "I've never had anybody fall overboard, so it was damned high adventure for me, too."

"Well, thank you!" she chirps and gives me a peck on the cheek.

Without another word, she skims off her top, drops her shorts and slides into the bed. Incredulous, I slip in next to her, touching her cool skin, caressing her breast, feeling the fever rising inside me.

And then I hear it. Up by the steering wheel, a mosquito starts his engine.

47

ONE LAST VICTORY

In the Sheridan Bar, a friend of mine, a runner, tells me he is going to compete in the Boomerang Road Race. He is going to race especially to beat Bill Sands. On the face of it, this seems a humble ambition. When I describe Bill Sands, you will know why.

Sands is one of those tall, gangly guys who just looks clumsy in his soul. However, he is a pro jock, a ski patroller, and he does move with a certain animal grace. I guess he looks decent enough, but he just doesn't look like he can do much running. When I started running seriously ("You call that serious running?" he once asked), he would invite me to run this half-marathon or that little 10K in Montrose. I declined, feeling better about running alone. I would surprise him one day.

Because he was a good friend and insulted me about my running, I knew I would enter a race against Sands. I would stalk him, jockeying for position on the terrain, gauging my strength so that at the very last second, I would hurl myself through the mountain air and across the finish line to embarrass and humiliate him in front of his peers.

I could see the headline in *The Telluride Times*: *VASS CRUSHES SANDS IN FOOTRACE*. His macho friends would then razz Sands endlessly and eventually, unable to stand the constant humiliation from his buddies, he would quit his coveted job on the ski mountain, sell his home and move his wife and kids back to Annapolis.

Don't get me wrong. I like Sands. He has been my friend for years. I have dined with him and his lady, and I have watched his children grow up. We have skied together. We have discussed world economics and town politics. And we have laughed.

Sands has a low, gravelly kind of voice. When he laughs, the laugh seems like it wants to come out and fly away on the breeze but it can't. It is a tight, uneven little chuckle held prisoner deep in his chest. When I laugh, it is an amplified fingernail across a blackboard. For years, Sands and I created distinct harmonies laughing.

In spite of our friendship, or because of it, I want to kill him in a race, to leave him face down in the asphalt, bleeding, humiliated, spiritually broken, a shell, his tight little chuckle seized in his throat, reduced to a gurgle.

In preparing for this glorious victory, I train hard, up the Tomboy Road, up Black Bear and Bear Creek. Society Turn and the Idarado Mine become my haunts, each day pressing on, always beating Sands in my mind's eye. Before the race is over, I will own Bill Sands' soul.

On I run, losing weight, getting more fit. Then the day arrives. This will be the race. The Ski Patrol Race, also called the Boomerang Road Race, is one of those events that only mountain men can think up. Starting and finishing in Telluride, the race is a loop 8.5 miles long, winding 1,000 feet above the valley floor. A mile from the start, just enough time to get warm, you start to climb the mountainside on the Boomerang Road up and out of the valley. It is steep, 1,000 feet of elevation in one mile. Then several small up-hills, then to the highway down Lawson Hill and back to town to drink beer and recover at Johnny Steven's place.

My strategy is simple. I will just hold even with Sands on the hills, all the time taunting him on the flats to eventually hurl myself through the air across the finish line ahead of him. The hurling part will be accompanied by the eagle-scream of victory I have practiced over and over in the isolated reaches of the upper Tomboy Road and Black Bear. After several beers, all of us competitors will point and giggle at the wimp, Bill Sands, and I will stroll home, flushed with good health and the ultimate victory over my friend.

Race day is a bright Saturday morning. I slip into my blue nylon running outfit saved for this occasion. Because of a vestigial potbelly, I have refrained, while training, from wearing anything tight. After training as hard as I have, I now deserve to wear something slick and clingy. Looking at the born athlete in the bathroom mirror, I notice that in a real running uniform, the potbelly is still there.

"What the hell, it is just Sands you're after. No big deal." The born athlete smiles back at me with a thumbs-up signal, sucks in his stomach and leaves for the race.

The ski patrollers are standing around in the front yard near the starting line, telling inside jokes, ragging on each other, comparing knee operation scars and all. I pick Sands out easily, taller than the rest, chuckling in his gravelly way. His running outfit does not match.

"You doing it today, huh, Bubba?" He smiles at me and shakes my hand. Old friends for sure, but if he thinks he can get mercy from me by being nice, he is sadly mistaken. My resolve hardens. Even Sands can't sell me out of the winning idea. I will hurt him before this day is over.

I take a good, close look at him. I memorize his face, knowing this is the best he will look all day. I want to compare the before and after and relish the disintegration of his personality. As we line up across the main street, Sands is beside me, right here where I can watch him. "How convenient," I think.

At the starting gun, Sands takes off like a black track star on a jailbreak. The next time I see him is over an hour later. He has run his race and is swilling his second beer by the time I finish. He looks cool and fit and happy, standing around with the rest of the real men, chuckling that little gravelly chuckle.

I hurt. I wheeze, spit, burn and gag my way around the course.

After a beer, I go home to lie on the floor and stare at the ceiling. Where had I gone wrong? I was slow getting off the start line, I know that. On the flat, I paced faster than I should have and ran out of breath. Part of the uphill I even walked. Walked, mind you!

On the downhill, my knees hurt. On the highway back in, I couldn't even catch Tom Taylor, who, when I tried to pass him, let out a big grunt and took off like a hemorrhoidal antelope.

There was no screech of victory for Vestigial Potbelly. Trying to get Sands was the mistake I made. My karma got me. Sands is my buddy. I shouldn't have hated my buddy and tried to humiliate and degrade him.

"It was all in good fun though," I say to my karma.

Karma screams, "And that's why you finished dead last? You were just lucky there was one beer left." Karma is being difficult.

"But, they are all pro jocks," I scream back. "They all get up in the middle of the night and do 5,000 pushups!"

Karma points her finger right at my heart, where it hurts, and says in an even tone, "You are not only a lousy athlete, you are an idiot. You can only do 10 pushups. What are you doing running against those guys? Especially Sands, who can run to Montrose for a quart of milk?"

"I can do 15 pushups," I say under my breath.

"Ten," she says in a flat voice.

I have to admit, Karma is right.

I decide to quit running. If I can't beat Sands, or even Tom Taylor, there is no purpose in running anymore.

I just can't quit though. Sands will never let me do that. He will look at me and then, well, you know, chuckle. I borrow a cane, lie in bed for a few days, and drag around town for a month accepting everyone's sympathy. It is a wonderful way to end a running career. Everyone buys the act, even Sands. He clucks sympathetically and gives me his exercise program drawn on a sheet of notebook paper.

I am still looking for some sport I can beat him at. Vestigial Potbelly ain't done yet. And to my friend who intends to beat Sands in the Ski Patrol Race, here is a piece of free advice: When you step up beside Bill Sands at the starting line, take a good look at his face. Notice the lack of worry lines, a clear complexion reflecting the good life and blue eyes that twinkle with confidence. Take a good look and commit the face to memory for that will be the last time you see the front side of my friend Sands for over an hour.

48
HOT TUB

In the Sheridan Bar, a petite, dark-haired woman moves up beside me. Janelle is lithe and lovely and expensively dressed, but she has a worn look. She smiles wanly, "Hi, Bubba, how was your week?"

"It was wonderful. I couldn't wait for it to be over," I say blandly.

"Yeah, I had one of those. I'm just bushed. Wanna go to the elevator?"

"Let's."

We walk quickly from the bar and wend our way to the side door, through the hotel lobby and into the elevator. She punches the third-floor button and the doors close. At the moment the vertical strip of light disappears, she produces a brown vial and carefully spoons a toot of cocaine into each of my nostrils. The door opens on the top floor. She presses the down button and toots up. In less than two minutes, we are back at the bar finishing the drinks we had left.

After a few minutes, she turns to me, "What are you doing tonight?"

"I don't know. I haven't got to tonight yet. Why?"

"Why don't you come home with me and we'll fix some dinner, get out of this mess."

"Sounds wonderful." We push through the drinkers to the door and climb into her new four-wheel drive. We speed off up the hill to her ski house perched precariously at the very top of a steep street. The vehicle whines; the clawing front wheels throw snowballs into the air. In moments, we are inside her aerie.

"Have you seen my house, Bubba?" she asks.

"Only while it was under construction. I've not seen it finished."

"I'll show it to you later. Let's get in the hot tub."

"Right on, babe."

A circular staircase leads up to a large white room: carpet, walls, and furniture, white everything. The couches and chairs are covered with snowy lamb's wool, soft and sensual. Floor-to-ceiling mirrors on opposing walls reflect and repeat themselves into infinity, thousands of images of the pristine room and everything in it. In the geographic middle of the room is a large scarlet tub big enough for six people, a red island in a white lake.

The water is already bubbling, flowing around the tub. Little translucent flotillas attack and retreat from the whirlpool at the end.

We strip in silence. In the soft lighting, I watch the woman undress with delicate, graceful motions, curling her fingers around a strap and the belt, shrugging out of her sweater.

The only thing better than a well-dressed woman is a well-undressed woman, I think. She's lovely. Nude, we slide into the hot tub, easing down into the hot water, feeling it burn momentarily. My muscles relax and my mind fades; there is just no way to stay tense in this womb of red and white.

Man, this is sinful. The husband has a woman and a home here in paradise, and I'm using both while he's down in Dallas trying to get here for the weekend. The expensive wife is here, lonely and balling whomever she pleases and killing herself with drugs and booze.

We lie in the warm water flank to flank, covered to the neck, the bubbles making circles around the surface beneath our chins.

"This is just too wonderful," I whisper. "Do you spend much time here?"

"Not enough. I get tired of being alone. I read here sometimes."

"Why are you in Telluride if you are lonely? Why not Dallas?"

"It's so phony. My husband's in the oil and gas business, and all he does is work. At least here it's beautiful and I know more people here in a year than I knew in Dallas in five. It's fun here. I like the people. You never know what's going to happen on any given night. Each day is a surprise. I think that's why," she answers dreamily, eyes closed, head back.

We loll in silence; the water caresses us.

This is a meditational form, I decide. It is hard to think about anything with bubbling hot water up to your neck. After a half-hour, I stand up and reach for a towel. "I'm done."

"Me, too." She stands, beautifully wet.

As she steps from the tub, drops of water fall and disappear into the soft rug. She gracefully wraps herself in a striped towel and tucks in the corner, locking the cloth over her hard breasts.

"Let me help you dry." I unlock the towel and begin to dry her slowly, methodically. She stands straight, watching me through lidded eyes, a slight smile playing around the corners of her mouth. I leisurely towel her shoulders and back, over her breasts, down her flat belly, around her tan buttocks and legs.

"You have a lovely tan," I say under my breath, fully occupied by the drying. I like women. I like women's skin. I like to make women feel good. I could never figure why women are so difficult for me on a daily basis. Then, on my knees in front of Janelle, drying her calves and feet, I drop the towel in a heap and kiss her belly, slowly, softly.

She breathes deeply and lets it go with a sigh. My tongue traces small circles on her tan abdomen under her ribs. With agonizing slowness, I drop lower and lower. She grabs my hair.

"Wait," she whispers and leads me to the fur-covered couch. She stretches full length on the fur, her tan aglow from the flush beneath. I take her toes in my mouth slide my tongue between and around each one. She watches intently, giggles and tries to pull her foot away. She squirms, her eyes glisten, and her breaths come sharply. As I progress upward and suck on her kneecap, she giggles and jumps around on the fur.

"OhGoddon'tdothat! It … tickles … !"

I laugh.

I look sideways into the mirrored wall and see an infinity of two bodies suspended in a pristine world like two puppies cavorting in a snowbound playground.

A downstairs door opens and the yells and drunken laughter of new partiers tumbles its way up the stairway. Stop. Wait. Are they coming up here?

Janelle wriggles away, grabs a towel and puts it between her legs. "Get dressed!" she orders. I do quickly. Then we sit on the couch as if in innocent conversation.

"That was wonderful. I don't know where you came from, but I want to be with you for repeat performances," Janelle says. "We have a house in Costa Rica. Let's go there for a couple of weeks. Then I'll go back to Dallas and check in. What do you think about spending a couple of weeks on the beach?"

"It sounds spectacular." I take a deep breath. "But I can't make it."

"Why not? Don't you like me?"

"I like you a lot and love to be with you, especially away from Telluride. It'd be a helluva romp." The idea is insanely compelling, screwing on the beach in the Central American moonlight with the gentle surf lapping at one's soul.

"But, I can't."

Her gaze is steady and challenging. "Why not?"

"Because I'm broke. Just lost a deal. I don't have two nickels to rub together. If it cost a dollar to get to Phoenix, I couldn't get outta sight."

She scowls. "Jesus Christ, you guys here are all frauds. You are beautiful but empty. You fuck us and leave us wanting more, then disappear. The only ones who have money here are old farts with limp dicks and huge egos. If it weren't for the mountains, I would never come back." Her anger is the anger of the rich: super-critical, everlasting and superior. She breathes heavily and shakes her head. "I hate all you guys!"

She toots up, descends the stairs and disappears downward into the noise.

I decide I need a bump but the toot left with her.

Sitting on the couch, if I move my head in a certain way, I can see my repeating images in the mirrors. If I move my head a different way, the room is empty.

49

THE COCAINE TRAIN

The Rev was a child evangelist who preached through Missouri. He became a lawyer, and before coming here, he lived on an island in the Caribbean helping natives through the morass of local laws. His most compelling trait is his ability to stand in the middle of a room and vibrate a magnetic force field around himself that draws in men and women alike. He easily pulls me in and becomes my friend and attorney.

Dabbling in politics, he is now our local district attorney.

The Rev always has his choice of any woman who comes within his force field and the woman he is currently with, while not wonderfully beautiful, oozes a sexual vibe that stops ogling men in their tracks. "She is a sorceress," the Rev tells me.

"I understand," I say. "I know all about women sorceresses."

Cocaine is taking its toll on the best and brightest, even those sworn to prosecute it. When you snort coke, the first thing that goes is your judgment; the second thing is your morality. It is the perfect cure for insecurity. The most insecure people become the worst addicts.

Everybody who can afford it, steal it or smuggle it does all the white powder available on any given day or night. The town is short of spending money because of it. It is God's way of telling you that you have too much money.

For the rich, the expense doesn't seem to make much difference in their lives but the unrich get it by street dealing. (Hey, Bubba, you need a grrrr? A hundred bucks?)

Smart people are smuggling cocaine in by airplane, ship, automobile and pickup truck. By my calculation, $250,000 in cold cash leaves the town every year.

It is common knowledge around the law enforcement community that Telluride is wide open when it comes to tooting up. It happens at restaurant tables, bathroom and makeup mirrors, elevators, coffee tables, public bathrooms and parking places on the main street with the dome light on.

In private meetings with town officials about licenses or approvals, the opening motion says the bullet goes around first; everyone there inhales a little spoonful and then the meeting begins. While nobody says one has to toot up the officials, it is street knowledge of every supplicant that passing the bullet has to happen first.

When the undercover narcs come to town, they are usually easy to spot, and the word flies around like static electricity. The street dealers leave the valley on sudden vacations. But the narcs come anyway and the druggies trust strangers that arrive in the form of tourists, and then they get a free ride to jail. Or disbarred.

At a French restaurant, after an elegant meal and aperitifs, the Rev, his girlfriend and a gentleman named Auburn, who slid over from an adjoining table, talk about the town and its attractions to people ready to move from their comfortable city life. In Auburn's case, Phoenix. After a half-hour talking about the peaks, skiing, summer and winter play, their conversation turns to the open drug use in the town.

The expensively dressed man sitting with them says to the Rev and his sexy woman of the moment, "You know, you are such nice people, and it is good to make new friends in this wonderful place. I'm thinking about buying a house here. I'm not ever leaving. Can you help me do that?"

"Sure I can," the Rev answers. "I handle lots of real estate contracts. When are you thinking about moving here? I am busy, but I can make room for you."

"Let's talk about fees. Are you expensive?"

"Nah. This is the mountains; everyone's fees are low. Trade-outs are common. That Citroen sitting at the curb belonged to my client who had to go away for a while and he gave it to me."

"Since you might take things in trade and you both are such nice people and you have been super nice to me, I'll tell you what I will do," Auburn says. "I can get you a kilo for half price, five large."

"Hey, man, I have no idea what to do with a ki of coke."

Sexy Woman chimes in, "There's always a market in Detroit!"

The Rev freezes. "Come with me," he says sharply.

Outside, he says, "That guy taped our conversation. He recorded the whole thing. I know it."

"Oh," she says angrily. "Why are you so paranoid? You are just so suspicious of everyone. He just wants to make friends. He said he is moving here and he needs a lawyer, someone who knows the town, to help him out. He is just trying to be friends with us."

"Bullshit. He's a narc."

Later that week I step from my office on the main street to see my friend braced against a police car, hands on the roof, feet spread, head lowered, being frisked by a plainclothes cop. His girlfriend hovers, her arms folded, looking grim, watching her life change right before her eyes.

The arresting officer makes headlines. The Rev, our local district attorney and my personal lawyer, loses his law license for seven years.

50
AIDS COMES TO TOWN

The favorite gay man in town is Christopher, a soft, charming, effeminate, polite, handsome and declared member of the other persuasion. Everybody loves Christopher. As it turned out, a third of the town had.

AIDS crashes into town like a hot comet and impacts somewhere close to Christopher's hot tub. It seems he likes men and women equally, and they reciprocate readily. So, when the AIDS word sneaks into town from the outside, panic ensues.

"Go to the clinic and get tested," is whispered at light speed, and the medical clinic becomes crowded with perhaps a hundred or more "loving friends" to check if they have caught a gift that keeps on giving. Everyone is surprised at how successful Christopher has been in his quest for friends. In the clinic waiting room, his friends do not look at each other but find their shoes suddenly art objects to be appreciated with new eyes.

Death feels imminent from a disease that dare not speak its name. Foreboding hangs over the town like street dust, a deathwatch.

Waiting for test results to come back, the victims quickly truncate their desires. Horny propositions are rejected outright or assignations delayed indefinitely. Bar attendance is reduced to tourists who know nothing of the local plague that gnaws at the brains of the locals. Sex becomes an imponderable. Nobody gets laid.

When the test results finally come back, sighs of relief roll down the main street like puffy spring breezes. Fear dissolves, hot tubs are rewarmed, parties resume. Drug sales recover. Condom sales go way up.

Christopher goes away to get treated. He never comes home.

51
INTERIOR SCROLL

Walking quickly across the main street, the county coroner hauls up in front of my little house. With a familiar and mischievous grin, he asks, "Hey, you want to meet a porn star?"

The Telluride Film Festival is a world-class event, loved by Hollywood, and considered one of the top three film festivals in the world, famed for its exclusivity and remoteness. The weather is perfect for this year's town event playing host to the rich and famous.

I look up. He is in charge of the airport pickup crew, those volunteers who drive to the Montrose airport and ferry the film festival guests to the high country where they can bathe in an additional 15 minutes of fame.

"Hell yeah, tell me about it!"

"A woman's coming in for a special event at the Sheridan Opera House and we need someone to meet her plane."

"So what's the porn star stuff about?"

"She's from Andy Warhol's group in New York— 'Happenings' and that performance art stuff. I guess she made some pretty explicit fuck movies."

"Hell yeah, I'll do that. I'll borrow Rosalie's red Cadillac and go see her for myself."

"Good. Here are the instructions." He hands me a manila envelope. "She's coming in tomorrow afternoon. Also, some French director—Agnes Varda—she's on the same plane. Pick her up, too."

During the hour and a half drive out of the mountains into the flatlands, I wheel the red Caddy through the canyon curves and ponder the possibility that I might get lucky here.

I think about the most unseemly aspects of the film business. Pornography is cheap art, filmed sexual exploits of cast members with equipment the size of baseball bats and gynecological close-ups that fill a 30-foot movie screen and turns vaginas into pink landscapes and actors who can't speak a line convincingly but can screw for hours in overwarm warehouses with a blasé crew watching, directing, filming, changing rolls, moving lights and furniture all the while drinking coffee and directing them. Fluffers stand by in case the man in the scene goes limp. The fluffers fall to orally and get him started again and filming resumes. Time is money.

Yeah, it is just this kind of pick-up luck that can start the fleshly adventures. If she is pretty as porn stars often are, I'll try to get something started. Obviously she will be dressed in a sexy outfit that broadcasts her profession to an entranced public, her breasts haughty, her butt firm, round, and inviting. Probably blond and perfectly proportioned with blue eyes and a flirty vibe. It could happen. I could get lucky here. But then there was always the size thing. It would be like following Gen. George Patton into battle; it could be a tough act to follow but, as Callard used to say with an evil smile, "A man has to do his duty."

The Montrose airport is one of those country landing fields with the bare minimum of amenities: one runway, a barn-like terminal, one gate and one urinal in the men's room.

The passengers file off the plane and walk quickly across the tarmac. I watch carefully to spot my prize and not blow this opportunity to rise to my level of greatness. As each woman enters the terminal, I dismiss her as not possible, too big, too fat, not sexy, bad hair, black hair, not blond, no high heels, no great legs, not in the league, not a player. Just by elimination, the last woman to come through the door has to be her. She is the only one left.

She is in a loose fitting, print housedress, the kind your granny wears, with men's dress silk stockings pulled high over her calves and shoes from the Salvation Army store. She is tall; her face is plain and unremarkable, simply bland, brown hair, dark eyes that scan us greeters in a disinterested, superior way, the New York indifferent way.

My fantasy evaporates. I step up to her. "Are you Carole Lee?"

"Are you my driver?"

"Yes, ma'am. We're parked at the curb."

"Good. Grab my bag," she says curtly.

I'll grab your bag, bitch. Do you know who I am? I own the most successful business in the center of the universe, and you reduce me to a grunt? Now I need a fluffer. "Wait here. I have another passenger to pickup," I say coldly.

Standing near the Colorado Highlights poster, a smallish lady looking very European scans anxiously around the terminal.

"Are you Miz Varda?"

She smiles quickly, "*Oui.*"

"Please come with me. And welcome to the Telluride Film Festival!"

"*Oh, merci.*"

She is a small, plain woman with a round face and an aura of style and breeding, an educated vibe, trim, black hair in a helmet cut, plainly, but expensively dressed in slacks, black jacket, flat shoes. She moves with a deliberate grace and confidence.

I put the bitch in the back seat and have the French lady sit up front with me.

Passing through that part of town where the worst of American culture settles in to do business—the fast-food joints, gas stations and parts stores, the small, free-standing offices of semicompetent lawyers and used car lots with strings of flipping flags—Agnes looks out the window and around the car with a sense of discovery. "I cannot beelieeve I am 'ere. I cannot beelieeve I am een a Cadillac!" Her sense of wonder is palpable. "Amereeca …," she breathes.

As we roll back toward the mountains through the farm fields and grazing land, the Uncompahgre River flows fitfully along, protected by the cottonwood trees lined up like a thin army along the banks. The San Juan Mountains rise beyond the closer mesas like a long, low-jagged banner. It is a spectacular day, enough to impress the locals never mind the innocent eyes of tourists, the sunbeams brightly making hard shadows. Puffy white clouds hang out like groupies over the peaks showing off with light snow on their highest points.

My passengers are silent for a long time. Agnes turns and speaks over her shoulder, "Are you een motion peecture business?"

"Yes," Porno answers in a serious voice.

"What kind of motion peectures you do?"

"I write and produce art films in New York."

"I like New York. Where een New York?"

"Soho."

"What are your subject?"

Porno's voice turns haughty. "Art!" she snaps.

A long silence as we all watch the passing scenery unfold like a TV travelogue. When the mountain peaks fill our windshield, Porno asks, "Where did you come from?"

"I come from Paree today. I just feenish my filming of two years. I just have a telephone call from my office, and they say I am invite to thees festival. Now I am 'ere. I cannot belieeve thees." She smiles slightly as if embarrassed.

"So what were you shooting there?"

"A film about women. Eet's the hardest thing I 'ave done. The crew 'ave 15 people. I feenish yesterday. Eet's done now. I get to rest. But I'm so tired. Eet's a long travel."

A long quiet from the back seat. The Cadillac thrums along the two-lane highway. From the back, "What size film are you shooting?"

Agnes looks puzzled. "Thirty-five meeleemeeter. What size do you work?" she asks politely.

Long pause. Finally, "Super eight."

Silence prevails as the red Cadillac and its two moviemakers slide over the top and up the canyons to the jewel of the Rockies where, for the next few days, everyone would be important except the locals who would glory in the reflected neon light of Tinsel Town, rubbing up against the stars and the wannabes and the nameless, faceless cinema freaks who always angle for their place in the sun, maneuver to find a producer, no matter how small, to press into their unwilling hands a film script which visitors and locals alike carry with them at all times just in case one is unexpectedly thigh to thigh in a hot tub with a real somebody.

The next day, the festival head of security walks up with a bit of worry hanging on his face. "Hey, Bubba, would you do us a favor and be a monitor in tonight's special event? You're older, and we're going to have young guys attending and we don't know how rowdy they'll be. We don't know exactly what the event is about, but this woman has a reputation for getting kind of dirty. She's done porn movies. Can you be there to keep these crazies calmed down? They know you. You'll have an official armband and all."

"You bet."

This ought to be fun. I'll go monitor the wild ones at midnight in the Opera House starring a live pornography star just to see it. If it is the woman I picked up at the airport, she had better be good with the makeup and dress in something besides a thin housedress patterned with little blue flower buds.

The small jewel of the Sheridan Opera House is full before midnight. Every seat is taken as it always is during these festivals. The early arrivals—men, young and middle-aged—sit in the first two rows. The stage looms over them. They talk excitedly, half drunk, loudly laughing, whooping and making dirty comments to each other.

From my station in the balcony, I look down on an empty stage and the audience settling in for a risqué show, restless in anticipation of an event where unpredictability is the promise.

The boys in the front rows are acting up. I have no idea what to do with them. Go down there and shush them like first-graders? I'm not a cop. I have no power, just an armband. Behind them sits a hundred middle-class film buffs waiting to see a happening, chatting, smiling, looking around, searching for famous faces from the movie business.

A back curtain rustles and Porno strolls to center stage wrapped in a white bedsheet. She is carrying a galvanized bucket with a stick in it and a jug of clear liquid. Without a word, she drops the sheet and stands nude above the audience. From the first two rows, all eyes stare up directly into youknowwhere. Her brown triangle mesmerizes the men who fall silent as if they have never seen a naked woman before. Especially that part. Without a word, she lifts the jug and pours water into a bucket and stirs it with a stick. After a minute of stirring, her breasts jiggling with the effort, she drops the stick on the floor, reaches into the bucket, pulls out a handful of mud and begins to smear it over her very ordinary body. She coats her thighs, then her flabby belly, upper arms and neck.

And then she speaks. "Women," she declaims in a dramatic voice that swings out over the audience like a flying anvil, "are the victims of men. Men are the enemy of women." Her voice shakes; her eyes are angry.

Watching an unlovely naked woman who hates men, covered with mud, standing stock-still on stage, her breasts sagging, her skin lumpy, her attitude ragged, is not exactly doing it for me. In the audience, no one moves—not a twitch, a smile or a frown. The picture becomes a freeze frame, a still photograph of passive faces. Breathing stops. Complete silence.

And then, slightly bending her knees outward, her hand goes to her crotch, fingers into her vagina. I panic. Oh, God, she is going to pull out a bloody tampon and throw it into the audience. What the hell am I supposed to do with the uproar that follows that trick?

Instead, she carefully pulls out an accordion-folded strip of paper a foot long from inside her nether regions. And she begins to read about the injustices of the film industry, the users and profit-makers, the frauds, the casting agents that expect blow jobs from actresses, the studios that don't recognize original talent.

This won't last long, I think. It'll be over soon and the Opera House, now stone silent and entranced, will return to normal where a person can take a deep breath and look around and search for stars again.

As she reads, her hands move down the paper to her crotch until, nearly touching her pubic hair, she pulls on the rickrack paper, and it unfolds some more with a small zttttt sound.

"... of the vagina in many ways—physically, conceptually, as a sculptural form, an architectural referent, the sources of sacred knowledge, ecstasy, birth passage, transformation," she broadcasts.

Zttttt ... .

More paper unfolds until she can read it directly in front of her face. The paper strip curls down several feet in an arc that disappears between her legs.

"... The vagina is an opaque chamber of which the serpent was an outward model: enlivened by its passage from the visible to the invisible, a spiraled coil ringed with the shape of desire ... ."

She reads down the folded lecture until her hands are even with her navel.

Zttttt ... .

My misery starts deep in my stomach, just a small bubble of a giggle. Then it comes up, the bubble expanding, out of control, a gut laugh that refuses to be contained. I bite my lip hard. I cannot be a monitor and set a bad example. I cannot laugh. The men and women in the hall sit immobile, listening hard, their eyes never leaving the nude woman on stage raging against the injustices of the world, reading from a long, folded strip of paper that disappears into her dark pussy. A loooong piece of paper. This show is a wonderful put-on and the audience is buying it, playing their passive part, absorbing it, seriously living it.

Zttttt ... .

I bite my lip harder and taste blood. But I can't stop the hurt in my chest and convulsive laughter that is winning out against responsibility. I shoot for the fire escape exit and out to the alley. My uncontrolled hoots explode into the cool night and continue for hours.

The next year, I receive a mailer from Porno. It headlines her new book, *More Than Meat Joy*, and her credits list *Interior Scroll* at the Telluride Film Festival. It breaks me up all over again.

Zttttt … !

52

IDARADO

This Saturday morning is transparently clear. The gray peaks appear as scissor cutouts appliqued on dark blue construction paper.

The sun leaps above the sharp peaks and pauses for a while to look around and take in the scenery. Before sunrise, the mountain sides are rocky and dark, blue, forbidding, raggedly outlined in aspen trees and evergreens with vertical boulevards of lighter bare rock, avalanche chutes slashed into the sides that are snow-filled for much of the year. When the sun comes out, the blue-black peaks no longer close over the valley. The mountains retreat a few hundred yards and the valley opens up, becomes amenable and then downright welcoming. The morning transforms the high country from dour wife to wicked, loving mistress.

I have spent years talking to hundreds of dreamers, scammers and trust funders, each with big dreams, small pocketbooks and no follow-through. There are always BS artists trolling to get something for nothing—some scrap of local information that allows him or her to prowl around the market and steal a deal, test out his or her real estate chops, buy a piece of heaven under market price, screw an ignorant local. Obviously, the locals snatch up the good deals first. The best deals never reach the open market.

The man who walks into my office is a fireplug, built like me but younger. He is very confident. "My name is Bob Carson. I'm a real estate broker in Fort Worth, and I represent an investors group. We are looking around up here for something to do."

"Good to meet you Bob. My name is Jerry Vass."

"I know," he says. "I got your name and bio from the president of the Idarado Mining Company."

"Oh?" We shake hands. His grip is strong, nearly hurtful. "Well, Bob, have a seat. So what did you see that you liked?"

"Me and my people have a serious interest in buying the Idarado Mine property." He stretches back in his chair and crosses his legs. "I called the president of the firm and he told me to deal with you. Said you were the only person he trusted in Telluride, that you had always honored your agreements with him and were a man of your word. He said everyone else in town had spent years trying to screw his company out of something. He said this town believes it is so special that ordinary business ethics, things like contracts and handshakes, mean nothing; that the philosophy here is 'what's mine is mine and what's yours is mine.'"

"Man, he should know," I say. "The problem is that town council thinks because this is chosen place in the universe and they think they have more power than they do. Council members do the best they can, but they don't know anything about business. As a result, they do what they want without regard for the ethical norms of business because they don't know what those norms are."

He smiles. "That seems to be the same everywhere. I watch the town government in Fort Worth and they think the same thing." He looks around the spare office. His steady gaze returns to me.

"They are fun to watch," I say. "In the last election, the candidates for the town council were a carpenter, an artist, the town idiot, a knee-jerk liberal, a fascist with property interests, an ex-drug smuggler, an Olympic class ski racer, a promiscuous, bleach-blond, real estate saleswoman and an epileptic, nymphomaniac, paranoid schizophrenic owner of a children's store that is never open.

"The politics are childish and full of passion," I continue, "often accomplishing nothing except college dorm debates without conclusion or action. A question the size of a new parking plan or transportation system can go unanswered forever. It is a town full of dreamers, hippies, paradise seekers, sybarites and hedonists, and combined, not enough managerial brains to run a used car lot. Just kids in their sandbox playing town. The debates are rancorous. Simple questions become difficult; difficult questions become impossible."

This rant has become a set piece for me, told hundreds of times. I pour us some black coffee.

He takes a sip and makes a face. "Well, it takes all kinds. These small towns all have quirky government." He takes a deep breath. "We are interested in the development possibilities of the mine property. It holds a lot of hello for us. We like the town and think there is an exciting long-term future here. My group is three moneymen and me, but we need someone on the ground here that we can trust; someone who knows their way around; knows the locals, the government, the power structure, where the bodies are buried. But there will be a lot of work to get the property rezoned to new uses. Are you interested in working with us?"

"I'm always interested in new projects that affect the town. What do you have in mind?"

"Based on what Idarado's president says, you are the best candidate. How would you like to be the fifth person in our partnership? I'm the packager; you will be the man on the ground here, the local management, if you will. The moneymen will use their statements to borrow the down-stroke based on the strength of their holdings, which is easy for them to do. We will split the profit five ways. If you become part of our group, you are in for 20 percent ownership if we get a deal together." He pauses, watching me carefully. "How much do you know about the property?"

Shrugging, "I know something about it. I'm not an expert, but I have hiked over much of the property. I have bought land from them in the past, and we've always gotten along well."

Watching me, he takes a sip of coffee and makes a face.

I continue, "If you are going to buy the whole mine property and operations, what they own is very complicated inventory. Some of it is fee simple property; there is a bunch of patented mining claims, obviously, and senior water rights—the most senior water rights, in fact. There are the mills and mine infrastructure, 350 miles of tunnels, and rights of way and tailings ponds and homes and town lots, mountains and valleys and streams. God, you name it. It is everything everywhere. About 10,000 acres worth that go from this end of our valley under and over the ridgelines 8 miles to the Ouray side. There are tunnels through the mountains that come out over there. Miners used to enter on that side. Like on this side, there is a mill and a medical clinic in Ouray, too. And some town lots.

"The mine has been shut down for a couple of years but they keep maintenance men on-site. I'm not sure what the ownership situation is since it closed, but Newmont Mining owns the Idarado. And I think that maybe Homestake owns a bit of it."

A long silence follows. Carson looks at the ceiling, then he squints suspiciously at the coffee cup. He nods.

"What're the local politics like?"

"Well, the town has 1,450 folks, give or take, depending on the time of year. The political power map is a series of concentric circles. In the center are 50 or so people I call the 'operators.' They actually make the town run. Businesspeople and old-timers, mostly. They know where the levers are, which ones to pull to get things done.

"Outside that ring are the locals, people who have lived here, say, six years or more. They have some influence on the center ring, and if you get enough of them together, they can have a great effect. But it takes a big issue like dog leash laws or rezoning to get their attention. Mostly they want to hike and ski and drink and do dope and play in the mountains and not be bothered by politics.

"The third ring is the seasonal visitors and tourists who bring in the fresh supplies of money but have no influence. No issue is taken too seriously unless you are talking about the people's toys or some kind of development—rezoning, architectural style, open space, tree cutting, density, building heights. These are, by definition, hot buttons. Real estate people, especially brokers and developers, are looked upon as land rapists, liars and public enemies. Rezoning issues become instantly hot. Many of the locals distrust anyone with a normal haircut and would just as soon have us leave town so they can do drugs without someone looking over their shoulder.

"The long-hairs change the day they knock up their wives and have to go to work to feed the kid that is the result of drug-pumped sex. The recognition that humans eat every day of the week, including Sundays, drives them straight. They cut their hair, shave and go into real estate and become the greediest, most pro-development people in town. Six percent of the population has a real estate license. Just a handful of us make any money at it though."

Carson nods as if he has heard it all before. "Are you one of the town operators?"

"Sometimes. But actually, I try to stay out of it. I'm 10 years older than the people in government, so they don't listen to me very much."

"So what do you think?" he asks.

"I'm interested, of course."

"All right. Here is the next step: Can you put together the maps and information and come to Fort Worth and show it to the other partners and explain it all?"

"Look," I say, "I can do the land part, but I don't know anything about mine works and mills and all that industrial stuff. But I can get you a general property inventory that you can work with."

"That'll do for now. Be aware that we have to hurry and get this deal done. We don't want a bunch of competitors coming out of the woodwork. This is between us. It can't go out of this room, you understand?"

"Of course. If I couldn't keep secrets, half this town would be in jail and I would've been dead years ago."

He laughs and waves from the doorway, "See you in Fort Worth."

I don't know if this is a real deal or not, but I estimate that the Idarado is worth at least $10 million. My fifth is $2 million. To invest nothing but time in research and a plane ticket to Texas in exchange for $2 million is my kind of deal.

On the drive from the airport into Fort Worth, Carson and I exchange small talk about the hot weather, the new skyscrapers downtown, the bright future of the city, now considered the poor cousin to richer and fancier Dallas but catching up fast, soon to become glittery and polished smooth by the gushing, frothy river of oil and gas money.

Nearing the city, he turns to me with a steady look. "I was in the Marines. Were you in the military?"

"Yeah, I spent four years in the Navy. Thirty-nine months as a deep-water sailor on a destroyer. I controlled naval gunfire."

"Do you scare easily?" Carson asks.

Now that's a weird question for a business deal.

"I don't know. Been in a couple of bar fights. I think I have a normal reaction to physical danger; depends on the situation. But I try not to test it. I tend to get my ass kicked in fights. Why do you ask?"

"Have you ever heard of one of our backers, a guy named Cullen Davis?"

"No."

"He is the richest man ever tried for murder."

"Never heard of him. Who'd he kill?"

"At trial, they said he shot his stepdaughter and his wife's boyfriend. Wounded the wife, Priscilla. Had big trials but he was acquitted. He's one of the money partners. You're going to meet him this morning and I have to tell you upfront, if he doesn't like the way he's treated, he'll threaten to kill you."

I laugh. "Bob, you are pulling my leg!" This is Texas of course. The whole state is confused on whether to brag about having the largest midgets in the world or the smallest.

"Have you ever read the book *Blood Will Tell*?"

"Never heard of it.

"It's the story of Cullen and the murders and trials and acquittals and everything," Carson says. "Read it. He was acquitted for the murders and walked, but then he put out a contract on his divorce judge. He did a little time for that."

We work our way through the traffic in silence. So what the hell does that mean to me? What does it mean to the deal? What does it mean to Telluride? I have no idea. I am perfectly comfortable with deals if everything is clear-cut, simple, easy to understand and explain. But partners with an accused murderer? Who could think this up?

Cullen Davis is a thin, little man—150 pounds of whip thong. He is dressed western: snappy shirt, boot cut pants, the obligatory Texas fancy cowboy boots, high-finish western hat. No amount of expensive dress can change his lean stature. His dark eyes are cold and hold a challenge; his demeanor and vibe exude total control of himself and his surroundings. Here is true Texas Rich in his native camouflage.

The other two moneymen are ordinary-looking, even forgettable, but presumably they have the juice to make a deal happen.

After standing at a whiteboard for two hours lecturing on the land holdings, poring over maps and aerial photos, discussing the inventory of the deal, I need to pee.

When I return to the room, Carson stands up and says brightly, "I've made lunch reservations at the Colonial Country Club." He points at me: "You go with Cullen." Then he commands the other two: "You guys ride with me."

Cullen stands and squints at Carson. "Why are we going to the Colonial?"

"I thought it would be nice to show our best country club lifestyle to our guest from Colorado. They don't have much of it up there," Carson says with a hint of a smile

On the drive across town, Cullen and I make small talk, but not much. There are long silences. I am careful about what I say, feeling my way along, not getting too far out there with my opinions, letting the scene play out. Caution seems called for as when one pets a notoriously bad dog. Go ahead and pet but keep your fingers tucked in.

Fort Worth's elite meets at the Colonial Country Club. The 18-hole course hosts championship golf and lays verdant and quiet behind the stately, pristine white clubhouse that impressively sprouts pure white columns.

As we pull into the parking lot, I see Cullen stare at a buxom blond woman as we pass. His face goes hard. She speaks closely to a trim and tan young man in white clothes and golf cap. She leans close to him. Her hand touches his arm.

The walk into the restaurant is pure show business. The place is crammed with a stylish lunch crowd; there are diners as far as the eye can see. Cullen and I follow the maître d' and a hundred heads turn in unison to watch the small man with the big walk. A murmur ripples around the tables like a radio wave. Eyes follow us as we curve our way to a round corner table with seven seats.

Carson arrives with the other two partners and says with a big smile and a twinkle in his eye, "Cullen, I just saw Priscilla in the parking lot talking with the club pro."

Out of the corner of my eye, I watch Cullen. The tiniest twitch shows around his thin lips.

Was this THE Cullen Davis? Couldn't be. There is no way this could be the same guy. This cocky little man, a murderer? I seriously doubt it. Seriously.

Carson is putting me on to keep me off balance, perhaps to kid with me, show his lighter side or see how I'll react. Potential partners have all kinds of subtle tests for each other.

After we five partners sit, two women arrive and we are introduced to the other partners' wives. An uneasy feeling comes in my stomach. This is a serious breach. I would never invite outsiders to a business meeting. Why are they here? Lunch with their husbands? Lunch with the famous Cullen Davis?

A wife seats herself between Cullen and me. From my seat, I look past her squarely onto the top of his head; he picks at his salad. His head is small; his dark hair shot through with gray with a lighter balding spot. He concentrates on his vegetables, his eyes hidden.

I watch him carefully and try to read the man beneath. He looks smaller without his hat. Ordinary. He slowly raises his gaze and catches me staring. We lock eyes and have one of those moments that rarely happen between strangers, a silent communication that reveals what both are thinking as if written on the walls behind us.

I meet his level gaze and I'm certain he reads my question: Is this man I'm staring at, eating lunch with, this smallish man who looks so ordinary, is he a child killer? A man that can execute a 12-year-old girl with a shot to the head? A point-blank execution? Is he capable of that? Is that a real man?

In that cold, challenging moment, our eyes exchange messages for five, six, seven, eight, nine long seconds. In that instant, I know and he knows I know. I see the answer in his icy eyes: I am going into business with an accused cold-blooded killer.

We drive back to the conference room and with little fanfare, the partners agree to buy the Idarado, agree on the 20 percent ownership to each partner. The deal is done quickly in a purely Texas fashion, just like the movies. We shake hands all around. Cullen's handshake is perfunctory and without energy. He puts on his hat, nods to me. "Thanks for flying down," he says, then turns and leaves.

Carson drives me back to the airport.

"I was sure you were kidding me about Cullen Davis."

"Yeah, he is really something. Kind of dangerous, I think, but he has settled down a lot since he did time. You should have seen him before he went to trial. A cockier guy you never met. During the big golf tournaments at the Colonial, he would have a trailer dropped into the parking lot by helicopter where he would show porno movies day and night. Served drinks, had the ladies in. It was quite a show."

I shake my head. "Amazing" is all I can say.

The fanjet engine drones through the bumpy mountain air between Denver and Montrose. What is the right thing to do? I can still say, "No, I don't want to be in business with *un malo hombre.*"

But what happens with the property? Precious valley land that is now frozen in place can be released to private enterprise. The senior water rights can be deeded off to the Town of Telluride, securing their pure domestic water forever. We can redevelop the current land that now holds mobile homes into permanent, low-cost housing for the locals; the mill can become a tourist attraction. We don't need a medical clinic in our operation so we can give the clinic to the town. The acres of flat-topped tailings ponds can become home to light industry like lumberyards, equipment storage, machine shops, long-term storage for cars and other stuff that people have too much of. Hiking paths can be developed along the river, scenic overlooks approached by Black Bear and Tomboy roads that with some improvement can join the Million Dollar Highway from the other side of the peaks. It might be possible to use the mine locomotives and cars to go under the 13,000-foot peaks to bring skiers into the Telluride Ski Area from the Ouray side. And there will be jobs for the locals.

Is it worth abandoning all of this possibility just because I don't care for a partner? No. I'll be a partner and do what I can to complete the purchase.

I will then go to the town and ask them what their vision is and how we might work together to make the valley a better place to live and work, with a sense that there is a future besides skiing and cleaning toilets.

I buy the book *Blood Will Tell*. Cullen Davis and his wife, Priscilla, and her 12-year-old daughter lived in a very chic house in the very rich neighborhood of Fort Worth.

Cullen was separated from his wife when, the district attorney says, one summer night he donned a hippie wig, snuck into the house and, surprised that his stepdaughter was home, walked her downstairs and executed her. He waited, and when his wife and her lover came home, he shot and wounded Priscilla, then chased down and killed her boyfriend. In several trials that lasted for years and taxed the Texas legal system, a jury of his nonpeers acquitted him in Amarillo. He walked into free sunshine with the help of the famous trial lawyer, Race Horse Haines, only to be sent to prison for an attempt to hire the assassination of the judge who handled his combative divorce.

In Telluride, nobody has a whiff of what is happening to the Idarado property. My first look at the purchase agreement is a surprise. It isn't a real estate deal; it is a stock deal: $13.5 million for 80 percent of the Idarado stock; Homestake keeps the rest. My estimate of $10 million was off by a third. My piece is $2.7 million in carried interest plus a fifth of the profits. It is, by orders of magnitude, the largest land deal in the valley to date.

The locals hate mines and mining. They ignore the fact that Telluride wouldn't exist without those money-hungry folks who crept over the wilderness passes a hundred years ago, hip deep in snow, in search of gold and found it in the peaks of the San Juans. The local tree-huggers who complain the loudest also fail to realize that their self-congratulatory lifestyle— everything they live in, eat, wear, and drive—comes from the earth, the only original source of money and food. Mining the mountains' resources made our country the richest in the world.

They hate Idarado, its mine tailings, the detritus of rusty equipment, the mine shafts that leave scars down the sides of mountains, the prospect holes of the 1880s, the broken tram A-frames that carried the ore from the high tunnels down to the mills, the hills of crushed rock left over after the extraction of its treasure of gold, silver, copper, lead and zinc, leaving weird-colored lagoons in the valley. It was the largest base-metals mine in the state, processing 1,700 tons of ore every day at the Pandora Mill 2 miles up canyon from the town.

What for this generation is an eyesore, to me is part of the beauty of the place: a rough and ready environment when Telluride was home to a wilder west, where whorehouses and bars, gamblers and illuminati met for good times and illicit love, or at least temporary like. It was the big city with bright lights for the immigrants who made up half of the 5,000 workers in the area, a place where the stamp mills could be heard around the clock rhythmically pounding rock into sand; donkeys and mules crowding the muddy main street strung together with a mile of coiled tram cable, each one snaking to the animal behind, creating a necklace of 20 pack animals that wound its way upward to the high mines.

The save-the-whales crowd could only see the damage; they could not see the history behind it, so they did everything they could to wreak retribution on the mining company for what they saw as reckless destruction of a beautiful environment. Indeed, the company and those that preceded it built the schools, the hospitals, the clinics and the clubs that still exist today. They paid 85 percent of the total taxes in the county, and the newcomers are now the happy beneficiaries of the mine's contributions when, for a hundred years, mining was the only game in town.

Nowadays, real estate brokers and developers are the most disliked folks in the valley, considered to be crooks by the free thinkers—Democrats, hippies and liberals—who make up most of the population. I can live with their disapproval since they are jealous of anyone who makes money the old-fashioned way.

Even with terminal envy in play, developers must also have some feeling for doing the right thing, to be socially responsible to your friends and enemies alike. I will make sure that we work responsibly on the Idarado.

In Fort Worth, everyone signs the purchase contracts, and the adventure is on. The closing is 90 days away. I don't realize what an adventure it will be.

53
AMERICAN HERO

When The Great White Hunter arrives from a city in Texas or California, he sees the endless San Juan Mountains rolling in from the horizon, crag on crag. He visualizes that out there in those blue valleys and high slopes are grizzlies, mountain cats and herds of elk, the bulls patrolling the cows. Daydreaming, he sees himself stalking, crawling silently through the pine needle carpet under the dark trees; a well-used muzzleloader is slung over his back and he's cold, shivering in the light snow mixed with rain that soaks the heat out of him. He sees himself fighting for survival out there 50 miles from the nearest wagon track. He sees himself as a mountain man in gray buckskins made smooth with bear grease and months of rain and dust and animal blood. He sees himself as the Great Western Pioneer Hero carrying on the tradition of soldier-hunter, protecting and feeding the little woman (who has a touch of asthma) and the hungry, thinly dressed kids back at the cabin with a sod roof. In his mind, the Great White Hunter can see his cabin, rough-cut logs chinked with adobe and the tiny curl of wood smoke from the crude river-rock chimney. The little house (a day's horse ride from the nearest neighbor) grows from the wooded bank of the white leaping river that sometimes roils with hungry native trout. In tough times, like now, he can't catch enough to feed his hungry children.

He needs a kill today. If he doesn't kill today, tomorrow may be too late, his body fuel drained by the effort of the hunt for the ever-elusive wapiti and the strain of surviving the high Rockies where one mistake can kill a man.

That's what he sees on the widescreen of his mind.

The reality is that he awakens in his million dollar home in the valley, enjoys a leisurely breakfast of bacon, eggs and toast just the right color, dons his down-filled Gore-Tex jacket and his waterproof boots, makes sure his answering machine is turned on, drives one block to pick up a thermos of hot coffee and some fresh Baked in Telluride éclairs, carefully carries them to his pickup truck with the 450 engine and mag wheels. Then he motors to the edge of town and parks on the shoulder of the main highway.

He walks a half-mile and waits under a tree, sips sweetened coffee and munches his pastry. He cannot entertain the idea that an elk with the same brains and equipment was hunting humans. Great White Hunter wouldn't be here if he thought an elk with a hunting rifle was hunting him. He would be at home, safely tucked inside his cowardice.

A magnificent specimen of a bull elk with a huge rack walks into range as he does every morning at this time to lick a salt block that has been left out for him by his benevolent neighbors.

The man unsheathes his custom-made, 30.06 hunting rifle with inlaid stock and loaded with the silver-tipped factory bullets, 220 grains of high penetration killing power. He centers the elk's tan bulk in his variable power telescopic sight, estimates the range and adjusts his aim inside the sight picture using the adjustable ranging crosshairs. He knows he cannot miss for he has spent thousands of dollars buying superb equipment to kill this elk. He squeezes the trigger and the rifle bucks. He does not miss. The regal animal snorts in shock and stumbles at the first shot, turns and runs uphill for a short way. Then the bull elk that we locals have admired for years and have considered part of our extended natural family crashes dead, inside the city limits of Greater Telluride.

The Great White Hunter then strolls back to his shiny truck, drives over to the dead animal, pulls it into the bed with an electric winch and drives back to his new, electrically heated, 5,000-square-foot home.

He feels good about today's hunt. Didn't get too tired. Didn't have to walk far. Didn't have to get wet or cold. Didn't have to worry about whether the rifle would work or if the gunpowder was dry. Didn't have to crawl anywhere. Didn't have to stay out overnight freezing in a lumpy sleeping bag. Didn't have to miss Geraldo's TV special on wife swapping among the middle classes. Didn't have to drive far and didn't get the truck stuck. Didn't have to worry about the little woman back at the house. Didn't have to worry about the victory Budweiser freezing.

And screw these overeducated, elitist, bleeding-heart liberal, knee-jerk environmentalist, mountain snobs who think that wild animals running free are beautiful. How perverse. Don't they know that killing big animals compensates for short dicks? What do they know about the hunter's spontaneous orgasm when a big animal falls defeated into a heap? Real men take game when and wherever they see it. Even town pets.

54

THE THREAT

A week after the purchase agreement is signed, the Idarado contract of sale becomes public knowledge and everyone in town knows that I am involved as a full partner. I stay low and continue to refine my development presentation for the initial steps, that is, work with the town and the county commissioners to help them understand what we have in mind and listen to what they have in mind.

I pick up the phone; it is the mayor of Telluride.

"Hey, Bubba," he says. "How ya doin'?"

"Perfect. How're you?"

"I'm good. Hey, we had a town board meeting last night and discussed the Idarado purchase at length. We decided that you will give us the Pandora Village land so we can build low-cost housing."

"Yeah, I'm gonna deed it right over to you." I burst out laughing. "And I'm gonna turn the valley into a water park!"

This is one of the mayor's jokes. He isn't a great joke teller, but he tries. "What are you going to do with it?" I ask. "Park the trucks and snowplows there? It is the most valuable land in the valley."

"No, we are going to build low-cost housing there," he says. "We need low-cost housing for the support people: the teachers, the cops and the lodge cleaners."

I say, "So, you decided we are to give you the land. Are you kidding? I don't think I understand what you mean? Do you mean buy it from us?"

"Not exactly. We think we can take the property through a condemnation proceeding. Our lawyers say we can prove a compelling need for local housing for the good of the town."

I feel my temper rising but for a change, I stay calm, my voice measured.

"Let me get this straight," I continue. "We've never had a meeting on this subject. You have never seen our plan that doesn't exist yet. Do you intend to take this land away from us by a legal action?"

"Yes. We don't need to see your plan. All you developers and real estate types are only in it for the money and screw the town and screw the people. For you, it is just for the money! We know you, Bubba. It's just for the money!"

"Mr. Mayor, I am not used to being threatened and I'm not intimidated by your jackleg lawyers."

"Well," he says firmly, "that is our position. You can deed it to us or we'll take it."

"That's a pretty clear threat. I take it seriously. Hold on for a sec and let me think about this." This is a sharp turn I did not expect. I always knew we would have to give something up but in exchange for something of value. "Are you sure you want to go this way? Force us to fight you in court for something we already own?"

"You can just deed it to us and save yourselves the trouble of a court fight," he answers.

"Mr. Mayor, we Telluriders are used to screwing outsiders. You forget yourself; I'm a local. I was here years before you arrived. This isn't the way we treat each other."

"We want the Pandora Village and we will have it one way or another. It's up to you."

My anger rose up like a standing bear. "Understand this, Mr. Mayor: The day you file a legal action against us, I, the Bubba Ram, will personally cut off the town's water supply."

"What do you mean?"

"That pure cold water that the town drinks? It's ours. It flows from our mine tunnels and we own all the rights—ALL the senior rights. The old Idarado allowed the town to use it as a courtesy but they never granted the town the water rights. It was a loan from the same Idarado management you have worked so hard to screw over in the past years. But we are not the old Idarado."

Silence.

"John, I was a citizen of the town before you flunked out of junior college, man, and I won't be threatened by you or anyone. I'm not an outsider; I am a local. I may not be able to beat you in court; I may not even show up there to defend our rights. But your citizens will be drinking muddy water out of the river until it clogs shut those old wooden pipes."

"You can't do that!" he screams.

"I'll do it on the day you file your action, I promise you." My temper bursts its dam. "You people think you are so goddamn powerful that you can take whatever you want. Well, not from me. You can tell my friends, the town board members, this: Tell them verbatim. Use these words: They can collectively and individually stick their condemnation idea right up their asses until they choke on something hairy!"

"Well, I'm sorry you feel that way. I was just trying to help the town."

"Bullshit, Mr. Mayor. You are trying to aggrandize yourself and your jerky, small town office. Everyone wants to leave his or her mark on Telluride for posterity. That's what you are trying to do—get famous, get popular and get congratulations on the street by fucking a big company. If you fuck with me, you will have to drink your bourbon straight at the Elks Club because there won't be any water."

Click. I hang up the phone.

Telluride. I hate this place and the small people in it. I hate the mountains and the overeducated small thinkers who believe this town is the whole world, the center of the universe, the be-all and end-all. I hate six months of winter and I hate cross-country skiing and wet sleeping bags and I hate scraping ice from my windshield and slipping and sliding on icy sidewalks walking to the post office and, most of all, the same tired old ski stories.

The people I love now are the visitors from the real world, the big world with honest-to-god horizons and warm sunshine and rain and live-and-let-live outlooks, where people smile and don't ask you how long you have lived in town, as if years of residence is a substitute for common sense. Telluride has lost its sense of adventure, of wildness, of attachment to the Old West where government was fair and brushes with it were rare, where it didn't try to control everyone's life.

I'm out. The big world is waiting. I've spent 20 years here. Learned a lot. I preceded all of these people except for a dozen or so old-timers. Moved here for the freedom. But now that is gone, consumed by the arrogance of people who ski 150 days a year, never served their country, never managed a business, never missed a meal, never lost big, never went broke, never worked without reward, relied on Daddy to pay the tuition, make their bail and send checks in the mail. They have never been punched squarely in the mouth, never bled from violence, never worked 12-hour days year after year with no hope of change, and never leave town to see what real life is like. These are the sheltered elite. These are the people who now run the town and try to run everyone's life. And they are doing it. They love the power that makes the citizens offer them cocaine bumps in the Sheridan elevator, buy them drinks at the bar and send them invitations to all the high-end parties. Even carrying all of their useless baggage, they believe that they are greatly superior to everyone who lives outside the valley. They believe that small thinking is what people worldwide do, but in the valley, we only generate big ideas. Ridiculous.

In a few weeks, oil prices plummet, and the bottom falls out of the oil and gas business. Texas goes broke. Once wealthy Texans now work for wages. My money partners go broke, too. At the same moment, the Idarado is declared a SuperFund site by the Environmental Protection Agency, which creates an unlimited liability for the company, obligating Idarado to an unknown and endless cost to clean up after a century of mining operations. The kicker is that whoever owns the property has the full liability whether or not they are responsible for past environmental degradation. If they own it today, they are the ones who pay.

Now my partners are broke; the mine is a SuperFund site; the liability is not only unlimited, it is immeasurable. Everything stops. Not only do my partners refuse to honor the purchase agreement, they don't have the money to honor the agreement even if they want to.

I am now trapped, stuck with this white elephant. My stomach hurts. I need this deal like a mattress made of bellybutton lint.

I hold my breath to see what happens next. This is going to be bad for everyone: my partners, the town, its people, and me. On the bright side, I'm sure the Idarado people will certainly turn and walk away from the purchase contract. There is no reason for them to contest our default; it will only tie up their property, remove it from the market so they can't sell it to someone else for as long as their lawsuit lasts, which could be years.

But Idarado won't abandon the deal. They sue the partners—everybody except me—for specific performance, that is, force us buyers to execute the contract to buy the mine as written, to gag up the $13 million and take ownership that includes the limitless liability of the tailings ponds. Idarado management does not include me in the defaulters; they know I have no money. If they win against me, they will get nothing. Whatever their reasoning, I love them for leaving me out.

Months later, I look across the street from the courthouse steps at my tiny, elderly lady. She is a pitiful structure: tarpaper siding of phony brick, black and battered tin roof patched where ice dams have frayed her edges. She waits patiently for new paint on her gingerbread trim, garish makeup for an old woman beaten up by a hundred merciless mountain winters and a hundred summers only slightly more merciful.

Color. What should the new trim color be? azul? Too Mexican. Red? Fades in the intense sunlight. Orange? Garish. Maybe a light purple, something fun and challenging. Maybe blue, the same blue as the shady side of snowdrifts. That would fit right in with winter.

The heavy courthouse door behind me squeals open and Morey Stein joins me on the stoop, his soft, effeminate hands fold around the pipe safety railing. He looks up main street and smiles munificently.

"Great town, isn't it?"

"Fantastic town. A power point in the universe."

There is a long silence as we take in the scenery: the aspen trees golden and shimmering up and down the valley, the visual chorus of yellows and oranges that sometimes shouts its importance above the silly patter of mere earthlings, zoning, money, politics, affairs, dishonesty, hypocrisy, drugs. A deep apathy overtakes me. The town is now just another tourist stop in a universe filled with unimaginative thinkers fighting to protect their tiny space in a tiny society, captured and fascinated by the physical beauty of a place, held in place to survive as best they can just to remain here and eschew the trappings of wealth, revolting against the city life, abandoning all those civilized morays they inherited from their parents. They now love money, cut corners and give only lip service to their former simple-life philosophies. They court the rich, genuflect to the dollar god, fuck the stars, take the advice of jacklegged lawyers and build their preciously spoiled children new, solar-heated schools. This downgrade into Middle American life is disgusting. The society has moved from the Old West mindset filled with adventure and random excitement and honor into the money-grasping, rich-American mindset that stretches and finally breaks the back of fairness. And I helped create this disaster. All this time I thought I was doing the right thing.

As the organizer and chairman of the first planning and zoning commission, I had a clean map to work on. Instead of prohibiting trailers and A-frames, I should have fought for them. Instead of writing a sign code that tightly restricted sizes and forbade neon altogether, I should have fought for the history-based idea of crudely painted signs any size, anywhere—even hanging over the sidewalks and into the streets as the original 19th century businesses did. The street, once gap-toothed, is now homogenized in a faux-Victorian showpiece of buildings of equal heights, a flat silhouette with predictable architecture, a show of fine, even teeth that never existed in the old town that was built with upchuck construction by rough carpenters who could throw up a building anywhere. Now, new buildings are slick brick with carefully proportioned windows and regular margins and tasteful colors with pseudo-Victorian trim designed by Disney. And they are as boring as roadkill.

The town's wrinkled and weather-beaten charm is gone forever. Now the town is just a dot on the tourist map—just another place to drive to, stay for a day, cruise down one side of the main street and up the other, order an overpriced hamburger, take a piss, change film, shoot a picture of the cute buildings with Momma and the peaks behind her, then get her back in the car and continue the San Juan Skyway tour to Ouray or Durango.

"So, Bubba Ram, what are you doing?" Stein asks.

"I'm picking trim paint for my house."

"What color are you going to use?"

"Dunno yet."

Long silence.

"You still with that gorgeous girl?"

"No. She went away. Went back east to live with her lover. I think she is getting married. She's been gone a couple of years now. I live alone."

"Oh … sorry. That has to be painful."

"Nah. Good riddance. I can now get a worry-free night's sleep. She was a pain in the ass."

He shakes his head. "They all are, Bubba. They all are." He pats me on the shoulder. "Well, see you around the campus," he says happily, steps down and turns toward the Sheridan Hotel.

I miss Crazy Shirley terribly as I have every day. Now we could leave together and never come back. We could have a perfect, loving life. I could buy another Big Red. We could be in nirvana. She could drive up in her orange Beetle with her two cats, run to me, kiss me passionately and say, "God, I've missed you. I love you. Let's make love."

I look down empty Colorado Avenue toward the open end of the canyon, west toward the desert and the lowering clouds tinged with pink.

High billows of red dust are blowing in from the Colorado Plateau, that part of the western desert torn by antique river beds and dead civilizations, protected by walled cities of vertical, varnished rock and impertinent blue mountains punching through the scaly crust of sunburned sand that now lifts high on the wind into the tattered clouds that boil toward us.

The wind will race up canyon soon, bow the aspens over and roil the street dust that flies above the stores and people, onward toward the mine and the upper end of the canyon, obscuring the blue sky, rolling garbage cans and flitting scrap paper in swirls along the now-perfect pavement with true square curbs and gutters. The tourists will groan and turn away from the raw threat, hide their eyes from one more awesome display of alpine weather. The women's headscarves will flip inside out, their feathers blowing backwards, exposing the embarrassing, unsightly realities of their roots and rear ends like chickens that turn away from the wind.

The incoming wall of wind lifts loose dirt from the valley floor. Across the street, I see a woman, a wife, who walks quickly up the main street. She waves and smiles broadly, her eyes lifting into mine. I wave back with a small tip of my hand, and I cross the street and follow her.

I feel the tiniest stirring of air in my hair. Then a wall of red wind slaps both Telluride and me with the sunburned, sandpapery hand of God.

55

CITY OF LOVE

Boulder, City of Women. I think of Boulder as East Telluride: same attitudes of holier-than-thou, my-mythical-athletic-God-is-better-than-yours town. But I have an appointment there.

The Dodge van has made the trip so many times, knows the road so well, that it steers itself through the five mountain passes out to where the Great Plains yield ungracefully to the rough rape of the Rockies. The full penetration of the peaks into the flat prairie is so violent that the vaginal folds of the foothills turn back on themselves.

This is an important meeting with a wealthy woman in her 40s with short blond hair above a skillfully maintained youthful face, lovely breasts, a full luscious mouth, gray, untruthful eyes and a yen to screw in the afternoon. The wife of an oil and gas man in Wichita, she is rich in her own right and feels she is privileged to do whatever she wants without regard for small and restrictive contracts like marriage.

As I slip the buttons of her blouse, Telluride and Crazy Shirley never cross my mind.

ACKNOWLEDGMENTS

For this author, writing and publishing a book is a team effort. Without a backup of sophisticated readers and editors, our books would never see the light of day. As a guy who has been writing for 35 years, I still don't know how to do it well. I flunked the same high school English course three times and finally graduated on a social promotion. "Get that troublemaker out of here," the principal said.

First Readers:

I am forever indebted to these smart, educated friends: Susan Dollar, Barbara Lofquist, Richard Gehman, Traci HalesVass and Jules Hinton for their insightful criticisms and nit-picky corrections. They were a huge help.

Editor:

My daughter, Rachel Vass, was the valiant senior editor for this work. She has been a wonderful production partner in books and movies for three decades. She is really good. She saves me every time.

My co-author on **Soft Selling in a Hard World** and **Decoding the BS of Business**, life companion, friend and bed-buddy for 25 years, Iris Herrin is my guiding light, keeps me out of trouble, tolerates insanities, makes me "act right" at parties and knows damn near everything. She is the deep keel to my otherwise shallow-draft boat. I love her desperately.

Books by Jerry VASS

SLEEPING BIG IN SMALLVILLE
A Telluride Story

ISBN 978-0-9629610-5-2/Book

ISBN 978-0-9629610-6-9/eBook

SOFT SELLING IN A HARD WORLD
2ⁿᵈ Edition Revised and Updated
Plain Talk on the Art of Persuasion
An Essential Handbook for Professionals
and Small Business Owners
80,000 in print

ISBN 978-076240401-8

DECODING THE BS OF BUSINESS
Selling to Executives
Plain Talk for Professionals

ISBN 0-962610-2-7

All are available in text and eBook at amazon.com

ABOUT THE AUTHOR

A Southerner by birth, a Westerner by choice, Jerry Vass has learned and then abandoned a half dozen trades and professions. He has travelled the world, is a professional photographer and is a survivor of near-death experiences.

With a shiver, he says, "I am the luckiest man I ever met. I have lived the American dream. I am crazy about my wife, love my friends and, at 79, feel terrific—maybe even bulletproof. I know it won't last forever, but for now, life is perfect."

He writes to entertain his friends (they know who they are): to make them laugh in a world where there aren't enough giggles. Jerry and Iris live on Butler Beach south of Saint Augustine, Florida, happily without kids or dogs.

You may contact him directly at **sleepingbig@vass.com**

Made in the USA
Charleston, SC
02 March 2015